MISTLETOE BRIDES

ANNA CAMPBELL

Serenade Publishing

ISBN: 978-1-925980-93-6

Cover design: By Hang Le

Print editions published by Serenade Publishing
www.serenadepublishing.com

HER CHRISTMAS EARL

No good deed goes unpunished...

To save her hen-witted sister from scandal, Philippa Sanders ventures into a rake's bedroom – and into his power. Now her reputation hangs by a thread and only a hurried marriage can rescue her. Is the Earl of Erskine the heartless libertine the world believes? Or will Philippa discover unexpected honor in a man notorious for his wild ways?

Blair Hume, the dissolute Earl of Erskine, has had his eye on the intriguing Miss Sanders since he arrived at this deadly dull house party. Now a reckless act delivers this beguiling woman into his hands as a delightful Christmas gift. Is fate offering him a fleeting Yuletide diversion? Or will this Christmas Eve encounter spark a passion that lasts a lifetime?

A PIRATE FOR CHRISTMAS

Pursued by the pirate...

Bess Farrar might be an innocent village miss, but she knows enough about the world to doubt Lord Channing's motives when he kisses her the very day they meet. After all, local gossip insists that before this dashing rake became an earl, he sailed the Seven Seas as a ruthless pirate.

Bewitched by the vicar's daughter...

Until he unexpectedly inherits a title, staunchly honorable Scotsman Rory Beaton has devoted his adventurous life to the Royal Navy. But he sets his course for tempestuous new waters when he meets lovely, sparkling Bess Farrar. Now this daring mariner will do whatever it takes to convince the spirited lassie to launch herself into his arms and set sail into the sunset.

A Christmas marked by mayhem.

Wooing his vivacious lady, the new Earl of Channing finds himself embroiled with matchmaking villagers, an eccentric vicar, mistaken identities, a snowstorm, scandal, and a rascally donkey. Life at sea was never this exciting. The gallant naval captain's first land-locked Christmas promises hijinks, danger, and passion – and a breathtaking chance to win the love of a lifetime.

PRAISE FOR ANNA CAMPBELL

"*The Seduction of Lord Stone* is romantic, emotional, sexy and funny. In fact, everything I have come to expect from Anna Campbell. I'm looking forward to reading the other Dashing Widows' stories." —*RakesandRascals.com*

"With her marvelous combination of humor and poignancy Anna Campbell writes in such a way that every story of hers has a special meaning and remains like a sentimental keepsake with those fortunate enough to read her work!" —*JeneratedReviews.com*

"*Lord Garson's Bride* is a well written and passionate story that touched my heart and sent my emotions on a rollercoaster ride. I particularly recommend this book for fans of convenient marriages, and those who enjoy seeing a deserving character find out that love is lovelier the second time around." —*Roses Are Blue Reviews*

"Campbell immediately hooks readers, then deftly reels them in with a spellbinding love story fueled by an addictive mixture of sharp wit, lush sensuality, and a wealth of well-delineated characters."—*Booklist, starred review, on A Scoundrel by Moonlight*

"With its superbly nuanced characters, impeccably crafted historical setting, and graceful writing shot through with scintillating wit, Campbell's latest lusciously sensual, flawlessly written historical Regency ... will have romance readers sighing happily with satisfaction."—*Booklist, Starred Review, on What a Duke Dares*

"Campbell makes the Regency period pop in the appealing third Sons of Sin novel. Romantic fireworks, the constraints of custom, and witty banter are combined in this sweet and successful story."—*Publishers Weekly on What a Duke Dares*

"Campbell is exceptionally talented, especially with plots that challenge the reader, and emotions and characters that are complex and memorable."—*Sarah Wendell, Smart Bitches Trashy Books, on A Rake's Midnight Kiss*

"A lovely, lovely book that will touch your heart and remind you why you read romance."—*Liz Carlyle, New York Times bestselling author on What a Duke Dares*

"Campbell holds readers captive with her highly intense, emotional, sizzling and dark romances. She instinctually knows how to play on her readers' fantasies to create a romantic, deep-sigh tale."—*RT Book Reviews, Top Pick, on Captive of Sin*

"Don't miss this novel - it speaks to the wild drama of the heart, creating a love story that really does transcend class."—*Eloisa James, New York Times bestselling author, on Tempt the Devil*

"*Seven Nights in A Rogue's Bed* is a lush, sensuous treat. I was enthralled from the first page to the last and still wanted more."—*Laura Lee Guhrke, New York Times bestselling author*

"No one does lovely, dark romance or lovely, dark heroes like Anna Campbell. I love her books."—*Sarah MacLean, New York Times bestselling author*

"It isn't just the sensuality she weaves into her story that makes Campbell a fan favorite, it's also her strong, three-dimensional characters, sharp dialogue and deft plotting. Campbell intuitively knows how to balance the key elements of the genre and give readers an irresistible, memorable read."—*RT Book Reviews, Top Pick, on Midnight's Wild Passion*

"Anna Campbell is an amazing, daring new voice in romance."—*Lorraine Heath, New York Times bestselling author*

"Ms. Campbell's gorgeous writing a true thing of beauty..."—*Joyfully Reviewed*

"She's the mistress of dark, sexy and brooding and takes us into the dens of iniquity with humor and class."—*Bookseller-Publisher Australia*

"Anna Campbell is a master at drawing a reader in from the very first page and keeping them captivated the whole book through. Ms. Campbell's books are all on my keeper shelf and *Midnight's Wild Passion* will join them proudly. *Midnight's Wild Passion* is a smoothly sensual delight that was a joy to read and I cannot wait to revisit Antonia and Nicholas's romance again."—*Joyfully Reviewed*

"Ms. Campbell gives us...the steamy sex scenes, a heroine whose backbone is pure steel and a stupendous tale of lust and love and you too cannot help but fall in love with this tantalizing novel."—*Coffee Time Romance*

"Anna Campbell offers us again, a lush, intimate, seductive read. I am in awe of the way she keeps the focus tight on the hero and heroine, almost achingly so. Nothing else really exists in this world, but the two main characters. Intimate, sensual story with a hero that will take your breath away."—*Historical Romance Books & More*

ALSO BY ANNA CAMPBELL

Claiming the Courtesan

Untouched

Tempt the Devil

Captive of Sin

My Reckless Surrender

Midnight's Wild Passion

The Sons of Sin series:

Seven Nights in a Rogue's Bed

Days of Rakes and Roses

A Rake's Midnight Kiss

What a Duke Dares

A Scoundrel by Moonlight

Three Proposals and a Scandal

The Dashing Widows:

The Seduction of Lord Stone

Tempting Mr. Townsend

Winning Lord West

Pursuing Lord Pascal

Charming Sir Charles

Catching Captain Nash

Lord Garson's Bride

The Lairds Most Likely:

The Laird's Willful Lass

The Laird's Christmas Kiss

The Highlander's Lost Lady

The Highlander's Defiant Captive

The Highlander's Christmas Quest

Christmas Stories:

The Winter Wife

Her Christmas Earl

A Pirate for Christmas

Mistletoe and the Major

A Match Made in Mistletoe

The Christmas Stranger

Other Books:

These Haunted Hearts

Stranded with the Scottish Earl

HER CHRISTMAS EARL

CHAPTER ONE

Hartley Manor, Wiltshire, Christmas Eve, 1823

Her heart racing, Philippa Sanders inched the massive oak door that led into the bedroom open. She prayed that nobody emerged into the lamplit corridor and caught her in a place where no lady of good reputation should be. Especially near midnight.

Quick and silent as a cat, she slipped into the shadowy room and carefully closed the door after her. In the stillness, the latch's snick resounded like a gunshot.

Her breath jammed in her throat, and she stood still and trembling, waiting for someone to investigate the noise. But the rambling old house remained quiet. She sucked in some desperately needed air and berated herself for being a jumpy widgeon.

The room, as she'd known it would be, was empty. Before coming here, she'd checked that Lord Erskine remained downstairs, carousing with his drunken cronies. If the last three nights were any indication, his flirtation with the brandy bottle would continue into the early hours. That left Philippa plenty of time to search his belongings undisturbed.

The thought did little to calm her nerves. Should anyone catch her alone in a gentleman's bedchamber, worse, such a notorious gentleman, there would be the devil to pay.

If only the stakes weren't so high. If only her sister Amelia wasn't such a ninnyhammer. If only Erskine wasn't a man who turned even sensible women silly.

Philippa sighed and straightened away from the door. "If only" wouldn't help. It was imperative that she found and destroyed the compromising letter her henwitted sister sent Erskine before her engagement to Mr. Gerald Fox had been announced last night.

Then Philippa would take to her heels and never think about the rakish Lord Erskine again.

By the light of the fire blazing in the hearth, she surveyed her surroundings with a jaundiced air. The chamber was large and luxurious. Her aunt must be trying to turn Lord Erskine up sweet, in the hope that he'd offer for her horse-faced daughter Caroline.

Given the trouble his libertine lordship had caused,

Philippa almost wished her vile cousin on him. Over the last few days, she'd observed him closely. She couldn't approve of the cynical light in his eyes and the way he arrogantly assumed that any chit in his vicinity must swoon at his merest word.

However Philippa wouldn't be female without admitting that he was a spectacular specimen of masculinity.

She'd worried that it might take too long to locate the letter, or that he might carry it with him as a trophy, but her gaze immediately fell on a beautiful mahogany writing slope left open on the window seat. She could hardly believe her luck. Pulses kicking with relief, she rushed toward the window.

Then stopped on a horrified gasp when she heard the doorknob squeak as it turned.

Lord save her...

Frantically she dived across the few feet of floor to the dressing room. She had time to notice dark coats hanging from rows of pegs and shelves neatly stacked with clothing. Hands shaking, she tugged the door closed until she cowered in thick darkness. Thick darkness redolent with leather and soap and sandalwood—and something undefined that teased her senses.

Dizzy with fear and that unfamiliar but pleasant scent, she silently prayed that whoever had come in would finish what they were doing and go. Much as she strained, she couldn't hear a thing, even with her ear pressed to the door. The thick wood blocked all sound, just as it blocked all light.

The dressing room door jerked open, unbalancing her. She only just saved herself from tumbling to the floor in an undignified heap. As she stared up at the figure looming above her, panic hammered through her, turned her blood to ice.

"What have we here?" The Scottish burr in the deep drawl brushed across her nerves like sandpaper.

Sick with dread, Philippa lurched away, crowding against the coats lined against the back wall.

This was beyond awful. What must he think? What might he do?

Lord Erskine's chest was bare, and a white shirt dangled from one elegant hand. The wall lamp near the doorway spilled gold over a terrifying expanse of gleaming skin. His lordship's sardonic green gaze focused on her.

His calmness only built her fright. One would imagine that he was accustomed to discovering well-bred virgins huddled amongst his undergarments. Curse him, he probably was. Philippa had only met Blair Hume three days ago, but like most of the nation, she knew his reputation for subverting even the most virtuous ladies.

"My lord—" Desperately she struggled not to stare at his impressive chest with its scattering of dark hair.

"Miss Philippa Sanders." With unconcealed irony, he bowed. "To what do I owe the pleasure?"

To her horror, he stepped into the confined space. The dressing room had been tiny before. Now it was suffocating. Her heart pounded with fear. That cursed elusive scent made her head swim as she wedged herself into the wall, wishing she could disappear altogether.

Still his tall body remained scant inches away. Surely it was only in her imagination that a subtle heat radiated out to envelop her.

"I mistook the room," she stammered.

She made the error of glancing at his chest. Broad. Powerful. Sculpted with muscle. She gulped for air. Watching the farm workers without their shirts from a distance wasn't at all the same as facing down a half-dressed rake in his bedroom.

A wry smile curled the rake's thin, expressive lips. "By a whole wing, apparently."

She straightened and glared at him, struggling to ignore the way his thick black hair was ruffled and his eyes devoured her. A gentleman would pretend to believe her, however feeble her lie.

Clearly Lord Erskine was no gentleman.

"It's late," she said with hard-won steadiness, telling herself that if she kept her head, she might yet escape unscathed. By Lord Erskine or by scandal. "I must return to my room."

He didn't step aside to let her pass. Definitely no gentleman. "Not quite yet."

Meeting his gaze required every ounce of faltering

courage. "Not before you return my sister's letter at any rate."

Surprisingly he laughed. "Huzzah, Miss Sanders. I knew there was more to you than the little shadow glowering at me from the corner."

Philippa flushed with chagrin. She'd had no idea this darling of the ton had noticed her, let alone remarked her disapproval. "My lord, I insist that you give me Amelia's letter immediately."

"Or what?" Dark eyebrows tilted in supercilious inquiry. At least he'd stopped staring at her like he meant to gobble her up like a Christmas bonbon. "You'll unfold all my shirts and stamp on them?"

Welcome anger bolstered her defiance. "A man of honor would return the letter."

"I'm afraid that's impossible."

"Why?" Her fists clenched at her sides as the urge to clout him thundered through her. "What do you intend to do with it?"

His smile broadened, and in spite of irritation, frustration and fear, his male beauty made her throat tighten. No wonder Amelia had made such a fool of herself over him. Right now, even clever, pragmatic Philippa Sanders felt a little giddy to have all that glorious virility focused on her humble self.

"I intend to do precisely nothing, my sweet little Yuletide burglar."

Her eyes narrowed. "What does that mean?"

His smile intensified. "It means that I burned it immediately after I read it."

She drew her first full breath in what felt like days. Since Amelia's tearful confession of her arrant stupidity, apprehension had knotted Philippa's belly. If Erskine wanted to cause trouble, he could use her sister's letter to spark an awful scandal—not to mention scupper Amelia's newly minted engagement to a nice young man of substantial means.

Philippa paused, knowing she owed Lord Erskine her heartfelt thanks for his unexpected chivalry and, even more urgently, an apology for invading his room. But her response sounded grudging, even in her own ears. "That was…generous of you."

The mocking smile didn't fade. "I'm glad you think so."

All night, anger had lurked beneath her fear. Firstly at Amelia for being such a rattlebrain and creating this mess, then at herself for getting caught. Most futile of all was her anger at Lord Erskine for coming in at such an inopportune moment. Although at least now she knew what had happened to the letter. "I must go."

"No rush, my fascinating Miss Sanders." He shifted closer, and the light behind him lent his face a suddenly sinister expression.

"I'm not your Miss Sanders," she snapped with a resurgence of dread.

A chill trickled down her spine. Awareness of her

own danger swamped any gratitude for Amelia's reprieve.

"Not yet, at any rate," he said mildly, pulling the door shut behind him.

Darkness wrapped around them. Rage and terror spurred Philippa to surge forward, shoving hard at Lord Erskine. Her hands met smooth, warm skin and an immovable male body. The silky hair on his chest created soft friction against her palms. "Let me out of here."

"Devil take you, do you never say please?" He shifted to break the contact, but not nearly quickly enough for her peace of mind.

As he leaned away, she pushed past him to tug madly at the doorknob, but even using both hands, she couldn't budge it. As she struggled, her shoulder brushed Erskine's arm. To her surprise, he made no attempt to hinder her departure. If he intended seduction, he was insultingly half-hearted.

Hardly surprising. She wasn't nearly beautiful enough to appeal to that famous connoisseur of female loveliness, Blair Hume.

She told herself she didn't mind. And didn't believe it for a minute.

"Stop this nonsense immediately and open the door," she demanded breathlessly.

"Have I persuaded you against breaking into anyone else's room?" he asked without shifting. "Especially if the anyone else is a man."

Shock made her hand drop away from the doorknob. "You're trying to teach me a *lesson?*" she hissed incredulously.

That familiar soft laugh played up and down her backbone like music, and she realized with an unwelcome frisson that the evocative scent filling the room was Lord Erskine's own. The intimacy of recognizing his personal essence scared her more than being trapped with a rake.

"I am indeed." In the tight space, she was close enough to hear him draw breath. More encroaching intimacy. "Step aside and I'll set you free, chastened but unharmed. And hopefully a little wiser."

Her snort was derisive. If her mother had heard the unmannerly response, she'd have a fit. But then so much of what Philippa did gave her mother the vapors. "Who on earth do you think you are? What a cheek."

"Miss Sanders, I feel some humility is called for." He still sounded as though he found her endlessly diverting. "If you're as clever as you think you are, you wouldn't be stuck here with a rake, while your sister sleeps comfortably in her own bed, safely beyond scandal's reach."

The comment's justice rankled. "You're a very annoying man," she muttered, wishing to heaven she'd left Amelia to solve her own problems.

"Undoubtedly," he said without inflection. "But that doesn't mean I'm wrong about you needing to temper valor with discretion."

She bit back a blistering response about profligate libertines following their own advice and waited impatiently for him to let her out. She very much feared that if she spent much longer with the irritating Earl of Erskine, she'd strangle him with one of his neck cloths.

For what seemed a ridiculous length of time, Erskine rattled the doorknob.

"Stop playing games," she said sharply, tired of his antics. He might find his teasing funny. She just wanted to leave this room, and say goodnight, and never see him again. "Unlock the door and let me out."

He stopped tugging on the doorknob. A fraught silence fell. For the first time when he spoke, no trace of humor warmed his deep voice.

"It's stuck."

"I don't believe you." The girl's voice was impressively flat and steady.

Erskine should have guessed that the self-possessed Miss Philippa Sanders wouldn't have hysterics when she learned she was confined with a rake. He didn't need any light to know that disapproval weighted that direct brown gaze. For the last three days, he'd suffered that solemn, critical stare every time guests and family gathered together.

Although she couldn't see him, he shrugged. "That is, of course, your privilege."

From the moment he'd seen her in this closet, reluctant excitement had thrummed in his veins. Although surely the small, brown-haired woman with uncompromising dark brows would strike most sane men as prim or dour.

Apparently he wasn't sane.

Since their introduction, he'd wanted to shake this girl's unnatural composure. Miss Sanders awoke all his worst impulses. Not since his schooldays had he wanted to pull a girl's plait or put a mouse down her back, just to stop her treating him like a member of some inferior species.

Erskine had grown up considerably from the boy who used such unproductive tactics on the pretty baker's daughter. He'd immediately recognized that his urge to upset Miss Sanders's calmness was similarly based in seeking her attention, if only in displeasure. And the heat swirling in his blood since she'd touched his bare chest was distinctly adult.

While he didn't understand the fascination, he made a habit of being honest with himself. This observant little sparrow drew him in a way the fashionable and sophisticated London ladies never had. He was yet to work out why.

This attraction's inexplicable nature added to its power. In all this sprawling house, the only person who stirred a shred of interest was the woman regarding him the way she'd regard a worm in an apple.

An unusual experience for a man generally considered irresistible to the fairer sex.

He'd been right to suspect that more went on beneath her quiet exterior than she wanted the world to know. In the last five minutes, she'd displayed more spirit than she had in three days of staring him down. Perhaps he should have locked her in a cupboard the first day.

"You've got a key. Or you've clicked the lock somehow."

She didn't sound frightened, for which he was heartily grateful. Instead she sounded like a schoolmistress scolding a lazy pupil for sloppy arithmetic.

Good God, Erskine was in a bad way. Something in that stern voice made him want to grab her and kiss her, until she lost the breath to berate him. "You're not a very trusting soul, are you?"

Her sigh conveyed endless irritation. "Lord Erskine, you needn't persist in this foolishness. You have my word that I will never invade another man's bedchamber."

He bit back an invitation to invade his bedchamber any time she fancied.

When he didn't respond, she went on, still as if speaking to someone slow on the uptake. "Pray unlock the door. No harm has been done. My sister's honor is safe because you destroyed the letter. You obviously realized that she'd written to you on a foolish impulse."

Actually the beauteous Amelia's letter had been incendiary in the extreme and had offered privileges nobody but a husband had the right to claim. Erskine spared a sympathetic thought for the chit's fiancé. Mr. Gerald Fox put his pretty beloved high on a pedestal, a pedestal from which she was likely to topple before long.

Erskine kept his voice light, although he wondered if Amelia's younger sister had any inkling of the letter's contents. "So all is squared away, and you go your merry way, with your uncharitable assessment of me intact."

He didn't see her frown, but he knew she did. He'd never been so attuned to a woman. And he hadn't even kissed her yet.

At the thought of holding her naked in his arms, hunger shuddered through him. While she didn't dress to display her body, he knew enough about women to guess what she'd look like out of that unfashionable blue frock. She might be slender, but the bosom curving beneath those discouragingly high collars was round and firm. He'd wager that description matched the rest of her.

Perhaps winter and this tedious house party encouraged a taste for more subtle attractions. Three days in her company had convinced Erskine that Philippa Sanders was a rare beauty indeed. He was just grateful that his blockheaded companions were too distracted by the false gold of her sister to notice.

"I hardly think you care about my opinion," she said in a repressive tone.

"I'm a sensitive soul."

"Clearly," she responded just as drily. "Now unlock the door." She paused and added a sugary edge to the next word. "*Please.*"

He laughed, wondering why her bossiness charmed him. He didn't in general like managing females, but something about this small, confident woman touched the heart he'd imagined immune to tenderness. "Did that hurt?"

Another of those delightful, dismissive snorts. "You've had your fun, my lord."

Not by a long shot, my dear. "Believe me, Miss Sanders, unless I can open this door, nothing will save you from the consequences of your foolishness. It seems fortune doesn't favor the brave."

He should be in a blind panic about what might happen, if they were discovered together in such a compromising situation. Somehow, he…wasn't.

"This isn't funny."

"I'm not laughing." He paused. "You're most welcome to search me if you believe I have a key."

Her faint gasp made him wonder if she too relived that searing moment when she'd touched him. "The door's really stuck?"

"It's really stuck."

He heard the faint rustle of her plain dark blue dress, the same dress she'd worn sitting across the table from him at dinner. Her expression had been critical, as she'd observed her overbearing cousin's attempts to captivate him. Caroline had been almost as busy making cow eyes at him as the beauteous Amelia.

When he'd accepted Sir Theodore Liddell's invitation, he hadn't realized matchmaking lay on the horizon. Although damn it, he should have. He was hardly a green boy when it came to ambitious parents.

Beside him, the doorknob rattled. Miss Sanders wasn't one to give up before she was well and truly defeated. He admired her stalwart soul. He'd mocked her bravery in sneaking into his room to steal her sister's letter, but it was a damned gallant act. An act that, unless they were very lucky, promised to have major repercussions.

As she moved, he caught a drift of her scent. Like Philippa Sanders, it was an intriguing mixture of tart and sweet. Lemon soap. And something warmer and earthier.

He couldn't let her continue battling with the door. Already she breathed in frantic little gasps. He placed his hand over hers. There was that same shock of connection that he'd felt when she flattened her palm on his bare chest. "Do you believe me now?"

"Yes." She sounded young and frightened, not at all like the assertive miss who had demanded the letter's return. "This is such a disaster. We can't stay here alone. What if someone finds us?"

CHAPTER TWO

Erskine didn't even consider sugarcoating his response. "We'll find ourselves in the middle of an almighty scandal."

"Please…please try and get the door open."

Her shaky request tugged at his heart. No, she didn't sound at all like the imperious chit so keen to put him in his place. Of course she was frightened. He was a stranger, and he could imagine what exaggerated stories she'd heard about his amorous exploits.

Hell, even without exaggeration, the truth was bad enough to terrify an innocent.

This tiny room wasn't his preferred venue for flirtation, but up to this point, unrepentant devil he was, he'd enjoyed himself. More, he hated to admit, than he had in years.

But because of that barely concealed fear in her voice, he accepted that he must make some genuine attempt to break free. With a muffled sigh, he stepped back, braced himself, and plowed his shoulder into the solid oak door.

Then bit back a decidedly unheroic groan.

Hartley Manor had been built for a more warlike age. It was designed to withstand trebuchets and cannons. A mere human shoulder, no matter how enthusiastically applied, hardly rattled the latch. All Erskine got for his trouble was a bruised arm.

Although Miss Sanders didn't speak, he felt her desperate hope that he'd get them out. Only that made him apply himself twice more to battering at the door. With equally disappointing results.

"It's useless." Miss Sanders paused, and for the first time, he heard a trace of warmth. "But thank you for trying. I can't imagine this is your idea of the nicest way to spend Christmas Eve either."

She'd think he was mad if he told her that right now, he couldn't think of another person he'd rather have with him. Was he getting old? He was only twenty-eight, but this last year or so, the parade of decadent pleasures had begun to pall.

As a younger man, he'd enjoyed kicking up his heels in London and shocking his straitlaced and tyrannical father back in Scotland. But since the old man's death two years ago, Erskine had a grim feeling that his hell-raising smacked of going through the motions. Nothing in ages had compared to the piquant thrill of knowing that he and Philippa Sanders were alone together—and that at last he might discover what lurked beneath her serene shell.

"Someone will come and get us."

Her laugh was hollow, but he admired her ability to squeeze amusement, however bleak, from their dilemma. He heard a faint bump as she slumped against the wall beside him. "That's what I'm afraid of."

"Odds are that it will be my valet Mills. He's the soul of discretion." With a master of such rackety reputation, Mills had to be.

"Does he wait up for you?" She sounded a little brighter. "Perhaps he'll check soon."

Erskine slid to the carpeted floor and leaned his head against the recalcitrant door. He extended his legs until his feet bumped the opposite wall.

Stupidly he hated to disappoint her. Absurd as it was, she awoke a faint chivalry in his black soul. "I gave him the night off."

"Oh."

More rustling. Then something soft dropped across his lap. "What's this?"

"A coat. It's getting colder."

It was. And he wasn't dressed for a winter night. He'd been in the process of preparing for bed when he'd caught his little burglar. It was yet another sign of his jaded mood that he'd forsaken the drunken buffoons in the dining room and come upstairs to sleep.

"Very sporting of you, Miss Sanders." He slipped the

coat over his shoulders. The wool was scratchy, but he appreciated the immediate warmth. "Considering that my arrogance in trying to teach you a lesson got us into this trouble."

"You meant well."

He almost laughed. Her generous response surprised him and sparked a faint gratification. He couldn't remember the last time anyone had said that to him. He couldn't remember the last time those words had accurately described his motives.

The irony was that Miss Sanders was right. He'd been horrified to discover her in his room. And doubly horrified at the salacious pictures invading his mind of how to take advantage of her presence. "You took an awful risk. What if you'd broken into the room of a man with no principles?"

Another laugh, self-mocking. "I thought I had."

His lips flattened. "In that case, you should be scared out of your mind."

More rustling and she dropped to sit. The restricted space meant that she ventured dangerously close. "I don't scare easily."

He didn't bother pointing out that only minutes ago, she'd sounded petrified. "I'll see you don't suffer any consequences."

"Very noble, my lord, but you're making promises you can't keep." Her words were heavy with discouragement. "If there are consequences, you'll face them, too."

The inevitable price an unmarried man and woman paid for spending an extended period alone together in a private place. Damn it, Miss Sanders sounded considerably more cut up about the prospect of marriage than he did. She spoke as if she'd rather face the hangman than a parson reading the wedding service.

To Hades with her, women all over England had tried to shackle him. He was rich. He was young. He was healthy—whatever the long-term effects of his rakish life. Society accounted him a dashed eligible fellow.

Then he reminded himself that he had no right to pique. They were stuck in this damned uncomfortable spot because he'd pretended to lock them in. He should have guessed that breaking the wicked habits of a lifetime and taking the high moral ground would only cause trouble.

"Hopefully Mills will find us before long." Except Mills wasn't likely to seek his master until morning. He knew better than to intrude upon the Earl of Erskine after midnight.

"You're taking this surprisingly well." She paused. "After all, I'm here uninvited."

"You were trying to save your sister from ruin."

"Amelia can be a twit. But if she settles to the match, I hope she and Gerald will be happy."

Erskine didn't respond. From what he'd seen of Miss Amelia Sanders, she was, at the very least, an unregenerate flirt. That stripling Gerald Fox would need to be considerably more awake than he currently was, if he intended to be master in his own house.

Erskine's silence must have conveyed criticism because Philippa spoke with more emphasis. "She's gone a bit silly with the success of her first season."

"It's your first season, too," he pointed out.

"I'm not the kind of girl that society takes to its heart," she said without resentment.

Regrettably that was true. Amelia Sanders was considered a diamond of the first water, and Erskine was connoisseur enough to admit that the girl was pretty in the conventional fashion. Blond and willowy with big blue eyes holding no more intelligence than a sheep's.

The younger sister, on the other hand, was well outside the common run of debutantes. Hardly surprising that those nincompoops infesting the capital's ballrooms hadn't discerned the treasure lurking beneath Philippa's direct manner.

He frowned through the darkness. His eyes had adjusted to the stygian gloom, but he'd give a hundred guineas for a candle. "That's society's loss."

She sat close enough for him to feel how she stiffened in response to his compliment. "Lord Erskine, no need to waste time flirting. I know I don't meet your standards."

She sounded repressive again. Unfortunately for her, he found her scoldings more appealing than another woman's praise. Besides, he'd much rather hear disapproval than fear in her voice.

Still, he was annoyed that she dismissed his sincere compliment as a rakish trick. "You'd meet the standards of any intelligent man." He paused. "Has nobody ever flirted with you before?"

Another dismissive snort. "I'm considered far too serious for anything as frivolous as flirting."

Erskine laughed, enchanted by her dry assessment of the world's opinion. "If you practiced, my dear Miss Sanders, I suspect you could become alarmingly proficient."

"The world mistakes you, my lord." For the first time, her voice held no wry note. "You're not the rapacious beast of legend. Instead, I think you might be kinder than you want to admit. You're trying very gallantly to distract me from our predicament."

Heat prickled his neck. When she called him kind, he felt about a thousand years old. Damn it, she must be at least twenty. He wasn't *that* much older than she was.

"Yes." He paused. "And no. You're so deuced convinced that nobody notices you."

"Nobody does." Not a hint of self-pity.

"I did."

"Really?" She didn't bother to hide her skepticism.

"Really."

"You hardly spoke to me."

He smiled into the darkness, encouraged to hear

she'd paid that much attention. "Whenever I approached you, you regarded me with complete disdain."

"I didn't," she said, shocked.

"You don't approve of me, Miss Sanders."

"I don't know you."

"No, you don't."

A prickly silence descended, and he heard the slide of fabric against the wall as she turned toward him. These soft, hellishly suggestive sounds of her body moving inside her clothing drove him crazy. He wondered if she wore one of his coats, too. The idea was arousing. The urge stirred to cross the mere inches between them and find out. But the memory of her earlier nervousness kept his hands at his sides.

This was a confounded odd encounter. He couldn't see Miss Sanders, but every other sense was alive to her. Her scent teased him. Fresh and innocent. And as alluring as Eve to Adam.

"You must think me odiously judgmental." Her voice was low.

He sighed. "I imagine that you listened to a lot of gossip before we met."

She shifted again. Dear God, he wished she'd stop doing that. Every time she moved, his restraint battled the urge to touch her. And if he manhandled her, that would only prove she was right to despise him.

"That makes me sound even worse. Not only am I

judgmental, I base my judgments on unreliable public report."

He laughed softly, charmed despite increasing discomfort. "You're awfully hard on yourself, aren't you?"

"You have no idea." Humor warmed her voice. "But you've behaved like a gentleman tonight, and I apologize for any unfavorable thoughts."

"I'm no saint," he was compelled to point out, much as he hoped to rise in her estimation.

Heaven help him, what had got into him? He never wanted a woman to think him a better man. He'd devoted his time to women who expected the worst of him, then generally got even less.

Philippa's sigh was breathy and alluring. Erskine fought the surging need to seize her in his arms. This tiny room transformed into a torture chamber.

"I assumed you set out to seduce my sister, but if that was so, you'd never have destroyed the letter. If nothing else, it would make a fine tool for blackmailing Amelia into doing what you wanted."

When she paused, he leaned forward. Damn it, moving closer filled his head with her intriguing scent. After tonight, he'd know her among a thousand, just by her fragrance.

"And you haven't been angry with me. When you should be."

He admitted the truth, even if it made him feel like an awkward schoolboy, instead of a worldly man with a history of too many lovers. "I always wanted the chance to talk to you."

The disbelief in her short laugh roused another of those unwelcome pangs in his chest. She was so convinced that she was of negligible interest. Erskine developed a hearty dislike for her overbearing mother and birdbrain sister.

"For a man renowned for his rakish ways, you're not very rakish."

"It's Christmas Eve. I'm taking a rest from wickedness." If she could see into his mind, she'd know that was far from true.

The girl sighed again, more heavily this time. "Surely it's well after midnight." She paused. "If you'd stayed downstairs as usual, I'd have been in and out of your room and you'd be none the wiser."

Unworthy pleasure flooded him. "So you've been watching me, too."

Another of those dry laughs. "You're very noticeable. You're the handsomest man I've ever seen." She stopped on a gasp, and he heard her squirm with embarrassment. Her damned wriggling would be the death of him. "Oh, no. Shoot me now."

He bit back a laugh, although her artless sincerity touched him. Sensual curiosity stirred. He was still a rake, no matter what good influence the lovely Miss Sanders exerted on his deplorable character. Could he translate her admiration for his looks into permission to touch?

Oh, he was a bad, bad man. At Christmas, and at every other time of the year.

A long and bristling silence fell. Then he heard a smothered sound near his shoulder.

Astonished, he turned in her direction, although he saw nothing through the blackness. "Is that a yawn? Good God, you can't possibly be bored."

Lord above, she was a tonic for his vanity. Yet again, he wondered why he liked her so much. She certainly didn't exert herself to flatter him. On the other hand, she'd been calm throughout this ordeal. The game would be up immediately if he'd been lumbered with a screaming female. They'd have no chance of avoiding discovery, if she'd started shrieking like a skinned cat. Not to mention that shrieking was damned wearing on a man's nerves.

Another yawn. "You'll think me the most rag-mannered hoyden in creation."

He wanted to tell her she was charming, but he recalled too well how she'd brushed over his last attempt to tell her she was exceptional. "Captivity after midnight with a man of shady reputation tests the bravest lady's nerves."

"I was nervous. I probably should still be." Another tormenting whisper of fabric as she settled more comfortably. "I was up at dawn to help my aunt with Christmas preparations. I'm awfully tired."

He'd lay good money that Amelia had stayed abed

until noon. "There's nothing much we can do except try and get some sleep."

A blatant lie. He could think of a hundred things he'd prefer to do.

He chanced sliding a fraction closer. "May I offer my shoulder as a pillow? We should make ourselves as comfortable as we can. We'll be warmer huddled together."

Very gently, expecting Miss Sanders to flinch away, he slid his arm around her straight shoulders and drew her down until her head rested on his shoulder. His heart gave a great thud of joy when she didn't move away. She wasn't wrapped in one of his coats, and the worn merino of her dress was soft to his touch. Nowhere near as soft, he was sure, as her skin. The thought didn't make him feel any sleepier.

"We shouldn't do this," she whispered, although nobody was within earshot.

"It's purely for self-preservation."

With her so close, a tantalizing female scent teased his senses. Tentatively so as not to alarm her, he brushed his cheek against her hair. It was as silky and thick as he'd imagined.

Miss Philippa Sanders might have a sharp tongue, but she proved a lusciously sweet armful. He tightened his hold, ignoring her half-hearted protest, and rested his head back against the wall.

However undeserving he might be, Christmas this year had provided glorious gifts.

CHAPTER THREE

Gradually Philippa surfaced from sleep. Beneath her ear, something pounded deep and steady like the ocean upon the shore. Whatever she rested upon was firm and warm. She murmured and rubbed her cheek against her lovely pillow. Lazy pleasure trickled through her as someone rhythmically stroked her hair.

Then she remembered where she was. And who she was with.

How bizarre to think that a man she'd hardly spoken two words to before tonight touched her with such tenderness.

How bizarre. How wrong. How…delightful.

"Dear heaven…" she muttered with less horror than a genuinely virtuous woman would muster.

When she made a token effort to sit up, Erskine's hold tightened. "Not yet."

How far she'd ventured from her safe little world. He hugged her into his side so she curved against him, her face buried in the front of his coat. One hand lay on his shoulder, and her legs curled beneath her, her thigh resting against his hip. The alien but delicious scent of a man surrounded her. Clean skin. Male musk. A touch of sandalwood.

Compared to her, Lord Erskine was so big. At their first meeting, she'd noted his height, but now, pressed to his hard body, she was overwhelmingly conscious of restrained power.

Any sensible girl would be terrified. Instead, Philippa stayed exactly where she was.

The sheer strangeness of how much she liked resting in Erskine's arms made her try yet again to sit up. This time he let her.

"I'm sorry." She raised trembling hands to her untidy hair.

How mortifying. She must have been wriggling all over him while she slept. Her hair was half collapsed around her face.

"No need to apologize." His voice was low and subtly insinuating. Or perhaps only her uneasy conscience made her think that.

"Did you sleep?"

"No."

Somehow that made it worse. That he'd remained alert while she'd felt easy enough to drift off into dreams. Dreams now wisps, but which left behind a trace of guilt.

"Was I asleep for long?"

"I'm guessing only an hour or so." Erskine's laugh was mocking. "Fear not, Miss Sanders. You didn't confess your darkest secrets in your sleep. You didn't molest me. Your innocence remains unsullied."

Except now she knew the touch of his hands and the scent of his skin. Now she knew how it felt to sleep beside him. A man of his experience might consider their interactions as pure as spring water. Philippa felt like she'd surrendered a corner of herself. She didn't like this vulnerability.

Erskine's arm still encircled her in a loose embrace that could have felt merely friendly, if not for her prickling awareness. She should insist that he release her, but curling up with her head on his shoulder had established an intimacy that made missish megrims too coy for words.

"Are you cold?" The softly accented voice was rich with concern. She'd once pegged him as a selfish, careless man, but tonight he'd been kinder than she deserved.

"No." If anything she was too warm. A blush rose in her cheeks. She struggled to sound calm and mature. It was fiendishly difficult. "Are you? I can get another coat."

"No, I'm fine."

Such a banal discussion, while all the time his touch

filtered through to her bones in a way she'd never experienced. Worse, she couldn't stop wondering what she'd do if he kissed her. Something about the late hour and the cramped room and, above all, the delicious warmth of his body, made her think of forbidden pleasures.

Given Erskine was such a rake, it seemed a pity not to sample his famous rakish skills. Unwelcome curiosity coiled like a snake. Curiosity, and a fatal yearning to play the wicked woman. Just once, before she resumed her life as beautiful Amelia Sanders's sensible, disregarded sister.

Philippa was never likely to have another adventure like this. The whole season, she'd trailed around London behind Amelia, making no impression at all. Now that Amelia had made a brilliant match, Philippa would return to the country and her dull but useful life, running her mother's modest estate. Perhaps in lonely old age, she'd look back on this encounter with a libertine and smile.

"Why don't you go back to sleep?" he suggested softly.

How horrified he'd be if he guessed the wanton pictures filling her mind. "No."

Although the idea of drawing on someone else's strength was so appealing. In the family, she kept things going, managed the farm, ordered the household. She'd always believed herself perfectly content. Until this brush with a scoundrel made her wonder if she'd settled for second best, only because it was easier for her mother and sister if Philippa undertook every necessary but unexciting task.

Discomfiting thoughts. Thoughts that did nothing to dilute her physical reaction to the man sharing this dangerously intimate space. It rankled that if he'd been trapped with Amelia or one of his glamorous London ladies, he'd do more than fling an avuncular arm across her shoulders.

"Aren't you tired?" she asked.

His laugh was a mere grunt. "I'm used to late nights. Unlike you, my innocent country lassie."

The darkness lent her courage to take issue with his remark. "You keep calling me innocent."

Another taut silence descended. Her comment overstepped the barrier separating polite strangers.

Well, mostly polite.

After a moment, he sighed and lifted his arm away from her. "It's a reminder that you're out of bounds."

With that, any pretense that only a jammed lock linked them melted away.

"If we're discovered, everybody will think that we've been up to no good." Philippa's voice faded to a whisper. But in this tiny room, there was no chance that he'd fail to hear, even if she was cowardly enough to hope he mightn't.

"Are you inviting me to ruin you?" he asked wryly. "Somehow I doubt it."

She raised her chin and told herself to be brave.

Some devil in her soul turned her into a person much more daring than her workaday self. Right now, she couldn't bear to think that she'd leave this closet with her curiosity unsatisfied.

"I'd like someone to kiss me." Her words emerged more steadily than she'd imagined possible. "Someone who knows what he's doing."

She flinched at Erskine's laugh. "To Hades with you, who else have you been kissing?"

It didn't occur to her to lie. "Prescott Wayne, the vicar's son, kissed me last year."

Danger hummed in the air. Lord Erskine's long body brushed hers as he shifted. One of the startling things about being so close to him was how physically aware she was of his every movement. She even heard the catch in his breath before he spoke. "You didn't enjoy the experience?"

"No, it was horrible." She shuddered, recalling the bad fish taste of Prescott's mouth and the sloppy suction of his lips.

"And you think I can do better?"

"I don't know." She paused, wondering if she was mad to pursue this. Then letting the devil inside her have its way, she pursued anyway. "I'd like grounds for comparison."

"Would you indeed, my little sparrow?"

She almost welcomed the surge of annoyance at his patronizing response. "Please forget I mentioned it."

Philippa slid away from him. Not far enough. His

big, strong hand closed around hers. She started as beguiling warmth flowed up her arm and through her body.

Oh, dear, she really was in trouble.

"I love that you look like a sparrow." His Scottish accent was more pronounced.

"I don't," she said glumly, wishing that she was as beautiful as her sister. Then this handsome rogue wouldn't hesitate to show her the kind of kisses that sent poets into raptures. "Sparrows are dull and as common as dirt."

His grip tightened. "You should look more closely. Sparrows are quite beautiful."

"Boring."

"Subtle."

Her pique faded. "You're full of clever answers. I suppose it's because you're used to persuading reluctant ladies."

"Are you so reluctant?" That velvety murmur was a seductive weapon.

A shiver rippled down her spine. To her surprise, it wasn't fear, but irresistible physical awareness. "You always have a ready reply."

"Not so ready. I've devoted three days of thought to the issue of kissing you."

She frowned into the darkness without trying to break his hold on her hand. "I'm an unremarkable woman from an undistinguished family. What interest can you have in me?"

"You underestimate yourself. If you made more effort to shine in company, I wouldn't be the only man to notice that your hair is like mahogany silk and that your eyes are large and sparkling and express your every thought."

Oh, no. She definitely didn't need him reading her thoughts. "In that case, I'm glad that we're in the dark and you can't see my face."

"I don't need light to see you. I've observed you very closely indeed, my lovely shy bird. From the moment I first saw you."

She tugged her hand free. "That can't be true."

"Of course it's true."

She heard the smile in his voice. If she'd thought that musical baritone appealing before, now she was close to melting into a pool of honey.

"Prove it."

She didn't know why she pushed this. Did she really want to confirm that he lied about seeing her? Something inside her blossomed at the idea that amongst the glittering throng at her uncle's Christmas party, this experienced man had singled her out.

"Yesterday, you wore a green dress. Today you're wearing a blue one. Whenever I've seen you, you've had a simple gold locket around your neck."

Shock jammed her response in her throat. Still he sounded like he smiled. She wished he wouldn't. She also wished she wasn't disappointed when he didn't try to recapture her hand.

"Shall I continue?" he asked gently.

"I feel…I feel a little overwhelmed." She reached up to fiddle with the locket she'd inherited from her grandmother. "Perhaps it's a rake's habit to note the details when he meets a woman."

Erskine laughed softly. "You're a suspicious chit."

He sounded as though he genuinely appreciated her. Her brief enchantment faded. Surely he mocked her. Or used dalliance to fill the dull minutes while they were stuck here. She wriggled away, feeling depressed at being Lord Erskine's stopgap.

"You're thinking too much," he murmured.

Every hair on her skin lifted in awareness. She heard the unspoken promise in his words. "You're dangerous."

"I've been a perfect gentleman."

"So far."

"I won't do anything you don't want me to."

That sounded ominous. Her stomach lurched with forbidden excitement. She moved further away, out of temptation's reach. Unfortunately in this glorified cupboard, that wasn't very far at all.

How mortifying that twenty years of respectability crumbled by the second. As yet, Lord Erskine hadn't gone beyond holding her hand and admitting that he'd noticed her. Imagine how cooperative she'd be if he tried a little harder to seduce her.

She swallowed to moisten a dry throat. "This has gone far enough."

"As you wish."

Curse him. He sounded like he didn't care.

Oh, she was a fool. Of course he didn't care. All his talk about the charms of quiet, brown-haired women was just that—talk. He must laugh himself silly to think that she swallowed this drivel about his interest.

As if a man like Lord Erskine would spare a glance for plain-spoken, plain-featured Philippa Sanders. She only had his attention now because there wasn't another candidate, and he must be bored, locked in this cupboard. He was probably wishing that Amelia had decided to retrieve her own letter.

The thought stung. As she meant it to. "Perhaps we shouldn't talk anymore."

She retreated further, bumping the base of a leather chest that filled the corner. How she'd love to stride away with pride intact. But of course, her pride wouldn't be wounded if she wasn't trapped with a sweet-tongued Don Juan.

Even so, she could get up. The room was small, but not so small that she had to huddle at Erskine's side. The thought had just crossed her mind when his hand brushed her cheek.

Every muscle went absolutely still. Even her heart stopped beating.

The tingling contact lasted a mere second. Then it was over.

She should shift. Protest. Make it clear that she had

no intentions of providing this rake with an amusing interval before his return to the fleshpots.

The fleeting tenderness in his touch kept her mute. Mute and waiting.

It felt like an eternity before he touched her face again, cupping her jaw in his large, capable hand. Still he was gentle, and his gentleness opened a rift in her heart. She'd never allowed herself to long, but this soft caress in the thick darkness made her yearn for a man's touch as she'd never yearned for anything in her life.

Such power a rake had.

But not even recalling the scandalous stories about Lord Erskine made her demur.

She trembled, waiting.

And still she waited.

Surely a rake wouldn't allow his prey a chance to reconsider her surrender.

Then the air vibrated in a way she couldn't define, and his lips glanced across hers. Her muffled response smacked of welcome rather than objection. His hand curled around her arm, and he drew her forward until she angled across his chest, perfectly placed for more kisses.

Another pause.

Before his lips met hers again, she was shaking as if she'd been left out in the snow instead of confined in this cozy den. She should tell him to stop. Kissing Lord Erskine was even more reckless than breaking into his room. But still that treacherous tenderness held her acquiescent.

Tenderness had been tragically rare in her life, and it lured like a warm fire on a cold night. Giving him silent permission to continue, she curled her hands over his shoulders. She behaved with shocking wantonness, but right now, she'd readily break any rule as long as this enchantment continued.

This time he lingered. Lord Erskine's lips were firm and cool. A hint of pressure here. A brief touch there. Everything deepening her need.

The intimacy was astonishing. She caught a hint of his breath, sweet with a rich hint of port. Lord Erskine's hand sweetly cradled her cheek, making her feel more fragile than glass.

Philippa remained in her right mind enough to recognize that, for all his careful handling, this was seduction. The moment he placed his lips on hers, all impulse to anything except pleasure had vanished.

Before she'd broken into his room, if anyone had suggested that she'd willingly kiss the reprobate Lord Erskine, she'd have laughed in their face. Now the prospect of more kisses made her giddy with excitement.

She pulled away a fraction to catch her breath. Her heart pounded a wild tarantella. And when he drew her back to him, her sigh sounded like yes.

Erskine kissed her again and again. Surprise lurked beneath her sensual delight. This rake's kisses were almost innocent. And astonishing. Prescott had grabbed her arms, holding her still as he thrust a slimy tongue into her mouth. It had been like eating a slug. Erskine's tongue touched her lips, tasting her delicately, never encroaching inside, although some wicked impulse inside her wished he would push further.

His kisses made her think of butterflies or feathers or silk. Nothing slug-like at all.

At first she appreciated his endless patience, but after an eternity of teasing, urgency subsumed uncertainty. Reaction settled hot and heavy and disturbing in the base of her belly. She longed for more. Although despite Prescott's clumsy efforts, she had no idea what "more" entailed.

Then Erskine began to kiss her face. Soft, quick kisses to brow and nose and chin. Across her cheeks. To the corners of her lips. More feathers and silk.

Instinctively she licked her lips as he moved on to trace the line of her cheekbones. Tasting him was astonishingly powerful, as though his essence seeped into her blood. She identified the flavors of wine and man and something that she guessed was desire.

Did Lord Erskine desire her?

Once the idea would have appalled her. Once she'd never have credited it was possible. Right now, trembling under a volley of sweet kisses, Philippa wondered if perhaps he did. It made no sense, but since she'd entered this dark cave of a room, the real world had lost its sway over her.

Still he tormented her. A dissatisfied sound welled up from her throat. Philippa wasn't stupid enough to yield more than kisses, and asking for more risked ruin indeed. But his touch made her restless and yearning. Her skin felt hot and tight, and her heart crashed over and over against her ribs.

His tantalizing seduction drove her mad, changed her into someone she didn't recognize. This panting girl who welcomed his touch was no longer purposeful, practical Philippa Sanders.

Another incoherent protest emerged. She parted her lips to drag in a shaky breath, and this time his mouth opened over hers. How did he know exactly where to place his lips when she couldn't see two inches in front of her face? The room was darker than a cellar in Hades.

He groaned into her mouth, and for the first time, she tasted him properly. His rich flavor overwhelmed her. Without thinking where this might lead, her tongue fluttered against his lips, seeking a response.

He groaned again, a sound of longing deep in his throat. At last his arms lashed around her.

She'd reached a stage of need where she wanted him to batter down her resistance, overcome her doubts, kiss her until all she knew was pleasure. The pleasure that still hovered out of reach, no matter how she enjoyed this dance of playful kisses, of advance and retreat, of pausing for permission, then relenting just as she reached the point of protest.

His mouth remained light on hers, although she felt the tension in his arms as he resisted the urge to tug her closer. How did she know this? Pure instinct. She was woefully inexperienced with a man. She was playing out of her class with a man of the world like Lord Erskine.

Which didn't mean she aimed to stop the game.

This time with intent, her tongue darted forward to touch his. Heat shuddered through her, sparking a fusillade of unfamiliar sensations. She shifted to relieve the building pressure between her legs.

Philippa might be innocent, but she wasn't stupid. Her body prepared itself for his. She'd grown up in the country. The mechanics of the sexual act were no mystery. But mechanics had no connection with the unprecedented responses rushing through her, softening her muscles, making her blood throb with need, weighting her breasts and belly with desire.

Heaven help her, he didn't need to drag her into his arms. The devilish purpose of that long, careful seduction now became clear. Philippa couldn't bear to be separated from him by even as much as an inch. She was the one who wantonly pressed forward.

He was irresistible, so warm, so big, so powerful. When her body slid against his, she felt the immediate change in him. His kiss shifted from exploration to unalloyed possession.

She should be terrified, but instead she felt desired. His tongue plunged between her lips, claiming her. His arms twined around her, so that she couldn't escape even if she wanted to.

He swung her until she sprawled across his lap, her face tilted toward his, her breasts crushed against his bare chest under the coat. What had begun like a game became as serious as life and death.

She felt dizzy with lack of air and the storm in her blood. The heaviness between her legs made her wriggle. If she'd ever doubted Erskine's interest, her position now left her in no doubt.

That was astonishing enough. What was even more astonishing was that she wanted him, too. She'd never experienced desire. She'd had no idea how it overwhelmed every consideration but physical need.

She moaned consent against his lips. She was too far gone for fear. There was only heat and hunger and his wild, wild kisses.

He tensed against her, but she gripped his shoulders. All that mattered was that he shared more of those shattering sensations. Then through the pounding in her ears, she heard the rattle of the lock. Before she could break away from Lord Erskine, someone flung open the door.

Keeping her in his lap, Lord Erskine twisted around at the interruption. In the glare of what felt like a hundred candles, Philippa blinked owlishly.

Then horrified shrieks split the night.

CHAPTER FOUR

Damn, damn, damn.

Erskine fought the urge to punch the wall, although this whole bloody mess was his fault. He'd locked himself in the dressing room with Miss Sanders. Then he hadn't had the sense to keep his hands to himself. Now here he was on the floor with an innocent girl in his arms, and the game was well and truly up.

But Philippa Sanders had been so sweet, so near, so utterly irresistible. The temptation had been over-whelming.

Which was no excuse for mauling her. And now exposing her to full-scale scandal.

Even through the thick door, he should have heard activity in the outer room. But Miss Sanders had so captivated him that he'd paid no whit of attention to anything else.

"Mamma, please hush," Philippa said urgently, and without effect. "You'll have everyone in here to see what the fuss is about."

"How could you? You wicked, wicked girl. How could you?" And a litany of similar complaints about her younger daughter's character and morals. All at top pitch.

Blast the harridan. Erskine would wager that they'd hear her in London. His grip on Philippa tightened, although it was too late for him to save her from trouble.

Behind the distraught parent's rotund figure, Amelia stood, hatred glittering in her icy blue eyes as she glared at her sister. Right now, Amelia looked ready to commit murder.

Erskine had always suspected that Amelia's angelic looks hid a nasty streak. He suppressed a shudder and thanked heaven that the elder Sanders girl had never appealed to him.

Mills, who held the key to the dressing room, raised his candelabra and greeted his master with a cool smile. "Merry Christmas, my lord."

Nothing shook Mills's composure, although a faint tightening around his eyes hinted that Mrs. Sanders' hysterics came close.

"Philippa, how could you do this? How? Oh, I can't even look at you!" Mrs. Sanders sucked in a noisy breath. "And still you sit there, basking in your sin."

Guilt punched Erskine in the gut as he realized that

he should have released Philippa the instant the door opened. Holding her was pure instinct, some rusty protective urge remaining from a boyhood of rescuing stray dogs and birds fallen from their nests. He thought he'd outgrown his need to shelter small, defenseless creatures. Apparently not. Philippa was a stalwart soul, but one glance at her wan, set face indicated that she needed protection.

Before he could apologize, she struggled free and stumbled to her feet. Feeling absurd on the floor before his accusers, he rose as well. In a futile attempt to shield her, he hovered at her shoulder. She sidled away, bumping into the leather trunk in the corner. Clearly she didn't appreciate his attempts to play the hero.

Damn it, why should she? He'd acted like a dunderhead.

Kissing Philippa, he'd felt invincible. Right now, facing down a wall of disapproval from his dressing room doorway, he felt like a rat in a trap.

"Mamma, there's a perfectly innocent explanation—"

"Don't bother lying, you nasty little cat." Amelia's contempt made Philippa recoil. "I should have guessed when you offered to help me that you pursued your own causes. You were so clever to hide your interest in Lord Erskine."

"Amelia—"

Erskine glanced at Philippa, then wished he hadn't. She looked utterly overcome. Unfortunately, however wounded and humiliated she appeared, she also appeared delectable and ruffled and thoroughly kissed. Her rich brown hair tumbled around her shoulders, and in her crushed dress, she looked little better than a gypsy. Her intentions may have been pure, whatever her sister thought, but Blind Freddie could see that physical contact had occurred behind that locked door.

Before anything else, he had to put a cork in the mother's damned caterwauling. "Mrs. Sanders, bringing the house's attention upon us can't be your intention."

To his surprise, the lady abruptly shut her mouth and turned accusatory blue eyes, eerily similar to her oldest daughter's, in his direction. Erskine frowned. Those eyes were completely dry and, until she glanced down in what he read as false humility, alight with calculation.

What the deuce was going on? Had he been caught by the oldest trick in the world? Suspicion soured his gut as he stared at Philippa.

He was under no illusions about his appeal to the ton's rapacious ladies. A single man of great fortune and distinguished lineage always attracted marriage-minded females. Since leaving university and taking his place in society, he'd been on guard. Since before that. The lassies on his Scottish estate were as awake as any English miss to the main chance.

But his doubt over Philippa's motives vanished almost as soon as it arose. He was the one who had locked them in, and he hadn't mistaken her dismay at the prospect of a scandal.

A glance at Mrs. Sanders told him that if Philippa hadn't realized the advantages of tonight's events, her doting mamma certainly had. Amelia continued to stare poison at her trembling sister.

"Just what are you doing in here, Mamma?" Philippa asked in a small voice.

Her mother regarded her youngest daughter with disfavor. "I couldn't sleep, and I wanted you to read to me. I was horrified to find your room empty. Naturally I went to Amelia and made her tell me where you were. I can hardly believe your brazen behavior."

Amelia's mouth pinched at the explanation. Erskine could imagine how unwillingly she'd revealed her sister's whereabouts. But Mrs. Sanders was a bully to the bootstraps. A self-centered little minx like Amelia could never withstand her mother's demands.

Wearing a startling scarlet dressing gown, his host Sir Theodore Liddell appeared at the bedroom door. Only moments behind him, Erskine's nitwit drinking companions crowded along the corridor, tripping over one another in tipsy eagerness to investigate the brouhaha.

"What's all this hullabaloo, Erskine? Is this some Christmas prank? Bit early in the morning for hijinks, don't you think?" Sir Theodore's jovial tone abruptly hardened as his eyes fell upon his cringing niece. "Good God, Philippa, what are you doing here?"

Any frail hope Erskine had harbored that he and Philippa might manage to sail through without attracting the world's notice shriveled. And he became increasingly convinced that Mrs. Sanders had manufactured this impromptu gathering.

He reached for Philippa's hand. For one sweet moment, her fingers curled around his. Despite the chaos buffeting him from all sides, brief peace filled his soul. Then that peace disintegrated as she withdrew her hand to twist it in her skirts in an agony of guilty remorse.

"U-Uncle, I know how this looks—" she stammered, sounding completely unlike the forthright woman who had demanded her sister's letter.

"Damned fishy is how it looks, Philippa, my girl," Sir Theodore snapped, an angry flush turning his cheeks as red as an overripe apple. "Just what in Hades are you doing in this reprobate's room at this hour? And why are you half-dressed?"

Erskine winced. The uncle showed as little propriety as the mother, even if he spoke from temper rather than calculation. Behind Mrs. Sanders, the drunken idiots audibly sniggered.

"Half-dressed?" With shaking hands, Philippa tugged at her clothes, although her uncle had exaggerated. However tempted he'd been to take matters further, Erskine had made sure that she stayed buttoned to the neck.

"My lord, your niece is blameless," Erskine said,

knowing nobody would believe him. But he couldn't bear to witness Philippa's shame. Especially when all she'd done was enjoy a few kisses. She was hardly the Jezebel that gossip would paint her once this story got out.

As it inevitably would.

Again he cursed his damned arrogance in shutting that door, although nothing could make him regret kissing her. That had been an unforgettable experience, whatever its price.

His defense of Philippa attracted Sir Theodore's wrath. "Look at her, with her hair falling about her like bloody Delilah." His voice lowered, but that only emphasized his outrage. "Erskine, I know the stories about you. Who doesn't? But I never heard of you ruining a girl of good family. This is abominable behavior, even for you."

Erskine hid another wince. Tonight he'd suffered an uncharacteristic impulse to do the right thing. Perhaps this was a lesson not to change his bad old ways.

"Your niece and I were trapped in the dressing room." His chilly tone would have done his stiff-necked father credit. "I will not have Miss Sanders's name sullied. She is respectably dressed. Her hair is untidy as a result of her struggle to open the door."

"A likely story," Sir Theodore sneered. "Even if it's true, that doesn't explain her presence in your bedamned bedroom."

"Uncle, I had good reason for being here," Philippa said shakily.

"Apart from brazen stupidity, I can't think what," her uncle retorted.

In silent pleading, Philippa's eyes fastened on Amelia. Erskine wasn't remotely surprised when Amelia failed to come to the rescue. Philippa, of course, was too honorable to tell tales. Odd how well he knew her, but he believed to his bones that she wouldn't betray her sister.

Although, to give Amelia the little credit she deserved, what was the point of confessing to the letter? Her lapse would only compound the scandal of her sister caught in a rake's bedroom.

Sir Theodore looked ready to explode. "I'm the closest thing that the brainless chit has to a father. I can't let this insult go unchallenged."

God above, could this get any worse? With every moment, Erskine found less room for maneuver. He had no intention of shooting Sir Theodore. The man was at least thirty years his senior. And if Erskine was any judge of men, the plump baronet had devoted most of those thirty years to drinking. The fellow couldn't hit a bull elephant at five paces.

With a horror that this time looked genuine, Mrs. Sanders abruptly ceased bawling and stared aghast at her brother. "Theodore, don't be a fool. In a duel, Erskine will make mincemeat of you."

The wrong thing to say. Tact apparently didn't run

in Philippa's family. Tact or good sense. Which was a sodding pity, considering Erskine's likely future.

Sir Theodore puffed up. "This is all your fault. You've let these girls run wild, Barbara. Although I always thought Philippa had a scrap of sense, unlike that twit Amelia."

"Uncle!" Amelia spluttered. "At least nobody's ever found me in a man's room after midnight."

Only for want of opportunity, Erskine felt like saying, remembering her letter. The problem was that hardened, selfish little flirts like Amelia kept an eye to their own advantage and rarely faced the consequences of their behavior. It was innocents like Philippa who were always caught out.

This had gone far enough. He drew himself up to his full height and shot a speaking glance at Mills. "We've provided enough Yuletide entertainment for your guests, Sir Theodore."

Erskine raised supercilious eyebrows at the louts in the doorway. He'd perfected the look years ago to squash the pretensions of social-climbing mushrooms. As usual, it succeeded. The boisterous young bucks shuffled back, muttering.

At a nod from Erskine, Mills closed the door and stood at the entrance like a tall, thin gatekeeper.

That left Philippa, Amelia, Mrs. Sanders, and Sir Theodore in his bedroom. A more manageable group, although Erskine wasn't deceived about his cronies' discretion. Before the day was out, the events of this Christmas Eve would be general gossip in London.

"Much better," he said calmly. There had been quite enough theatricals. "Sir Theodore, may I get you a brandy?"

The older man nodded, then frowned as though disappointed that the high drama descended into something resembling a family meeting. Even Mrs. Sanders seemed less inclined to histrionics, although her eyes retained their beady, acquisitive light.

"Just what do you intend to do about my little girl?" she asked, her show of concern for Philippa too late to convince. "She's ruined."

Mills shifted from the door—Erskine's dismissal had succeeded, the threat of invasion faded. The valet moved to the sideboard and poured generous brandies for Sir Theodore and his master. Then after a considering glance at Mrs. Sanders, one for that lady.

Erskine stepped next to Philippa and once more took her small, cold hand in his. His deliberately ostentatious gesture wouldn't be lost on her mother and uncle. Or her sister.

Ignoring Philippa's frantic attempts to pull away, he straightened and spoke words that yesterday hadn't been on his horizon. "Sir Theodore, would you honor me with your niece's hand in marriage?"

CHAPTER FIVE

For Philippa, the next four days became a nightmare from which she couldn't wake. She felt like a ghost in her uncle's house. Or like a prisoner in a dungeon. Again and again, she protested that under no circumstances would she marry Lord Erskine, yet still arrangements proceeded for the hurried wedding.

Why should her mother change a lifetime's habit and listen to her now? The triumph of capturing the elusive Scottish earl for her daughter made her mother deafer than usual to common sense.

Not that her triumph was untrammeled joy. Even as she prodded at Philippa to show some enthusiasm for this ill-judged match, she bewailed the fact that Lord Erskine had chosen the wrong daughter. How it irked her that the beautiful older sister would become a mere

Mrs., while plain little Philippa joined the ranks of the aristocracy.

Amelia's reaction to the engagement wasn't a surprise either, which made it no more pleasant to endure. Like their mother, she was convinced that Philippa had engineered this awful mess. In Amelia's mind, Lord Erskine had been ready to steal her away from her betrothed. Only Philippa's spite had stymied that glorious outcome.

As a result, Amelia retreated into a seething silence that Philippa correctly diagnosed as a first-class sulk. Even Mr. Fox noticed that his chosen bride had been elated on Christmas Eve and noticeably downcast and snappish since—and nobody would describe him as a perceptive gentleman.

The only blessing in the whole miserable situation was that, thanks to the almighty scandal, all guests not directly linked to the family had departed the house by Christmas night. Unfortunately that left Philippa with her betrothed, her nasty cousin Caroline, her sullen sister, a mother who ignored her every plea, and an aunt and uncle never much interested in her, who now treated her like she carried a contagious disease. Mr. Fox was kind, but a stranger, and he'd taken to retreating into the smoking room to avoid his grumpy fiancée.

Philippa tried to warn her sister about her behavior toward Mr. Fox and got no thanks for her trouble.

After that, she decided to let Amelia stew. Philippa had problems of her own.

It was all very well knowing that she was blameless —she refused to feel guilty for enjoying Erskine's kisses. He was a notable rake; he could probably make a saint kiss him back. But when the world viewed her as a scarlet woman, and, more galling, an overweening social climber, it became difficult to hold her head high.

Gossip had spread horrifically quickly. Even three days later, she shuddered to recall the ordeal of church on Christmas morning. She'd pretended not to hear the whispers from pew to pew when the Sanders and Liddell families arrived for the service. Under the battery of avid stares, Philippa had wanted to curl up and die. She didn't like being the center of attention, particularly attention bristling with malice and disapproval.

It irked her that Lord Erskine had taken his new circumstances in his stride. On Christmas morning, he'd been so cool under fire that she'd wanted to skin him alive. Almost as much as she wanted to skin him for setting this marriage in train without asking her first.

She'd been right all along. He was an arrogant swine.

Trapped in that dark dressing room, she'd wondered if he was a better man than she'd thought. And despite everything that had happened since, she'd never deny how marvelous his kisses were. Those moments in his arms had been astonishing, a rapturous experience that would fuel her dreams.

But by daylight, Lord Erskine returned to the supercilious creature she'd so disliked. And she was sick to death of the world acting as if in marrying him, she won some wonderful and completely undeserved prize. Just as she was sick of the pity and surprise directed at Erskine, when people heard of his sudden engagement.

Nobody apart from her mother and Amelia had the nerve to say it aloud, but Philippa knew that everyone thought such a plain girl was lucky to capture this rich, handsome man. The sly glances silently congratulating her on her clever game were almost worse than the pity.

Generally Philippa prided herself on her self-control. In her family, only her calmness and cool reason held their fragile world steady. Right now, she was ready to scream and throw china and slam doors like the most spoiled debutante. After four days of playing Lord Erskine's inadequate bride, she burned to end this horrible farce.

But devil take the man, despite a heavy fall of snow, he'd left for London on Boxing Day, and she hadn't seen him since. It was enough to make even the most complacent woman want to smash something. Preferably Blair Hume's thick skull.

His absence meant that she was yet to share her

plan for their mutual rescue. He'd written to her uncle since reaching London, she knew. Only because Sir Theodore, who spoke to her almost as rarely as Amelia did, had informed her at last night's dinner that Lord Erskine was expected back today, with the wedding to take place the following morning. The dizzying speed of events left Philippa queasy with helplessness. This was like being tied to the back of a runaway horse.

Well, this afternoon, the runaway horse submitted to the bridle. Philippa heard the quick, confident step approaching through the barren woodland behind the Chinese summerhouse. On wobbly legs, she rose from the wooden bench outside.

"My lord," she said flatly as her betrothed turned the corner of the icy gravel path. She curtsied briefly. When she straightened, she huddled into her old black winter coat, several seasons out of date but warm. Thick drifts of snow lay about them, and the cold was perishing. "You got my note."

"Apparently, or I wouldn't be here," Lord Erskine said lightly, although his green eyes were watchful. A faint smile hovered about his lips, and when he spoke, his breath clouded in the chilly air. "And good afternoon to you, Miss Sanders."

She blushed. She kept forgetting that he wasn't her enemy. He was a victim, too. She supposed a real fiancée would inquire after his health, ask about his journey. But of course, she was only the girl he'd been cornered into marrying. "Good afternoon."

He smiled fully, and despite her determination to end this travesty, her foolish heart skipped a beat. He really was a spectacular man. "Is this meeting wise?"

Wise? She suppressed a hollow laugh. She'd moved beyond the reach of anything resembling wisdom. Desperation had driven her to ask Mills to deliver the note requesting a private conversation. Over the last days, she'd come to approve of Mills. Nothing seemed to disconcert him, and he treated her with a sincere respect that she'd encountered nowhere else since Christmas Eve.

"My reputation couldn't get any worse," she said morosely, rubbing her gloved hands together to warm them.

Erskine's amusement drained away, leaving deep concern in its place. "Has it been bad?"

This time the hollow laugh escaped. "How long have you got?"

"I'm sorry, Philippa. I left you in a damned spot, but I had to get the special license. The sooner we're wed, the better for everyone." He didn't sound like the haughty rake she loathed. He sounded like the man who had been unfailingly good-natured, sharing a cupboard with a woman he'd never have chosen as his companion.

The man she'd kissed so ardently.

His apology soothed her resentment, although she'd spent the last four days cursing his high-handedness. She stifled a complaint about him calling her Philippa.

After all, if their marriage took place, he'd have rights to much more than the use of her Christian name.

She met his eyes, then wished she hadn't. If he'd been lethal to her common sense in the dark, here lit with gold in the late sun, he was devastating. He was dressed for the country in buff breeches and a dark blue coat that emphasized the breadth of his shoulders and his height. His thick dark hair was disheveled, as though he'd recently run his hand through it.

"That's…that's what I want to talk about." She wished she sounded more confident. But something in the way he studied her reminded her of his discomfiting kisses.

He watched her as though he guessed how unhappy and confused she'd been. "I know you're worried—"

She spoke quickly. "Can we go into the summerhouse? It's freezing, and I feel exposed out here." If anyone reported her meeting Lord Erskine, it would only add fuel to the catty gossip about her brazenness.

"Very well." He gestured for her to precede him up the shallow flight of stairs into the wooden pagoda. Even when determined to dislike him, she'd noted Lord Erskine's perfect manners.

He paused in the doorway as she subsided onto the red lacquer bench running around the room. The building, cleared of furniture and fabrics, felt cavernous and cold.

She'd chosen this place for its seclusion. She wanted a frank and uninterrupted discussion. Only now as she looked up at Lord Erskine's shadowed face did she question that decision. Something about the isolation and the pretty, empty room suggested a lovers' rendezvous.

The last impression she wanted to convey.

"Please sit down," she said shakily, staring down to where her hands twined together in her lap. It wasn't much warmer inside than it had been outside. "I'm sure you know why I asked you to meet me."

He stepped into the summerhouse, sitting beside her but not, she noted with relief, too close. "I'm hoping it's because you want more kisses."

She choked on appalled laughter as her gaze flickered away from his. Clearly the romantic isolation had struck him as well. "I wouldn't be so presumptuous."

"That's a pity. I've been thinking about kissing you ever since Christmas Eve. I enjoyed it. I'd very much like to do it again."

She gasped and stared at him. He appeared sincere, but of course, he couldn't be. "Stop it."

In the enclosed space, their voices echoed oddly. The sun on the snowdrifts outside created a white, eerie light inside.

Those slashing black brows lowered with displeasure. "If we're to marry, it's best if we're honest."

Philippa leaped to her feet and began to pace. Nervous energy made her steps quick and staccato so that the heels of her half-boots clicked across the chinoiserie tiles. "That's precisely it."

She sucked in a breath and told herself to be resolute. Which was harder than she'd expected when she'd skulked in her room plotting this meeting.

"What's precisely it, my love?"

The endearment, however meaningless, spoken in his soft Scottish burr made her shiver with a mixture of pleasure and discomfort. "Don't call me that."

He shrugged and lounged back against the sill, pushing the window behind him open a fraction. The breeze played with his hair, free to touch him when she wasn't. At her sides, her fingers curled as she bit back a surge of longing.

Seeing him again proved more...difficult than Philippa had expected. She hadn't counted on quite how many barriers their captivity had shattered. It must be her imagination, but her nostrils flared at a hint of his clean, sandalwood scent. Since Christmas Eve, sandalwood had haunted her dreams.

"What is it, Philippa?"

She stopped her restless pacing and leveled her shoulders like a soldier facing a cavalry charge. "We can't marry."

Although he maintained his casual pose, Erskine's muscles tightened with denial. Damn it, he wasn't backing out, and if he had his way, neither was she. "Of course we can."

That ruffled his sparrow's delicate feathers. Temper added color to cheeks that had been too pale when she'd met him outside in the snow. That neat, rounded body also seemed slighter than it had when he'd left for London.

Hell, he shouldn't have left her alone, but he hadn't had any choice. Still, he could imagine how her bloody awful family had treated her in his absence. After he married Philippa, he'd make damned sure that they showed more care.

In the days since he'd seen her, his uncharacteristic urge to protect this girl hadn't faded. He'd taken one look at the spiritless, unhappy young woman who had greeted him, and he'd wanted to punch someone. Then kiss her until she became once more the soft, passionate armful of a few nights ago.

"You're not listening, my lord." To his relief, she sounded much more like the girl who had challenged him in his room. "Nobody can force me to marry you."

Without straightening from his slouch, he arched his eyebrows. He knew his cool reaction threw her off balance. Just what he wanted while he worked out how to convince her against jilting him.

Erskine should have anticipated something like this. Despite her outward quietness, Philippa Sanders wasn't meek and obedient. Married life promised to be interesting. "You agreed—"

Her lips tightened. "Actually I don't believe I got in

a word that night you arranged everything with my uncle."

Dismay made him forget strategy and sit up. Good God, she was right. No wonder she was disgruntled. "Philippa, what a blasted dunderhead I am. I should have asked you."

His immediate capitulation seemed to mollify her, and some of her stiffness drained away. "You didn't have much chance."

He stood, covered the few feet separating them and dropped to one knee, seizing her hand. "Let me remedy that lack right now."

"You misunderstand," she said sharply, trying to pull free.

"I've never proposed before. I should do it properly, bonny lassie."

Color flamed in her cheeks. The wan creature of a few minutes ago became only a memory, thank God. "I pray you, Lord Erskine, please stop this."

He refused to give up. "My delightful Miss Sanders, darling Philippa, will you marry me tomorrow and make me the happiest of men?"

Her eyes narrowed, and she stopped fluttering. "This is such a joke to you, isn't it?" She rushed on before he could answer. "I don't know why you find it so amusing. You'll be trapped, too—although I suppose you intend to maintain your rakish ways and act as if I don't exist."

He frowned, all pretense at nonchalance evaporating. "That's not very flattering. To me or to you."

"Perhaps." Her voice bit. "But accurate."

He released her and rose, glaring. "A sweeping statement, considering how little you know of me."

She didn't retreat, although he'd used the tone that made grown men cower. "Surely you want to avoid this disaster as much as I do."

His vanity pricked under her open reluctance to marry him. "In honor, I can't—"

One hand made an emphatic gesture, negating his protests. "Honor will be poor comfort when we're condemned to a lifetime of misery."

"Please don't spare my feelings," he retorted, turning to stare out at the bleak wintry landscape.

Erskine fought to calm his breathing. This uncompromising girl tested his temper. Nobody tested his temper. He never cared enough about anything to get angry.

She sighed, and when next she spoke, she sounded less adamant. "I'm sorry. This isn't your fault. And… and I appreciate you stepping in to try and save me from ruin."

His lips twitched at her grudging thanks. Women generally worked like the devil to turn him up sweet. He must be mad, but her frankness appealed to him. "Was that apology painful?"

"A little," Philippa admitted after a pause. He heard

the soft click of her heels as she came up beside him. "Lord Erskine—"

He glanced at her. "Don't you think you should call me Blair?"

She no longer looked cross. Instead, she looked sweet and earnest and breathtakingly lovely with her pretty hair bundled in a loose knot. Her serious brown eyes focused on him, and emotion colored her ivory skin. With every moment he spent in this girl's company, he found himself more astonished that the world considered Amelia the beautiful Sanders sister.

Philippa's cheeks turned dusky rose, and when doubt pursed her lips, he couldn't help thinking of kisses. Privacy tested his restraint. He'd dearly love to haul her into his arms as he had in the dressing room. The only thing stopping him was that in her current frame of mind, she'd probably slap him.

To his surprise she didn't haver about using his Christian name. "Blair, if I jilt you, no blame will attach to you."

"Of course it will. I'll forever carry the reputation of a man who seduced an innocent girl and left her alone to bear the world's insult."

For the first time, a glimmer of genuine admiration sparked in her eyes. "Good heavens, I really did have you all wrong, didn't I?"

He shrugged, suddenly uncomfortable. "I'm not a good man, but there are some things even I won't do."

"All the more reason not to sacrifice yourself to a loveless union."

He floundered here. He hadn't expected his betrothed to want to cancel the wedding. When he'd received her note, he'd imagined she hoped to soothe her fears of marrying a stranger by deepening their acquaintance. Hopefully with a kiss or two. He hadn't lied about how the memory of her kisses had plagued him. "If I don't marry you, your life will be untenable."

She swung away and slumped onto the bench. "Life as your neglected wife will be untenable." Before he could argue, she raised one hand. Surprisingly, it was completely steady. "Now that Amelia's settled, I'll return home to run the family estate as I've done since my father's death. If I retreat to Essex and live as a blameless spinster, any scandal will eventually blow over."

He sat beside her, and this time when he took her gloved hand, she didn't withdraw. Satisfaction filled him at this small sign of trust. Inevitably, he recalled holding her hand in the dressing room. And the enchanting interlude that had followed. "Is that really what you want? To hide away for the rest of your life?"

He expected a heated response, but when she turned to him, tears swam in her huge dark eyes. It was the first time he'd seen her cry. Her misery punched him in the gut.

"At this stage, what I want doesn't matter. What matters is making the best of things."

He kept his voice calm, reasonable. With another woman, a demonstration of passion might persuade her to his point of view, but not with this one. The irony was that with every moment, his need to touch her grew.

"What about your mother and sister?" Distantly he wondered why he was so determined on maintaining their engagement. She was a sweet little thing, and she stirred his interest more than any other woman he could remember. But he enjoyed his freedom. Surely he should seize this chance for escape when she offered it. "What about your aunt and uncle? And your cousin? Your loss of reputation will affect everyone in your family. When we set the world on its ears, we did it with style, my love."

This time the endearment didn't turn her as stiff as a ruler. Instead her fingers tightened around his as though she sought reassurance.

His gut gave another of those unfamiliar lurches. He couldn't remember anyone turning to him in their troubles. Philippa's trust placed a weight upon his heart. It made him want to prove himself worthy. Why out of all Creation did this one girl rouse his rusty honor?

"People will forget," she mumbled without conviction.

"People never forget scandal. Believe me, I know." He made himself ask the question that hovered unspoken. "Do you dislike me so much?"

She frowned as if he made no sense, which went some small way toward soothing his bruised feelings. Dear God, he couldn't recall the last time he'd cared about a woman's opinion. His London friends would laugh their heads off at his dilemma. He was accounted a dab hand with the ladies. He'd believed that himself. Until he encountered Philippa Sanders. Who, apart from a few sizzling kisses, seemed completely immune to his vaunted charms.

"I don't know you."

He laughed, delighted despite himself. "Well, that's honest at least."

Her sternness didn't relent. "And you don't know me. Surely in a marriage, that's a recipe for disaster."

He shrugged. "I'm no expert on the institution." He paused. "But we have solid foundations."

"Like what?" she asked with such disbelief that he hid a wince.

"Well, whatever you think of me, I definitely like you. And physically we're compatible."

Her cheeks heated, and she avoided his eyes with delightful shyness. "A few kisses prove nothing."

His grip firmed. "This is where I can claim some expertise. We'll have no difficulties in the bedroom."

He heard her shocked gasp. "You're very blunt, my lord."

"You strike me as a woman who appreciates a direct approach." His voice deepened into sincerity. "I'm sorry, though, that you'll miss out on a courtship. If we had more time, I could convince you that we're very compatible indeed."

Her smile was faintly wistful. "I never expected anyone to court me."

Anger pricked him at how her dreadful family had disparaged her—and convinced her that they were right to do so. At that moment, he swore on his unlamented father's grave that she'd never feel insignificant again. "We'll postpone the courtship until after the wedding."

She still looked suspicious. "I'm surprised that you're taking this in such good spirit."

"I can imagine worse fates than being married to you."

"You speak rashly, my l…Blair." The tension eased around her eyes, and for the first time, he caught a glimpse of the intriguing humor he'd so enjoyed during their sojourn in his cupboard. "I might be bad tempered in the morning. I might slurp my soup."

It was a relief to hear her sounding more like his redoubtable companion in adversity than the unsure girl who had met him outside the summerhouse. "I might tramp mud into the carpets or feed the dogs under the table."

"Do you like dogs?"

"Of course." He smiled. "Do you?"

"Yes."

"Excellent. Something we have in common."

Her brief lightness faded. "You pretend that we can

win through on just a smile. Yet you must know we can't."

"A girl brave enough to break into a rake's bedroom is brave enough to approach our marriage as a grand adventure."

She studied him, her brown eyes troubled. "I think…I think it would help if you kissed me."

He regarded her with surprised admiration, even as heat stirred in his loins. She was indeed brave, his little sparrow. "Did you like it when I kissed you?"

"Yes," she confessed on a thread of sound.

"I'm glad." The urge to sweep her into his arms was nigh irresistible, but some strain of strategy in his compromised soul made him pause.

He couldn't blame her for hesitating to trust him. As she said, they were strangers. But if they were to make a success of life together, he needed to engage her interest on more than a physical level. "At least I was an improvement on Prescott Wayne."

Her eyes widened. "You remember?"

He should laugh, tease, treat her lightly, keep her guessing. But instead his words rang with unstrategic truth. "I remember everything you've ever said to me."

As reward for his unprecedented sincerity, cynicism shadowed her eyes. "I'm sure." She tilted her face in unmistakable invitation. "Will you kiss me?"

He placed a finger beneath her chin, keeping her turned toward him. She looked adorably earnest and remarkably tempting. They sat at a decorous distance.

Anything more would test fate—and his barely maintained principles. "Will you marry me?"

Her marked dark brows drew together. There was so much character in her face, she made conventionally pretty girls look dull in comparison. "It's a mistake."

"It's an opportunity." He released her, knowing he had her attention.

"You're a gambler."

He smiled down at her, feeling as if he played to gain a magnificent treasure. "Only when I know I'll win."

Her lips flattened. "You can't think I'm much of a prize."

"And there you'd be wrong."

She still looked troubled. "You're just saying nice things to get your way."

"I definitely intend to get my way. Especially when it's wicked."

Another wash of sweet color to her cheeks. "But I don't know anything about you."

"What do you want to know?"

He braced for questions about his affairs. He could imagine the gossip she'd heard. And for the first time in his chaotic, self-indulgent life, he was ashamed of those careless amours. Something about this pure, forthright girl made him examine the man he was and regret the dreams he'd forsaken as he became the notorious Earl of Erskine.

"Do you have a family?"

He drew a relieved breath. She wasn't calling him to account for his decadent life. Yet. "An older married sister with two daughters. A younger brother, still a bachelor, in the church. My mother lives in London."

He saw that his prosaic answer surprised her. "And where do you live?"

"Until now, mostly Erskine House in Berkeley Square. When I become a respectable married man, I suspect I'll spend more time on my estates in the Borders." He paused. "Although I'll have my wife's wishes to consider. Do you like the country?"

"Yes."

"Then I look forward to showing you my lands."

"You won't mind leaving London?"

Would he? Only a few days ago, he'd have sworn he'd never willingly abandon the capital's amusements. Call him a romantic fool, but at this moment, a cozy country idyll with his capable and kissable wife beckoned like paradise. "We can visit."

Impatience tightened her lips. "You're taking my consent for granted again."

"I think you and I have as much chance of making a go of things as anyone else," he said, knowing that if he revealed the depth of his desire, he'd frighten her.

He'd called her a sparrow. If he made the slightest untoward movement, his wild bird would fly away into the forest and he'd never find her again. And the strangest result of the last days was the certainty that if

Miss Philippa Sanders left his life, it would be immeasurably poorer.

She leveled that intelligent, thoughtful gaze upon him. He wondered what she saw. He wanted to tell her that she could trust him, but at this stage of their acquaintance, that statement was mere words. He had to prove himself true. The devil knew how.

Unexpected warmth softened her expression. "I hope you're right."

"Do I have your promise that you'll marry me tomorrow?"

They both recognized the question as deadly serious. Her coffee-colored eyes betrayed her responses. Denial. Fear. Then hard-won courage.

It took her so long to speak, he still wasn't sure that she'd agree. Although if she didn't, what future could she have?

After an agonizing interval, her thick eyelashes fluttered down. Her delicate throat moved as she swallowed. Just as he was about to beg like a complete blockhead for her answer, she spoke.

"Yes."

He struggled to hide his powerful satisfaction. This was insane. As she'd said, unforeseen circumstances compelled this marriage. But somewhere between discovering her in his room and this instant, he'd become reconciled to marrying her. Even if she didn't feel nearly so optimistic about their chances.

"I have your word?"

This time the response came with a hint of irritation. "Yes."

"Thank you." He ran his hand down her soft cheek, wanting to do more, knowing he couldn't, not yet.

When he stood, she stared up at him, mouth open with surprise. "Aren't you going to kiss me?"

Her disappointment was gratifying. Perhaps he had grounds for hope after all. He smiled at her. "Tomorrow."

Outraged, she jerked to her feet. "What?"

His smile broadened. "If you marry me tomorrow, I'll kiss you all you want."

Kiss her. And more. He could hardly wait. Instinct told him that right now he had the advantage. Kissing her would remove that advantage.

"That was a dirty trick." She sounded peeved, but the flicker of a dimple in her cheek indicated unwilling amusement.

"I'll show you more dirty tricks once we're married, my love."

His joke fell flat. Her expression turned worryingly somber. "I'm sure."

CHAPTER SIX

The sensation of being caught up in the whirlwind remained with Philippa after she left Lord Erskine—Blair—at the summerhouse. She accounted herself a determined person, someone who made up her mind and stuck to it. So how had he persuaded her to agree to the marriage when she'd arranged their meeting specifically to set him free?

More puzzling, why was he so set on doing the honorable thing?

How it grated that by far the most disappointing part of the encounter was that Blair hadn't kissed her. When on earth had his kisses become so important?

She returned to the house feeling irritable and frustrated and jumpy. A mood not improved when her mother caught her the instant she stepped in from the terrace and whisked her away for a dress fitting.

Philippa's disgrace didn't merit a new gown, but

nor could she marry an earl in a frock she'd worn for over a year. Her mother had enlisted the local seamstress to alter a dress Amelia disliked. Her sister's taste ran to frills and furbelows. So far, Philippa hadn't resisted her mother's choices as she'd been sure the wedding would never take place. Now it seemed she must make some effort not to look like a cheap fairing at the ceremony.

It was dark before she finally broke away from the fussing to retreat to her room. This was her last night in this shabby chamber. Tomorrow she'd share a bed with a man who remained an enigma, for all his unexpected kindness. To her astonishment, her nervous shiver at the thought contained a large dollop of excitement.

The door opened without a knock to reveal her cousin Caroline. The girl stared down her lengthy nose, increasing her unfortunate resemblance to a horse. "So this is where you're hiding."

Philippa settled more firmly into her chair, and her hands curled around the book that she hadn't been reading. Her haughty cousin didn't usually seek her company.

"What do you want?" she asked without enthusiasm.

Not waiting for an invitation, Caroline barged in. "Amelia wants to see you."

That was a good argument for staying just where she was. "I need to change for dinner."

Caroline scowled at her. "You've got ages yet." She paused. "Or are you too high and mighty to spare a few minutes for your family, now that you've trapped Erskine into marrying you?"

"Stop being so childish." If either her sister or cousin harbored a shred of sincere affection for Blair, Philippa might feel guilty about claiming his hand. "What's going on?"

"Amelia wants to make it up with you. She feels awful about the estrangement."

Philippa frowned. That didn't sound like the sister she knew. "Really?"

"Do you want to get married tomorrow without giving your only sister a chance to apologize?"

"So she's forgiven me?" Philippa asked, not bothering to hide her skepticism.

"She will if you come and talk to her now." Caroline paused. "If you don't, I fear that the breach may become permanent. Is that what you want?"

Despite Amelia's many sins against her, a feud wasn't what Philippa wanted. The thought of standing in the church tomorrow while her only sister stared daggers at her was too depressing for words. "No."

"Well, then." Caroline rushed forward to grab her arm, hauling her to her feet and sending the book thudding to the floor.

"Caroline!" Philippa protested, stretching to pick up *Persuasion*, but to no avail. Her cousin was considerably bigger and more powerful than she was.

"Stop whining," Caroline snapped. "You don't want to miss this chance to become friends again."

She couldn't remember a time when she and Amelia had been friends, but from long habit, Philippa gave in to her cousin. It suddenly struck her that her marriage to Lord Erskine might offer benefits beyond his obvious attractions. While she abandoned a home she loved, she'd also escape her relatives and their petty tyrannies.

Possibly Blair was another bully, but his behavior so far hinted at a reasonable man lurking beneath his rakish wiles. On the other hand, he'd very likely leave her alone once he became bored with her. If that happened, she'd find purpose elsewhere, just as she'd found purpose in running the Sanders estate.

The resolution proved less bracing than she'd intended.

With Philippa firmly in her grasp, Caroline bustled along the corridor, then down two flights of stairs to the ground floor. Breathlessly, Philippa asked several times about the hurry, but her cousin ignored her.

When they reached the library, Caroline paused outside the closed door and spoke in a piercing tone. "Oh, I do hope Amelia is here."

Philippa's confusion mounted. "You said she's waiting for me."

As she flung open the door, Caroline's grip on Philippa's arm tightened painfully. "There."

Soft lamplight lit the library that Philippa's uncle

used for gambling and drinking, but never for reading. His father, the previous baronet, had collected the books lining the walls. In the hour before dinner, it was usually empty. But even as Caroline shoved Philippa hard in the back, forcing her to stumble inside, she caught a flicker of movement at the far end of the long, narrow room.

Philippa stopped on a horrified gasp as her cousin crowded hard against her shoulder. Her eyes took in the scene before her mind could make sense of it.

In front of the hearth, lit to theatre by flickering flames, Blair stood with his hands around Amelia's slender waist. Her arms circling his neck, her sister leaned into the hard chest that Philippa knew, oh, too intimately.

"Blair?" Philippa asked uncertainly, struggling to keep her knees from folding. She took another unsteady step forward, this time without Caroline's encouragement.

At the sound of his name, Blair's head jerked up as if he'd been struck. Without shifting away from Amelia, he stared at Philippa, eyes dark with what looked like anguish.

"Hell—" he muttered, although in the fraught silence, she heard him perfectly.

Still clinging to him like a barnacle to a rock, Amelia turned toward Philippa, her expression alight with spite and triumph.

"I don't understand," Philippa said dully.

Truly her principal reaction was confusion. But other emotions hovered close, ready to rip her apart. Anger. Self-disgust for trusting this man. Unbearable hurt.

The hurt was the most puzzling of all. She'd only known Erskine a matter of days. How could his deceit crush her like this?

"What's to understand?" Amelia regarded her with contempt. "You can't imagine a mouse like you could hold the Earl of Erskine."

"Stop it!" With a total lack of chivalry, Erskine tried to tug Amelia's arms from around his neck. But she fought his attempts to free himself.

If he'd been prepared to hurt her, he could have broken away. But of course he wasn't willing to hurt Amelia, whatever wounds he inflicted on Philippa's aching heart.

"Blair, there's no point hiding the truth," Amelia said in a sickeningly sweet tone, pressing closer.

"You have to trust me, Philippa. This isn't what it looks like."

His voice was rough. With chagrin because she'd discovered his treachery? Or because this scene had some innocent explanation?

He stared over Amelia's ruffled gold head to where Philippa stood, struggling to accept what she saw. It shouldn't be so difficult. After all, she'd always known this man for a rake.

Amelia turned fully toward her, grasping Blair's

arm. Hectic color marked her cheeks. Proof of emotion? Certainly not proof of embarrassment. Her demeanor conveyed no shred of shame.

As if Caroline were no more significant than a fly, Philippa shook her off. Another shaky step forward, although what could she do when she reached the couple? Scratch out Amelia's eyes? Scratch out Blair's?

Her hands fisted at her sides, even as her urge for violence sank under desolation. What was the point of tantrums? If Blair wanted Amelia, Philippa couldn't do anything about it.

Oh, Blair. How could you make me like you, then betray me this way? It's too cruel.

"Devil take you, leave me be," he snapped at Amelia.

Amelia cried out in rage as he shook free and strode right up to Philippa, stopping mere inches from her. Instead of letting him go, Amelia staggered after him, clawing at his arm.

"Blair, it's too late," she gasped. "She knows now."

"Don't listen to her, Philippa lass." As he extended his hand in her direction, he sounded more Scottish than she'd ever heard him. Distantly she noticed that his hand was unsteady, but the knowledge offered no comfort. Even if he tried to escape Amelia's clutches, Philippa could have told him that what her sister stole, she kept. That had been true from the moment Amelia had snatched Philippa's first doll away from her.

"Don't—" Philippa retreated a pace before he could

touch her. She focused on Amelia and spoke in a raw voice. "What about Mr. Fox?"

Amelia attached herself to Blair's side. "He'll have to let me go. Just as you'll have to let Blair go."

How Philippa loathed hearing his Christian name on her sister's lips. This afternoon, she'd felt privileged to call him Blair. Now she felt cheap and stupid and shabby.

"But there will be a scandal." A stupid thing to worry about. Scandal had tarred this Christmas gathering from the moment Amelia had written to Erskine.

"Better a scandal than two broken hearts," Amelia said, visibly savoring the drama.

The urge to cry was nigh overwhelming. She'd had no reason to believe Erskine would be faithful. No reason to believe—except that fragile bond between them, woven in the darkness of a cold Christmas Eve. Better by far to discover his treachery before becoming his wife.

If only Philippa's despairing heart believed that she meant that.

But even as she stood trembling in the center of the library, shock receded. Her usually reliable mind started to work.

And her mind, as it was inclined to, questioned the evidence.

On the surface, it made perfect sense that sophisticated Lord Erskine would prefer her sister. But the man she came to know wasn't at all a careless, destructive rogue who rode roughshod over honor's demands. In fact, if Blair meant to jilt her, she'd offered him the perfect opportunity mere hours ago.

Yet despite her arguments, he'd stuck stubbornly to his commitment.

And if he was such a rogue, he'd had plenty of chances to have his way with Philippa, and still evade penalty, apart from some extra gossip linked to his already infamous name. He could have taken her in the dressing room. He could have pounced on her this afternoon.

She blushed to remember how she'd invited his caresses. And still he'd played the gentleman.

As confusion receded, Philippa met Blair's gaze. He didn't look like a man about to claim his darling. He looked like he struggled against a nightmare. His attention didn't shift from her, as if sheer force of will could convince Philippa to follow the ridiculous demands of her heart.

Were her growing suspicions of Amelia wishful thinking?

But this lovers' tryst felt staged. Something about the way Amelia grabbed Blair didn't ring true. As if she was terrified he'd run away. Not the behavior of a woman confident of a man's love.

As Philippa's silence continued, Blair tried once more to remove Amelia. Even now, he was too much of a gentleman to give her the jolly good shove she deserved.

"Philippa, I swear it's not as it looks." His hand remained extended. "I know how damning this appears, but I...*beg* of you, trust me."

Her bewilderment shattered. Whatever else she believed, she was sure of one truth. Blair Hume wasn't a man to beg.

If he could lower himself to plead, he wanted her and not her sister, however beautiful, however manipulative.

She sucked in what felt like the first clean air since she'd caught Amelia in Blair's arms. Even that was up for interpretation. He could have been trying to push her away, instead of holding her close.

"Let him go, Amelia," she said sharply. "It hasn't worked."

"Philippa?" Blair's voice was as shaky as minutes ago, hers had been. "You'll still marry me?"

Amelia had unwittingly done her a favor. At last, she felt in control of her life. She met Blair's troubled green gaze. "Of course I will."

Amelia paled and sidled closer to him. "You can't mean to hold him against his will."

Philippa found it in her to smile at her sister. How odd that this nasty little scene had shown her what she wanted from life. "You overdid the theatricals, sister," she said drily. "I hope you're saving some acting talent for when you stand up as my bridesmaid tomorrow morning."

Fury distorted Amelia's pretty face until she wasn't

pretty at all. Her eyes narrowed, and her lips thinned. This was genuine emotion, Philippa realized, not the false love she pretended for Blair.

"You will not have him!" Amelia finally released Blair to launch herself at Philippa, arms raised and hands extended into talons. Philippa gasped with fright and whipped her hands up to protect her face.

Amelia never made contact.

Slowly, Philippa lowered her arms while her sister abused her in language that would shame a stablehand.

"No, you don't, lassie." Erskine wrapped his arms around a struggling Amelia. "You've done enough damage."

"I...I don't know what this is all about," Caroline said shakily from behind Philippa. "Amelia, you're not behaving like a lady."

"Amelia, it's over," Philippa said quietly. "You're just making a fool of yourself."

"You stupid slut!" Amelia hissed, fighting Blair.

"That's enough!"

Blair's bark of command silenced Amelia. She twisted to fling herself sobbing into his arms. Philippa wondered if this was another ploy, then realized that her sister was genuinely distraught.

"You can let her go," Philippa said softly.

"She might attack you again."

Warmth filled Philippa. Nobody had ever worried about her before. Nobody had ever stepped in to save her. The fragile seedling of optimism that had unfurled when she'd decided to trust Blair sprouted a few more leaves.

If she was lucky, if she was right, that seedling might grow into a great tree that would shelter her for the rest of her life. She still felt like she launched herself into the void, but with every moment, her hope of a safe landing strengthened.

"I don't think so." The defiance had drained out of Amelia, and she hardly reacted when Philippa placed an arm around her. "I'll take you upstairs."

"Perhaps Miss Liddell can help her."

"None of this is my fault," Caroline insisted. She was an even worse actress than Amelia. "You can't blame me."

Ignoring her cousin, Philippa tightened her grip on her sister's suddenly fragile shoulders. "Amelia, come with me."

Amelia raised a tear-stained face to stare at her blankly. "What about Gerald?"

In Philippa's opinion, Mr. Fox deserved a better bride, but what could she say? "He doesn't know about this."

Amelia's expression sharpened. "You'll tell him. I would."

Impatience tightened Philippa's lips, and she met Blair's steady regard across her sister's blond head. Despite everything, she smiled at him, and he nodded in open approval.

The warmth in her heart surged anew. She couldn't

remember anyone ever approving of her before either.

Then she returned her attention to Amelia. "You have my word I won't."

Amelia started to cry again and slumped in Philippa's arms, playing the tragic heroine for all she was worth. "If he finds out about this, he'll hate me."

Blair still watched Philippa, and she felt a pang of longing for a private moment with him, to examine the miracle that had taken place between them. He'd asked her to trust him, and she had. It sounded simple, yet it was the most complicated, magnificent event in the world.

"Come upstairs, Amelia," she said again, wishing she wasn't parting, however temporarily, from the man she'd marry in the morning. "I'll put you to bed with a headache powder and a cup of tea, and nobody need be any wiser about what's happened."

Blair's mobile mouth quirked into a conspiratorial smile, as if he guessed how reluctantly she accompanied Amelia. Not long ago, Philippa had wondered if she'd ever smile again. Now she found herself once more smiling back. Silently his lips formed the word "tomorrow."

He caught her free hand in his. The strengthening heat of his touch flowed into her.

"I honor you," he whispered, bowing over her trembling fingers with a reverence that made her unruly heart cramp with yearning. His lips brushed her skin, sweet promise of caresses to come. She couldn't wait.

With a regret she noted and appreciated, he stepped back. Before she turned back to Amelia, she reached out to touch his cheek in a feather-light acknowledgment of the link between them.

Gently she coaxed her sniffling sister past Caroline and toward the door. Tomorrow would come quickly. Until then, it was enough to know that she and Blair had made an excellent start on their life together.

CHAPTER SEVEN

Candles lit the cavernous bedroom to gold, setting shadows dancing in the corners. Christmas greenery decked the walls, adding a festive touch.

Wearing a crimson dressing gown over his nakedness, Erskine quietly closed the door from the adjoining chamber. He stepped toward the huge four-poster in the center of the room. Carved oak columns stretched toward the high ceiling. Lords and ladies in faded gilt costumes pranced across the headboard. He guessed that some previous landlord of Salisbury's best inn, the Boar's Head, had bought the furnishings from a once-grand family. This particular bed wouldn't be out of place in Hampton Court.

Sitting against piled pillows in the midst of all this grandeur was one small woman wearing a plain white flannel nightgown. She clutched the blankets to her chest, and her expression brought Christians and lions to mind, with the Earl of Erskine playing the lion. He didn't need to see her slender throat move as she swallowed to know that the girl was petrified.

"My lord," Philippa whispered.

"My lady," he responded, smiling in what he hoped was a reassuring fashion. The impulse rose to take her in his arms and tell her everything would be fine, but he beat it back. He had a horrible feeling that if he touched her right now, she'd shriek louder than her mother had on Christmas Eve.

His bride had been quiet all day. She'd hardly eaten at the wedding breakfast, and appreciating how difficult the last days had been, he'd given her a few hours alone on the journey from Hartley Manor. He'd ridden through the cold afternoon, while she'd traveled inside his luxurious carriage.

Now that he noted how scared she looked—much more frightened than earlier—he wondered if he'd have done better to keep her company. On her own, she'd clearly tormented herself with imaginary terrors. They'd stopped for dinner at an inn along the way, but the place had been busy and private conversation had been impossible.

Aware that tonight he set the tone for his future, he diverted from his path. He veered toward the sideboard, set out with delicacies and, more importantly, a decanter of claret.

"Would you like something to eat?" Her pale face

and glittering eyes told him that he needed to work up to discussing anything important.

She shook her head. Her hair lay loose around her shoulders. He'd never seen her hair undone, although it had been beguilingly untidy by the time they left his dressing room.

The flowing curtain of mahogany transformed her into a mysterious and sensual creature. A dryad or a fairy. There was a masculine satisfaction in knowing that only he had seen this secret, enchanting version of his wife. Watching him with her characteristic gravity, she was beautiful beyond fantasy. And he'd fantasized a lot.

What a lucky devil he was.

Which made what he did now even more important. He'd always approached bed sport with a light heart, if heart was involved at all. How strange to recognize that despite his experience, tonight he was a novice like his bride. Never had getting everything right mattered so much. He respected Philippa's strength, but despite her strength, she was delicate. And she'd been shockingly undervalued by the people who should love her the most. At this moment, he made the silent vow that he'd never let her down.

Erskine poured claret for both of them and approached the bed, sitting to face her. Her mysterious dark eyes widened at his nearness, but at least she didn't shrink away. He passed his wife a glass of wine.

His wife...

He liked the sound of that. It made him feel disgracefully proprietorial.

With his marriage, he claimed his place in the world in a way that he never had before. He remembered his overbearing father dismissing him as a wastrel with his dying breath. But now Blair Hume was a married man who looked forward to creating a family.

Perhaps he'd start that family this very night.

Another male thrill coursed through him.

"Shall we toast our wedding?"

"Yes," she said. Still quiet.

He smiled and raised his claret in her direction. *His wife...*

He'd always known it was his duty to marry. But there was nothing of duty in what he contemplated doing tonight and everything of longing and desire and, God willing, joy. "To our happiness."

After a hesitation that jabbed at his heart, she took a sip. "Should I lie down?"

He hid a wince at the stoic little question. He'd hoped the memory of their kisses might ease her fears. That had been too optimistic.

Erskine kept smiling, wishing she'd smile back the way she'd smiled yesterday afternoon, as if he set the sun shining in the sky.

"Shall we talk for a few moments first?" The flash of relief in her eyes pricked his vanity. "Do you know what's going to happen?"

"My...my mother told me last night."

Bloody hell. He could imagine how that had gone. No wonder his bride looked ready to bolt. "What did she say?"

Philippa blushed and studied her claret as if it held the answers to every eternal question. "That you'd hurt me. That I must submit. That this is a wife's lot, and I'm paying for Eve's sin."

To blazes with the old bat. "Have some more wine."

Her gaze darted up to meet his. "Will it help if I'm foxed?"

"It will help if you're not expecting me to torture you," he said shortly, yet again damning his harridan of a mother-in-law. "I swear it won't be as bad as you think."

He hoped to Hades he spoke the truth. He'd never taken an innocent girl to his bed before. The thought of Philippa's ardent kisses bolstered his confidence.

With understanding and patience, the roué who still lurked beneath the new husband was certain that he and this woman could scale the heights of pleasure. The prospect of those heights made him hotter than the fire in the hearth.

"I hope not."

He almost laughed. That cautious response was very much hers. She'd never butter a man up with meaningless flattery. "You trusted me yesterday. Will you trust me now?"

Another of those heart-stopping hesitations before she nodded and drank a little more wine. "I'll try."

A surge of fondness and gratitude jammed his throat so his voice turned husky. "I can't tell you what it meant when you believed me yesterday."

It was the first chance they'd had to discuss that harrowing scene in the library. He couldn't think of another woman who would have stood by him. He still hardly believed that she had.

At that moment, his decision to marry Philippa Sanders had become his choice rather than something he did for honor's sake. He'd always wanted and liked her, but her stalwart faith had rocketed his feelings into a new universe.

"I know Amelia."

"But you don't know me."

"When I had a chance to think, I assumed that she must have tricked you." Philippa no longer sounded likely to faint away at his slightest move, thank God. "After all, if you wanted Amelia, you'd have proposed to her."

He fought back another, stronger urge to sweep Philippa into his arms. "What a fortunate fellow I am, to have such a level-headed wife."

That drew the first hint of a smile from her, a tiny twitch of her lush mouth. He'd kissed that mouth. He knew how delicious it was. With an eagerness that would have astonished him five days ago, he looked forward to kissing it again.

Soon. But not yet. Not until the wary light left her big brown eyes.

From where she leaned against the stacked pillows, she regarded him steadily. "I didn't feel very level-headed when I walked into the library."

"Perhaps not." His gut knotted at the memory of the distress on her face. He'd been so sure she'd believe he was up to his bad old tricks. Given his reputation and their brief acquaintance, why would she think anything else? "Amelia sent me a note saying you needed to see me. When I got there, she must have listened for your cousin outside because she didn't touch me until just before you appeared. Then she was like a blasted octopus, all arms, and I couldn't control what she did with any of them. I should have been suspicious when the note wasn't directly from you."

"I guessed the truth might be something like that." She paused. "I was so glad to leave Hartley Manor. Thank you for deciding not to stay there tonight."

"I thought you'd feel more comfortable away from curious eyes." He drank some wine. Befitting this hostelry's exorbitant prices, its quality wouldn't disgrace his own cellars.

"Oh, I do," she said fervently, coaxing a laugh from him. She once more sounded like the delightful woman he'd discovered after a jammed door delivered his destiny. "There's so much we need to talk about."

He damn well wanted more from tonight than conversation, but he could already see that taking things slowly eased her into her new role. "Not all at once, surely," he said mildly, not feeling mild at all.

"Maybe not, but I'd like to know where we're going after Salisbury. London or your estates in Scotland?"

"Whatever you prefer." He shrugged as he set his glass on the nightstand. "Scotland at Christmas can be bleak, but beautiful. There's London, but perhaps you've had your fill of Town. We could stay here. Or perhaps you'd like to travel. I cheated you out of a courtship. The least I can do is offer you a honeymoon. I am a man of some fortune. The world, my dear, is your oyster."

He saw the precise moment when she realized that her old, circumscribed life was over. Excitement sparked in her eyes, and for the first time tonight, she smiled properly. "Perhaps I'll like being a countess after all."

"I hope so." He risked touching the hand resting open at her side. When he'd come in, she'd gripped the covers like a shield. Now her fingers lay loose and relaxed.

He waited in an agony of suspense for her to withdraw. How his raffish friends would guffaw to see the famous libertine in such a lather about touching a lady's *hand*.

His heart gave a mighty thud of thankfulness when she curled her fingers around his. She took another sip of wine. Whether it was the warm room or the claret or his presence—he dearly hoped it was his presence— she looked considerably more spirited than she had earlier.

"When you were so kind to your sister yesterday, you impressed the hell out of me. She tried to do you a very bad turn." And him, he thought with a shudder. Thank heaven Philippa had invaded his room on Christmas Eve and not Amelia. The idea of a lifetime with Amelia Sanders brought him out in a cold sweat.

"She's not as bad as you might think. Amelia has always been discontented and unhappy. My mother has encouraged her to think that because she's pretty, she doesn't need to be anything else."

Erskine could imagine. Although understanding didn't make Amelia's spiteful little games any more forgivable.

He lifted his wife's hand and kissed the spot below her wedding ring, glinting bright gold in the light. "You're too good for her."

And for me.

But she was his, however undeserving he was. He had a piece of paper to prove it. And it was time he introduced her to some of the benefits of married life.

He unlaced her fingers from her wineglass and placed it on the nightstand. She'd nearly emptied the glass, thank goodness. He leaned in and placed his lips softly on hers. She released a little huff of surprise, but didn't draw away.

Because her mother had told her to submit? Or because she wanted him to kiss her? He prayed it was the latter.

Exquisitely aware of her innocence, he kissed her

chastely, rediscovering the satiny texture of her lips and her tart, intriguing taste. To support his weight, he splayed his hands on the counterpane. With encouragement from the claret, she'd stopped acting as if he was about to devour her, but he knew he hadn't banished her fears.

After an interval both delightful and frustrating, she pressed forward with a breathy sigh. Reluctantly he withdrew. He lifted one hand to brush his thumb across her plump, glistening lips, pulling the lower one down to reveal a glimpse of straight white teeth. Her eyes were as dark as a starless night. He could dive into her gaze and never come up for air.

Puzzlement creased her forehead. "You kissed me."

She didn't sound entirely pleased. A tender smile curved his lips. "I promised I would, remember?"

"After I married you."

He said what he must, although every word cut like a razor. "I'm prepared to wait."

The faint line remained between her dark brows. "You don't have to."

He bit back a sigh and cupped her cheek. "We're strangers, Philippa. I want you, but I'm not a barbarian. If you're not ready, I can give you more time."

For a prickling interval, she studied his face in silence. He struggled to convey patience and understanding, although she must also see his barely contained hunger.

He steeled himself to retreat to the room next door.

Or perhaps she'd relent and let him sleep beside her. Holding her in his arms without possessing her would be torture, but still it seemed preferable to the lonely hell of a night without her.

Reluctantly Erskine withdrew his hand and straightened. He told himself that this was for the best. No man of honor could expect his wife to welcome him tonight, whatever rights this morning's ceremony had conferred.

Which wasn't much consolation when he faced a cold bed.

"Sleep well, Philippa."

In the light of candles and fire, her eyes turned even darker. He shifted away slowly, like a man going to his execution. He knew he did the right thing, but the knowledge offered no satisfaction.

His wife remained very still, watching him, although her hands curled slowly into the sheets at her waist. He'd been trying very hard not to notice the way the nightgown molded over her breasts. Now his gaze dropped helplessly to where her nipples pressed, beaded like raspberries, against the white material. That image would torment him through a restless night, damn it.

He expected Philippa to look relieved or, best of all, grateful. He'd like her to be grateful. A grateful wife was likely to invite him to consummate their union sooner rather than later. Hopefully before he went completely mad wanting her.

He'd risen to his feet before she spoke. "I trusted you yesterday."

Because of that, he'd lay down his life for her. "Yes, you did. Thank you."

Without lowering her gaze, she bit her lip. He wasn't sure where she was going with this, but he'd much rather stay than leave, even if she only wanted to *talk.*

"You've always been kind to me."

It was his turn to frown. "You make me sound like an aged uncle."

A rueful smile twisted her lips. "You're nicer to me than Uncle Theodore ever was."

He didn't smile back, and his voice emerged with a bite that he regretted but couldn't contain. "Philippa, let me be frank—I don't feel remotely avuncular when I look at you." He sucked in a breath and spoke the words likely to terrify her into running back to her unpleasant mother. "The first time I saw you hovering in the shadows like a little ghost, I wanted you. I wanted you when we were trapped in the dressing room. That's why I kissed you. Every hour since then, I've wanted you more. Tonight I'm offering you a postponement, but I don't....I can't let you think that I'll accept a chaste marriage."

He waited for an appalled reaction, but she didn't flinch away. Neither, confound it, did she leap into his arms declaring overwhelming desire.

"I...see," she said slowly after a tense interval.

He stepped closer to the bed, even if it was a step he'd need to retrace when he left her. "Have I shocked you?"

"A little." She paused. "You have a husband's rights."

"I'm not a bully."

"No, you're not."

He should go. This awkward conversation just extended the torture.

Her eyes flickered away, and her hands stopped twisting at the sheets. Instead, she began to pluck nervously at them. Not much of an improvement.

Why the deuce was the chit nervous? Hadn't he just given her a reprieve? Surely that saintly act alone must cancel out a few of his sins in the heavenly register.

"It's late," he said regretfully, starting to feel like a fool standing in the middle of the room, gazing at Philippa like a dog slavering at a butcher shop window. He turned to leave.

"Don't go."

Erskine stopped, wondering if he'd heard her aright. Slowly he faced her. He couldn't read her expression. "What did you say?"

Her deep breath made her breasts swell voluptuously against her nightgown. He closed his eyes. God give him strength. She wasn't doing this to get him excited. Although he was undoubtedly getting excited.

She licked her lips. How he wished she wouldn't.

Philippa swallowed and spoke in a rusty whisper. "I said...don't go."

He braced his shoulders and told himself he could be strong. They had years to get this right. A wedding night was just another date on the calendar. "You don't want to sleep alone in a strange place? I can understand that."

Her eyes flashed with annoyance, surprising him. "No, I don't want to sleep alone. But that's not what I mean."

"What *do* you mean?"

Her lips tightened with displeasure. "You're the blasted rake. You work it out."

His heart kicking into an excited gallop, he stared at her without moving. It took him far too long to realize that while she looked uncertain, she also looked…interested.

He could work with interested, by God.

On an astonished laugh, he dived across the floor and onto the bed, dragging her into his arms. "Prepare to be ravished, lassie!"

Before Philippa could reply or, heaven forfend, change her mind, he captured her lips in a kiss that wasn't chaste at all.

CHAPTER EIGHT

*P*hilippa had time to snatch one shocked breath before Blair seized her in his arms and kissed her as if waiting another second would kill him. The sensation was overwhelming, like being caught up in a whirlwind or tumbling against the beach in a great wave. Compared to the sweet tenderness of his last kiss, this was closer to those wild, passionate moments they'd shared in his dressing room. As heat poured through her, she immediately softened against him and moaned in surrender.

Through the tumult, she was vaguely aware of him flinging away his dressing gown. When her seeking, stroking hands met warm skin, a thrill sizzled through her. She'd never touched anyone like this. A man's body offered a banquet of unsuspected pleasures. Blair was hard where she was soft; straight where she curved; powerful and potent. The musky scent of his skin flooded her senses.

She gave a soft protest when he drew her to her knees, interrupting her exploration. Then a gasp of shock mixed with excitement when he tugged her nightdress over her head and sent it flying through the air.

She had no time to feel self-conscious because he caught her up and kissed her with an enthusiasm that sent the blood pumping madly through her veins. She tasted claret on his breath.

He tipped her back against the bed and lifted his head to smile down at her with a masculine appreciation that made her tremble and sigh. "You're glorious, my darling."

She hadn't blushed when he flung off her nightdress. She blushed now at the awe in his tone. Once she might have argued with his remark. But staring into his glowing green eyes, for the first time in her life she felt genuinely beautiful. The experience was heady.

"Thanks to you, I feel glorious," she admitted with a touch of shyness, then leaned forward and kissed him. He gave a grunt of pleased surprise before he took charge with magnificent results.

On a groan of anticipation he settled above her, her legs framing his lean hips. His weight crushed her into the bed and stole her breath in an unfamiliar but wonderfully pleasing way. She ran her hands up and down his back, fascinated to feel the powerful muscles flex. More fiery kisses burned away her brief curiosity to see his nakedness. His tongue tangled with hers, his arms lashed her to his long, strong body.

For the first time, he touched her breasts. As response sizzled through her, she cried out in startled pleasure. Those long fingers rolled her nipples into hard, aching points. She trembled at her spiking reactions.

"Oh, Blair…"

He bent his head and took one yearning peak between his lips, sucking gently at first, then with more pressure. Another thrill jolted her, and a throbbing, impatient pulse set up between her legs. When he'd kissed her before, she thought she'd discovered desire, but compared to this conflagration of need, that had been a mere flicker.

Her trembling hands tangled in his thick dark hair, pressing him closer, asking for more of this exquisite torture. He made a wordless sound of appreciation deep in his throat and shifted his attention to her other nipple. Her restless, relentless excitement swelled.

Philippa spiraled toward something her mind didn't understand but which her body craved. She whimpered in desperation as the unknown goal remained beyond reach. The hot brush of Blair's skin, the scent of his body, his lips on her breast, the touch of his hands, nothing eased the coiling tension.

Blair raised his head to stare down at her stretched beneath him. In the candlelight, his expression was stark with need. She'd never imagined he could look like this. His green eyes glittered with hunger. The skin over his high Celtic cheekbones was taut. His mouth glistened from her kisses.

Instead of this new version of Blair terrifying her into retreat, another shiver of arousal ran through her. He was such a superb man.

And right now, he was hers to enjoy.

Emboldened, she began to explore his body, learning the hard lines of muscle and bone, the jut of his hip, the curve of his buttocks. Yesterday, even an hour ago, she'd have hesitated to touch him like this. But she was beyond holding back. He was her husband, and she wanted to claim every inch of him.

"I feel like I'm caught in a storm," she confessed, her voice husky.

"Me, too." He cupped her jaw and tilted her face for more soul-stealing kisses. He nipped her bottom lip and drew it between his teeth, sending another of those extraordinary jolts through her. "You make me tremble."

"I'm glad." Once she'd never have believed that plain Philippa Sanders could affect him so profoundly, but she couldn't mistake the ripples of reaction running through the body poised above hers.

Her hands tightened on his shoulders, and she raised her mouth to his. The knowledge that she had this experienced man of the world shaking with desire made her want to cry.

After her mother's cold account of the sexual act, she'd dreaded her husband's attentions. Now she began to suspect that her mother had neglected the most important information. The section about how her husband could drive her mad with anticipation. Blair's kisses had always promised pleasure rather than shame and submission.

Now the delight she found in his arms was astounding enough. Even more astounding was that yielding to Blair's passion was an act of heart as well as body. Every brush of his hand or glance of his lips lured her far beyond the physical realm.

"Oh, my beautiful sweetheart—" he groaned, grazing her neck with his teeth.

She cried out at the tingling response. Her eager hands tested the hard ladder of his ribs, his narrow hips, the powerful thighs. Daringly she ventured lower, toward the part of him that remained a mystery.

He groaned again as her hand brushed his rampant heat. Briefly cowardice defeated curiosity. She withdrew and linked her hands across his back. He buried his silky head in her shoulder and breathed in great gusts that shook her with their force. Their kisses in his dressing room hadn't prepared her for the powerful intimacy of lying beneath him.

"Should I stop?" Philippa asked shakily. Her inexperience made her feel suddenly awkward. She had no idea what a man liked a woman to do to him.

"Hell, no," he gasped on a warm puff of breath that set off a fusillade of sensation inside her.

"I may touch you?"

His laugh was edged, as if he was in pain. "Please."

"I don't want to hurt you."

Another difficult laugh. "I hurt with wanting you."

The jagged admission banished the last of her timidity. With more confidence, she curled her hand around him. He felt alive and strong and dauntingly big. How on earth would he fit inside her?

"Goodness gracious," she breathed, tentatively running her hand down the hot, satiny column, feeling vitality in the raised veins beneath her fingers.

Liquid heat flooded her at her bold forays. She shifted, feeling sleek and needy. More slowly, she moved her hand up until she brushed the swollen tip. He was damp, too.

As all the new experiences of the night crashed down upon her, she snatched her hand away.

She felt fretful, needy, hungry. This wasn't at all what she'd imagined after her mother's advice. She'd pictured herself lying back while he took control. This degree of involvement felt threatening, like she surrendered more than just her body. And however much she liked the man she'd married, she didn't yet trust him as the keeper of her soul.

She'd recognized Blair's emotional power over her yesterday when she'd seen him with Amelia. Now fear and desire battled for supremacy, and she wasn't sure which was stronger.

"Trust me," Erskine said softly. When he'd asked Philippa to trust him before this, she'd never failed him. Let her trust him now.

He'd never imagined that introducing his wife to pleasure could carry such importance. Dear God, let him do this right. Let him show this innocent, gallant girl bliss. As he rose above her and stared into her brilliant eyes, his desire for his wife burgeoned into an emotion strong enough to shake kingdoms.

He sucked in a shaky breath. Her scent filled his senses. Lemon and flowers. Arousal. A trace of sweat. The mixture was as intoxicating as brandy.

"Yes," she said simply, and relief struck him like a blow.

"I'll be gentle," he promised, praying that it was true.

His hand drifted down from her face, lingering to test the kick of her pulse at her collarbone. She had a beautiful body, small and slender and graceful with high, round breasts that fit his hands as if created for the purpose.

"Oh," she gasped as he kissed a particularly sensitive place on her neck. "I like that."

He loved the taste of her skin. Clean and fresh and warm with life. Tonight he awoke the sensuality that he'd always suspected lurked inside her. He loved watching her amazed wonder at every new experience. He loved watching her confidence build with every sizzling moment.

"Good," he whispered, fighting the urge to rush to fulfillment. Patience now would reap untold rewards. "I hope you like everything else I've got planned."

To his delighted surprise, she giggled. He'd never heard his serious little bride giggle before. He nuzzled his way across the slope of her breast, drawing in her scent, so much warmer and richer there. "You're quite delicious, you know."

"You sound like a hungry lion," she responded breathlessly, hooking her fingers over his shoulders.

At her touch, heat blasted him. "This lion wants to eat you," he growled.

He came down over her, balancing on flattened hands, and bent to kiss her. She met him readily, darting her tongue into his mouth with a daring that set his blood swirling with need.

The craving to slide into her tight velvety passage was overwhelming, but still he reined in his impulses. He wanted her so drunk with arousal when he took her that any pain became merely a fleeting distraction on the road to rapture.

"Can you feel how much I want you?" He brought her hand down. Excitement shuddered through him as she closed her fingers around him once more.

"I...I want you, too," Philippa admitted, caressing

him as she raised glittering eyes to his. He saw right to the pure depths of her soul. Through a wave of unfamiliar emotion, he offered up a prayer of gratitude to whatever powers had decreed this union.

Her hand flexed, setting off an explosion behind his eyes. For endless excruciating minutes, he bore her ministrations, gritting his teeth to stop himself from driving to culmination. He relished the intense concentration she devoted to his enjoyment. But he was only human, and this tentative, searing torment approached the limit of his endurance.

Erskine caught her hand and glanced a kiss across her knuckles. She was breathtakingly lovely with her creamy skin and drifting cascades of hair. His nostrils flared as he took in her hot scent. Her body told him it wanted him. "It's my turn to please you, my darling."

Erskine wasn't by nature prone to endearments, but something about Philippa made him want to call her every silly fond name he knew. He became completely starry-eyed over his young wife.

"You do," she admitted in a choked voice.

Deep emotion shone in her eyes. He wasn't alone in tipping over the edge of physical pleasure into something more profound. He'd had no idea what he'd invited the day he'd offered to marry this woman.

"I will." He spoke with the same decisive tone that he'd used for his wedding vows. "Let me show you what you've got in store for the next fifty years, sweetheart."

He palmed one round breast, bending his head to take the other nipple between his lips. As he sucked at the beaded peak, she whimpered and slid her hand up his chest. When she sank her nails into his skin, he groaned at the stinging mixture of pleasure and pain.

He raised his head and stared at her. "If you touch me, I'll lose control, and I need to make sure you enjoy this, darling."

Her brief uncertainty melted into a smile. "Can I touch you later?"

"Over and over and over."

"That's a promise?"

"Yes, it is." Paradise hovered so close. "Now, lie back and enjoy yourself. You vowed to obey me today."

"In hindsight, that seems a little rash."

He smiled, captivated. "Too late, sweeting."

He caressed and kissed her breasts until she bucked beneath him. Her every wriggle released more alluring scent into the air until he drowned in his wife's sweetness. She was so sensitive, she was close to shattering, but some selfish element in him wanted to share that final joy.

When she trembled beneath him, hot and feverish, he finally, finally ran his hand across her belly and touched her between her legs. Triumph thundered through him when he found her slick and ready.

Carefully he slid one long finger into her, testing the silky heat, the tight muscles clenching around him.

Another finger, gently stretching. She breathed in humid little gasps that fired his need.

He rose over her and parted her legs. "It's time, my darling wife."

Her dark eyes held the unconditional trust he'd waited so long to find. Very gradually, he eased into her. She was so primed, possession should be easy, but he'd never taken a virgin before. Somewhere the careless lover had transformed into a man who'd cut off his own balls before he hurt his wife.

He met the barrier of her innocence and paused, gasping for control. She sighed and curled her hands over his shoulders.

"Don't stop," she whispered, so low he barely heard her.

This act's power was unearthly. He'd thought himself a man who knew women. Yet this first night with his wife flung him into radiant, unknown space.

He could wait no longer. He wanted her so much. He tightened his hips and thrust.

She stiffened and whimpered. Her nails dug into his damp, bare skin.

Then on a cry, she arched to meet him, bringing him deeper. In unmistakable welcome, she contracted around him. This time her sigh was long and deep and saturated with enjoyment. She tipped back her head until her breasts brushed his chest. A proud smile teased her lush red lips.

"Oh, my darling," Erskine choked out and kissed

her with the powerful passion that he'd leashed all night.

"That's wonderful," she gasped, sliding beneath him in a way that threatened his tattered control.

For as long as he could bear, he kept still, letting her become accustomed to his body. Despite her unabashed welcome, he remained overwhelmingly conscious that she'd never done this before. Then slowly and tenderly, he moved. The glorious sensation threatened to incinerate him.

Again he thrust, more purposefully. This time she shifted, changing the angle, and his hunger sharpened to the verge of agony.

Still she stroked him, urged him on, told him with fluttering sighs and touches that she wanted more. He abandoned himself to the fierce, vital rhythm.

Fiery thunder shook his world as he claimed his wife. He'd think he acted the complete barbarian, if not for her whispered words of encouragement and delight. Those broken little murmurs of praise smashed restraint to oblivion.

She shuddered into her climax and cried out, the sound sharp and triumphant in the firelit room. Then with a mighty rush, Erskine lost himself in a release unlike anything he'd felt before.

He flooded her with his seed and forever united his life to hers.

CHAPTER NINE

When Philippa stirred from deep, dreamless sleep, her husband held her clasped tight to his powerful chest. Dull gray light edged the curtains, and the candles had burned down to puddles of wax. A shy glance up at Blair's face from where she lay tucked into the curve of his shoulder showed her that he was still asleep.

With those cynical green eyes closed, Blair looked younger. She realized with a start that this notorious libertine must be only a few years older than she was. At Hartley Manor, he'd seemed so impossibly beyond her in experience and sophistication that she'd felt a complete child in comparison.

After last night, she didn't feel like a child anymore. She felt like a woman.

A woman suffering the pangs of an excruciatingly guilty conscience. With morning, so much became painfully clear, and she cringed at how she'd wronged her husband.

Queasy with self-disgust, she eased away from Blair and gingerly sat up. As she pulled her nightdress over her head, her body twinged in unfamiliar places. A reminder that despite his care with her, she was unused to a man's possession. The faint discomfort only made her recall his gentleness, and how that gentleness had flared into a passion beyond imagination.

Blair had repaid her sins against him with breathtaking pleasure. But this morning she faced the stark truth that fate had dealt him an awful hand when Philippa Sanders broke into his room.

"Where do you think you're going?"

The drowsy baritone question from behind her made every muscle tense. Muscles already aching after the night's exertions.

It seemed her husband was a light sleeper. Curse him for stirring. She'd hoped to escape unnoticed.

Long fingers curled around her wrist above where her hand spread against the rumpled bed. As if she needed reminding of how uninhibited they'd been. Twice. Blair had woken her after midnight and used her slowly and sweetly with whispers of praise that her lonely soul had soaked up like a desert soaked up water.

The first time had been astonishing enough. That second time had threatened to break her heart.

"I thought I'd go and sleep in the next room," she mumbled, without looking at him.

He'd made such a gallant effort to pretend that this forced marriage hadn't blighted his life. But of course it must. Devilishly handsome rakes didn't willingly tie themselves to women undistinguished by either fortune or beauty.

How wrong her first impressions of him had been. Blair was the kindest man she knew. She didn't deserve him. And he certainly didn't deserve a disaster of a wife like her.

"Did you indeed?" Even with her back to him, she knew he studied her. Worse, he probably guessed that she'd woken unhappy. She was developing a healthy respect for his powers of perception. "Why?"

"I thought you might like some privacy."

She definitely wanted some time alone. Lying in his arms, she couldn't think, and she badly needed to think. There must be some way to release him from the prison of this marriage.

The bed dipped as he sat up and shifted closer. "I can think of something I'd like much more than privacy."

After last night, she thought she'd never blush again. She was wrong about that. "Do you want to do… that again?"

"Don't you?" He didn't sound sleepy anymore.

"As you wish." She blinked back tears and finally

made herself turn in his direction. She struggled to appear calm.

Apparently she failed.

"What is it, Philippa?" He frowned, more in puzzlement than irritation. "And don't tell me I'm imagining that there's something wrong."

She stopped on the verge of saying just that and glanced toward the glowing embers in the hearth. She couldn't bear to look at him. He was so beautiful, and seeing him only reminded her of how marvelous he'd made her feel last night.

"Please let me go," she said tonelessly.

His hold tightened, making her pulse leap under his fingers. "No."

Surprised she stared squarely at him for the first time since she'd woken. He didn't look annoyed, although even she admitted that she acted like a ninny-hammer. Instead he looked determined. Which was much more daunting than anger. "I thought you were joking about the obedience."

A faint smile teased his lips, but his eyes remained watchful. He raised the hand he held and kissed it. "That depends on what you intend to do next."

Even as reaction shivered through her, she closed her eyes against tears. If only he wasn't so considerate. If only he was the heartless rake she'd believed him to be. That man deserved to be saddled with a wife he didn't want and a life he hadn't planned. "Please—"

"Talk to me, Philippa."

He released her, but his kiss still tingled on her skin, reminder of the hundreds of kisses he'd given her last night. He'd been so good to her, so generous. And she wasn't worth his care.

"This marriage isn't what you wanted," she said in a choked voice.

To her surprise, he greeted that with a soft laugh. "I thought the issue might be something like that."

She waited for him to say that it didn't matter, to lie. Ever since they'd been caught together, he'd done his best to shield her from the consequences of her actions, but that didn't make him a willing participant in events.

When the silence extended, she opened her eyes, pique stirring beneath self-castigation. "You were trapped into marrying me."

He settled with a sigh against the headboard, his stare unwavering. An embroidered lady wearing a steepled head-dress peeped over his shoulder with faded eyes. "And now you're torturing yourself with guilt."

"I broke into your room. The blame is mine."

"Yes."

Another silence while she waited for him to say something conciliatory. When he didn't, she glared at him. "Now we're tied together for life."

The green eyes were unreadable as they rested on her face. "Do you mind?"

Blair was a wonderful man, and every day she

discovered new and intriguing facets of his character. Not to mention that when he touched her, he made her feel like a goddess. The promise of a lifetime in his bed made her want to skip and sing and turn cartwheels.

How on earth could she mind?

"Not for myself," she said, too shy to share the wanton thoughts running through her head.

"So you think I should mind?" he asked neutrally.

"If you'd been free to make your own decision, you'd never have chosen me for your wife."

A smile teased his lips. "That's true."

Oh, dear Lord in heaven. She was right. He did regret marrying her.

Philippa clenched her free hand in the tangled blankets as a jagged hole gaped in her heart. "So you've been forced into a situation not of your choosing. And it's my fault."

"Definitely."

Despite the justice of Blair's response, her lips flattened with displeasure. She didn't expect a declaration of eternal love, but this swift agreement with her bleak assessment irked her. "You should wish me to the devil."

The green eyes seemed to convey a message she couldn't read. Something unconnected to his hurtful words. "You know, when you put it like that, I suspect I should."

"But it's too late," she said in despair.

"Once the vows were spoken, it certainly was."

She bit her lip and told herself she'd cry when she was alone. Despite that exhortation, tears pricked at her eyes. She spoke the only words she could, knowing even as she did that they were utterly inadequate to the wrong she'd done him. "I'm so sorry."

"You know," Blair said musingly after a long while, "given all these grim facts you're so determined to enumerate, any sensible man should be as cranky as a dog with fleas this morning."

Miserably Philippa stared at him. Why did he have to be so handsome? Right now, his physical appeal felt like yet another attack on her wilting confidence.

"Yes, he…you should."

Another delay before he responded in the same thoughtful tone. "But you know—"

She braced for condemnation. Instead he relaxed back against the elaborate headboard with a casual air that left her bewildered.

The silence continued to the point where she wanted to scream.

"I know what?" she forced out.

"You know—" His lips stretched into a smile that set her foolish heart dancing, despite the morass of wretchedness. "Now I think about it, I'm not nearly as discontented about our wedding as I imagined I would be. When your uncle threatened to shoot me if I didn't do the right thing, I was sure that we'd got ourselves into a deuce of a coil."

Her wayward heart stumbled to a standstill. Open-mouthed with shock, she stared at her husband. She didn't trust what she thought she'd heard. "What does that mean?"

Amusement lit his eyes to emerald. "It means, wife, that I'd like to try and make this a true marriage."

She frowned. This seemed too good to be true. Handsome, profligate men didn't give up their sensual pleasures for the sake of plain little mice like Philippa Sanders. "You think I believe that?"

He leaned forward and cradled her face between his hands, sending her heart into another ridiculous jig. "I think you're creating monsters in your mind."

Desperately she searched his remarkable face for signs of deceit. "I don't want you to be unhappy."

"Believe me, after last night, no man could be unhappy. It's just not possible."

She blushed again. "There's more to marriage than bed sport."

He laughed with the hint of affectionate mockery, familiar from the night they were locked in the dressing room. "It's a start." When she didn't smile back, he continued. "And we've got more than that, Philippa. You know we have. I like you. I admire you. You're always interesting. In fact, I couldn't have chosen a better wife if I'd tried."

Relief flooded through her, and under the unabashed warmth in his eyes, her fit of futile guilt melted like ice in the sun. "Do...do you mean it?"

"Of course I do." He paused, and his expression

became serious. "Now the question is whether you're happy to go forward with me."

This time she didn't try to hold back her smile. "My lord, you demonstrated some essential husbandly skills last night. I look forward to sampling your other talents."

He laughed at her light response, which was just what she wanted. In a marriage so new, she couldn't burden him with the unprecedented emotions that had welled in her heart when he'd joined his body to hers.

Perhaps her feelings now were merely a virgin's romantic fancies, but staring into her husband's brilliant eyes, she wondered if she was halfway to falling in love with the scandalous Earl of Erskine.

More than halfway, she suspected, wondering why the idea didn't make her sick with fear.

Perhaps Philippa wasn't terrified because her husband's expression warned her of an impending demonstration of husbandly skills.

With sudden confidence that everything would turn out all right, despite their topsy-turvy beginnings, she leaned forward and eagerly pressed her lips to his. As he kissed her back with gratifying enthusiasm, she silently promised Blair that whatever happened, he'd never regret their marriage.

EPILOGUE

Hartley Manor, Wiltshire, Christmas Eve 1824

PHILIPPA'S LAUGH RANG with joy and excitement as Blair dashed up the long corridor and dragged her into their bedroom. It was the same room he'd slept in as a bachelor, when he'd so reluctantly attended Sir Theodore Liddell's last house party.

"Blair, they'll hear us." Her family must guess exactly what Lord Erskine and his countess planned for their "early night."

"Too bad." Blair turned to haul her into his arms, kissing her with a passion that had only grown more powerful since their wedding. When he raised his head, he regarded her with the narrow-eyed green glitter that warned her she was about to become very rumpled indeed. "Anyway, all attention is on the new Mr. and Mrs. Fox."

"I hope they'll be happy," Philippa said, although right now she hardly cared.

Blair shrugged, kicking the door shut behind him. The huge bedroom that had seemed so daunting last Christmas Eve was empty. Mills had swiftly learned to appear only when summoned. "Your sister looked almost human when she walked up the aisle this morning. Perhaps she's finally growing up."

"I hope so." It was true. Amelia had even complimented Philippa on how pretty she looked in her attendant's gown. With her sister, that was as close to an apology for her spite as Philippa was likely to get. "And my mother unbent enough to ask my opinion of the flowers in the church."

"Good God, much more of this, and I'll stop dreading family gatherings," Blair said wryly. "Which doesn't mean that once we've done the pretty for Christmas, we're staying past Boxing Day."

The Earl and Countess of Erskine had become country bumpkins of the most dedicated sort. They'd spent most of their year together on Blair's Scottish estates, and Philippa had never been happier.

When her husband edged her toward the wall, Philippa frowned. "Aren't we going to bed?"

He laughed. "What a hussy I married."

She blushed. Twelve months of dedicated carnal

education hadn't cured her of the habit. "You don't seem to mind."

Even in the early months of dazzling sensual discovery, she'd been sensible enough to wonder whether his interest would wane once her novelty faded. But he'd never shown any restlessness.

At first that had astonished her. But eventually she'd come to accept that she'd snared that rarest of beasts, the reformed rake. And the rake showed every sign of being content in his captivity.

"It's Christmas Eve. Time for good little boys to get what they've asked for." He took another step forward.

Frowning in puzzlement, she automatically took another step back. "But you've had me all year."

He stopped herding her like a stray calf and burst into laughter. "Oh, my bonny lassie, you are a treasure. I bless the day that door jammed."

Could her blush get any hotter? "Well, I'm beginning to think I married a lunatic."

He stopped laughing and focused that concentrated regard on her face. "Only beginning?"

She dug her heels in, refusing to budge. "What are you up to, Blair?"

He was still smiling. "I'm fulfilling a dream that's teased me for a year, my dear wife. Brace yourself."

"Brace—"

He flung open the door to the fatal dressing room, and she suddenly understood why he looked like a cat who had taken over a dairy.

His hand closing around hers, he pulled her into the confined space. Immediately Philippa was transported back to last Christmas Eve. A night of dread and uncertainty—and her introduction to the pleasure that had since become a rich strand in her life. Blair's subtle scent was part of her now, but in the small room, she was overwhelmingly aware, as on that first night, of his essence.

As he tugged the door shut, she noticed the lit candle on the trunk. She cast him a sardonic look. "You're better prepared this time."

"Practice makes perfect. I hope you're not expecting a leisurely wooing, my love."

Every time he called her his love, she suffered a pang, despite the radiant happiness of the life they'd built together. He used endearments all the time. Darling. Sweetheart. Dearest. But when he said "my love," she remembered that for all his attention and affection, he'd never said he loved her.

And poor, pathetic, yearning creature she was, she'd offer up her soul on a carving plate to him, if only he'd say the words. Even once.

Philippa shook off the bleakness. Her husband planned a wicked interlude. She refused to brood on what couldn't be and spoil what promised to prove a memorable encounter. "You're feeling the pinch?"

"Most definitely." His low, insinuating laugh made her shiver with familiar excitement.

His expression intent, he backed her toward the

closed door. She had fond memories of that door. The first time he'd kissed her, she'd been leaning against it.

He kissed her again, with a desperation that jangled with his light-hearted tone as he'd lured her in here. Eager hands tugged at her bodice, and they both sighed with satisfaction as he fondled her breasts. He slid her skirt higher, then with a couple of deft movements, her drawers fell to the floor. His exploring hand quickly discovered that she too was needy.

"Don't make me wait," she begged, clinging to his shoulder with one hand while she fumbled at the fall of his trousers. A year had taught her a few husband-managing skills of her own.

Soon her fingers curled around the heavy, virile weight. He groaned and tilted his hips forward. Anticipation fizzed like champagne in her blood.

Philippa moaned encouragement as he hitched her up against the door. The oak was hard against her back, then she was only aware of miraculous, hot fullness as Blair pushed inside her. Her body quickly adjusted to the unfamiliar angle, and pleasure forked through her like lightning. Through a year of nights and days, the glory of their joining had never faded.

Pressing his face into her hair, he began to move with relentless purpose, building the conflagration until she cried out and shook in his arms. For a long, shining time, she rode the waves of her delight. A liquid rush filled her womb before she tumbled back to her feet, legs near to collapse.

As she and Blair slid in a heap to the floor, he kissed her with more of that thrilling desperation. He mightn't love her, but he wanted her to the point of madness.

With a satisfied sigh, he leaned against the door, and she sprawled across him, too exhausted after her shuddering release to move. During the wild encounter, her hair had collapsed around her face, and she brushed it back as she fought to regain her breath.

Every time they made love, he turned her world to fire. His mere presence lit every day to flame.

He shifted to fasten his trousers, although she could have told him not to bother on her account. She loved every inch of his superb body. To her chagrin, she loved every inch of his soul, too. But that was her burden, and one she intended to bear in silence.

What point risking their happiness with demands for what he couldn't give?

Eventually the heart beneath her cheek calmed from its frantic race, and his breathing steadied. "That was…better than I imagined. And I'd imagined something unforgettable."

She stirred, but his grip tightened, keeping her close. When she raised her head, she expected to see triumph in his face. After all, she'd succumbed to his seduction without a hint of hesitation.

He didn't look like a conquering hero. Instead he looked strangely vulnerable.

Because of that expression, she could no longer

keep silent about the truth she'd discovered a month ago. "Blair, I'm going to have a baby."

She wasn't sure how he'd react, although she assumed he'd be pleased. But he straightened and stared at her, green eyes unreadable and long, expressive mouth unsmiling.

The pause extended. And extended.

Until Philippa shifted uncomfortably and moved away. She immediately felt the absence of his touch.

"Say something," she said, her voice fracturing. She wanted to return to their usual joking flirtation, but the words emerged as raw demand.

Still he stared at her.

Dear heaven, what was wrong? She frowned. "After what we've done all year, you can't pretend you're surprised," she said sharply. "It's not like I managed this by myself."

He swallowed, and his hands opened and closed on his thighs. "You don't sound pleased."

There was no trace of his familiar humor. Something moved in his eyes, something she didn't understand.

Her belly clenched with apprehension, although what could she do? She wanted this child with a fervor that astonished her.

"Of course I'm pleased," she snapped.

He tilted one black brow, his fierce expression lightening a fraction. "Really?"

"Yes." She glared at him, challenging him to object. "Are you?"

A shuddering breath expanded his chest. Somewhere in their passion, she'd tugged off his neck cloth, and his shirt lay open, revealing dark hair over the hard, powerful muscles of his torso.

"I love you," Blair said flatly. "I want you to be happy. If this baby makes you happy, then I'm overjoyed."

"Of course this baby makes me—" She faltered into an astounded silence. Surely there was some mistake. He couldn't have said what she thought he had. Particularly in such an unlover-like tone. Pregnancy must play with her mind. "What…what did you say?"

"I said I'm overjoyed. When is the child due?" he asked, sounding much more like himself. He hadn't sounded like himself when she'd heard him say that he loved her.

Still distracted, but unable to gather the courage to pursue the issue, she answered. "June or July, I think."

"And how are you feeling? Will you be able to travel tomorrow? We can stay here until the baby arrives, if you think it best."

In spite of the fraught moment, she couldn't restrain a dry laugh. "Now I know you must be excited about the baby, if you're offering to extend your time with my family."

He'd told her he loved her. Had he?

"I can't bear to lose you."

That was no surprise. He'd said things like that before. From their earliest days together, she'd been in no doubt that he valued her. Her qualms about trapping him in a marriage he didn't want hadn't lasted beyond the night in Salisbury.

Philippa basked in the way his overriding concern for her outweighed his male urge to procreate. Perhaps he might love her after all.

Still she shied away from asking him if she'd heard him right. What if she hadn't?

"You won't lose me. I'm as healthy as a horse. I haven't even been sick, although I gather I should have been by now."

"Should we go to London and see a doctor?" He sounded unsure. Again, not like himself. She rather liked seeing her lordly husband in a sweat. "Balcannon only has the village midwife."

The impressively competent village midwife on his estate had confirmed that Philippa was indeed expecting a child. "Let's wait and see."

The blankness receded from his expression. She realized now that his silence had been shock. His eyes brightened, and he smiled at her. "What a clever girl you are."

She sucked in a relieved breath. "Well, I had help."

"Yes, I take all the credit." He was definitely back to sounding like the man she lived with day in and day out. Not like the stranger who had told her he loved her.

"Not *all* the credit."

"A baby." His smile widened. She was reassured to see that he appeared remarkably cheerful. She dearly wanted him to look forward to this child with her. "In the summer."

She started to smile, too. After all, she was excited to start their family. "Yes."

"A little girl for me to spoil."

"Or a boy to continue the family name."

He gave a sudden shout of laughter. "Well, damnation, that's wonderful news!"

He reached out and seized her, hauling her into his arms for a kiss that combined passion with celebration. It was unlike any kiss he'd ever given her. Beneath the elation lurked something she'd never felt in him before.

Eventually she pulled away. "I'm so glad you're happy."

"Of course I'm happy."

He kissed her again, then stopped. "What's wrong? You're not getting into the spirit of things."

She was such a fool. Against all the odds, they were contented with their life. Now fate granted them the child she'd prayed for. Any reasonable woman would leave it at that. What was the point of crying after the moon?

But if it was true that Blair did indeed love her, her joy would be complete.

Philippa could stifle the question no longer. "Did… did you say you love me?"

"Of course," he said lightly.

"Don't joke." She grabbed his hands in a trembling grip. "I can't bear it if you joke about this."

He frowned. "Is losing your mind a symptom of having a baby? If so, we're going to have an interesting few months."

She swallowed to ease a tight throat. He acted as if all of this was so unimportant, yet the rest of her life hinged on what he said next. "Is it true?"

Blair sighed with impatience and tugged his hands free. "Philippa, what bat has got into your belfry? You know I love you."

"No, I don't," she said emphatically, shaking her head. "You've never told me."

He looked surprised. "I didn't know I had to. You must know you've had me in a complete spin from the moment I first saw you. It took me a while to identify the problem, but that's the result of my slow masculine brain. Not to mention that until I met you, I'd never been in love before."

If he kept saying things like this, she could almost forgive him for torturing her. Almost. "I know you want me."

He cast her an unimpressed glance. "Of course I want you. Even a girl only half as clever as you could work that out."

"That doesn't mean you love me," she said stubbornly, wondering why she argued, when she'd longed for his love every day of the last year.

He laughed drily. "In my case, it certainly means that."

"Tell me once more." She paused and swallowed again. She felt like a boulder the size of Ben Nevis blocked her throat. "Tell me like you mean it."

She prepared for another mocking response. But after a pause, he raised his hands to cradle her face so that she couldn't evade that searching stare. He'd touched her like this their first morning together as man and wife, when she'd been such an absurd muddle of doubts and confusion.

The light in his eyes warmed her to her bones. He beheld her as if she was the dearest treasure in the world, and he knew he was a lucky man to have her.

At that moment, whatever he said next, she believed he did love her. She thought she'd been happy before. But finally knowing that her husband returned her love made her feel like she stood in bright sun after a long, dark winter.

"Philippa Hume, my dearest wife, I love you with every beat of my heart and every breath I take." To her astonishment, his deep voice cracked with emotion. He sucked in an unsteady breath before he continued. "And to hear that you're having my baby makes me the happiest man since time began. I bless the day you came into my life, and I thank whatever grace allowed me to make you mine. You're the center of my life, and I worship the ground you walk on."

Oh, dear... Be careful what you wish for.

This was almost too much. She wasn't worthy. Moisture stung her eyes. It was her turn to be lost for words.

"There, I said it." He smiled at her with breathtaking tenderness as his thumbs brushed the tears from her lashes. "Don't you want to say something to me?"

Her laugh was husky. "How about, 'Kiss me, Blair'?"

"How about 'I love you, too' or something along those lines?" Her self-confident husband looked unsure. As ever when his feelings were strongly engaged, his brogue deepened. "I've just laid my soul at your feet. You could at least tell me whether you want it or not."

She gulped, struggling not to burst into tears. She was too happy to cry. But her silly eyes didn't seem to agree.

"I want it," she forced out.

His eyes sharpened on her face. "And?"

She could tease him again. But the moment was too profound for games. She turned her head to place a kiss on his broad, capable palm. "And I love you. I think I loved you from the first, too. I definitely knew I loved you on our wedding night."

"Oh, my darling…" He drew her into his arms and held her close to his thundering heart.

The tears she'd fought so long gushed out at last. "I'm crying all over you."

"I forgive you," he said, his voice rich with love, his embrace tightening.

"After everything, it seems too good to be true that I love you, and you love me, and we're having a baby," she muttered into his chest.

"Altogether a most satisfactory outcome," he said gently and kissed her with more of that heart-shattering tenderness. She was dazed with wonder when he finally raised his head. "Let's celebrate in bed."

Her laugh was unsteady. She was still in the grip of poignant emotion. "You're such a man."

Blair laughed back at her. "I am indeed."

He drew her up with him, his hands clasping hers with a firmness that she couldn't doubt. It seemed the marriage that had started so chaotically turned into a match made in heaven.

And if Philippa knew the expression on her husband's face—and she did—now a more physical form of heaven awaited. What a wonderful way to welcome the first Christmas Day of their married life.

Misty eyed, she watched him turn toward the door. Less misty eyed, she watched him tug uselessly at the doorknob. "Blair, don't play the fool. I loved reliving our courtship, but my plans for tonight involve more space than we've got here."

Instead of facing her, he slumped against the door, his shoulders shaking with laughter. "My darling lassie, history repeats itself. The door's jammed. We're stuck here until Mills comes to let us out."

She stared at him, not quite as horrified as she should have been. "Truly?"

He drew himself up and faced her. "On my honor, truly. I'd have thought your uncle would get the lock fixed after last year's fuss."

"Perhaps he's hoping to catch Caroline an earl, using the tactics that worked for me."

Blair gave a huff of laughter. "God help the poor fellow, whoever he is. But what the devil are we to do now?"

Philippa found herself smiling at her dark and dangerous husband as if he'd given her the best Christmas present in the world. After all, when he said he loved her, he had.

"It seems, beloved, that you and I must find some way to occupy ourselves until Mills comes to the rescue."

A PIRATE FOR CHRISTMAS

CHAPTER ONE

Penton Wyck, Northumberland, December 1822

It all started with the donkey.

In search of the star performer in the Christmas Eve play, Bess Farrar presented herself on Penton Abbey's doorstep. A cutting wind whistled around her, and the promise of snow tinged the air. She stamped her feet in their half-boots to restore some feeling to her toes.

As she waited an unacceptably long time for someone to answer her knock, she huddled into her coat and cursed landlords who took up residence in a community, then proceeded to ignore their obligations. The nativity celebrations were a longstanding tradition in Penton Wyck. Just as longstanding was the tradition that the lord of the manor provided the donkey.

The new earl wasn't going to wriggle out of his duty just by playing hard to get. Not if she had anything to say about it. And she certainly did.

Sighing, she stared up at the Abbey's impressive Elizabethan façade, noting the signs of neglect on the golden stone. How sad to see the beautiful old house so unloved. Everyone in the village had hoped that the new Lord Channing might be more vigorous and engaged in local life than the last. So far, indications were that he'd prove even less effective than his late brother, whose good intentions had fallen victim to lifelong ill health.

A pity that the new earl promised to be a disappointment. But what could one expect of a man reputed to be a pirate? And a Scottish one at that.

Eventually the heavy door inched open and bespectacled eyes peered out from the shadows. "His lordship isn't at home."

"Good afternoon." She straightened her shoulders and fixed the man with the gimlet stare that always brought recalcitrant parishioners into line. "My name is Elizabeth Farrar. My father is the vicar of St. Martin's."

As his lordship would know, if he took the trouble to show his face in church.

Strangely, her introduction appeared to puzzle the man, who wasn't a butler. His lordship was yet to employ any indoor staff. Another bone she had to pick with him. Many local livelihoods relied on finding work at the Abbey, and since the previous earl had moved to Italy for the sake of his health, there had been hardship in the village.

"*You're* Miss Farrar?" He sounded as if he didn't believe her.

"Yes."

"Um, good afternoon. And his lordship still isn't home."

"I'll wait."

"He's not expected back today."

Because young Will Potts worked in the stables and passed on any news about doings at the Abbey, she knew that was a lie. She glued a polite smile to her face, and kept her tone steady but determined. "I'd still like to wait."

The man, whoever he was, proved no more immune to that purposeful tone than the villagers. The heavy door gave a gothic creak as it eased fully open.

"Then please come in." His words were more welcoming than his tone.

On this gloomy afternoon, the great hall was dark and comfortless, and almost as cold as the front step. Nobody setting foot in this frigid stone cavern, barren of all decoration, would guess that Christmas was only a week away. "Surely his lordship wants a fire. This place is like a tomb."

The tall man in glasses and shirtsleeves was reed

thin and looked like he needed a good meal. That's what came of failing to hire a cook, Bess wanted to tell him—and his absent master.

He swallowed until his Adam's apple bobbed. "His lordship isn't here, I told you."

"I hope he returns before I freeze into a block of ice." She subsided onto one of two carved oak chairs set against the wall. The hall was mostly devoid of furniture, and in the dull light, the tall windows with their stained glass panels appeared more funereal than heraldic.

"If you leave a note, I promise to deliver it."

Her lips firmed as she shifted to find a comfortable spot on the unforgiving seat. The noble Earl of Channing didn't want visitors settling in. Indications were that he didn't want visitors at all.

Too bad for the noble Earl of Channing.

"So he can ignore it, the way he's ignored my other correspondence?" she asked sweetly.

The studious-looking man avoided her eyes. "His lordship has been busy since taking over, Miss Farrar."

Bess glanced around the dusty, empty room. "Not with domestic matters."

"His lordship—"

His lordship stormed in.

At least Bess assumed that the disheveled auburn-haired man who crashed through the door at the other end of the hall must be Penton Abbey's elusive new master. He stalked past her, brandishing a sheaf of papers.

"That blasted Farrar besom is hounding me again, Ned." His Scottish brogue added an exotic edge to his heated remarks. "I thought I asked you to put her off."

He didn't see her as his long stride ate up the tiled floor. In this gloom, it would be hard to make out an army, especially with the sky darkening for snow.

"Rory, for heaven's sake," the other man stammered, casting Bess an embarrassed glance.

Bess stood and performed a perfunctory curtsy. "Good afternoon, my lord."

He turned on her. He was as tall as his friend, but much more heavily muscled. A more formidable character altogether, she could already tell. "Just who the devil are you?"

She permitted herself a cool smile. "I believe I'm the blasted Farrar besom."

"Oh, hell," he muttered, staring at her thunderstruck. He looked as shocked as if one of these iron-hard oak chairs had stood up, bowed and asked him to dance.

She paused to take stock of the new lord of the manor. The previous earl, his brother, had died six months ago, and had been abroad for two years before that. Since his demise, tattle had run rife about Rory Beaton, the heir. Confused stories about a licentious rapscallion who had led a lawless life sailing the world's oceans.

Surveying him now, Bess was inclined to trust to rumor. From his ruffled red hair to his large booted feet, he was every inch a man who commanded the stage. Even more buccaneerish were the brilliant green eyes with their spark of devilry.

Never had she encountered anyone who so precisely fitted her image of a pirate, a wicked seducer, and a reckless adventurer.

She'd spent her life in peaceful Penton Wyck. It was perfectly natural that her heart should skip a beat in the presence of a notorious rascal.

Or so she told herself as she raised her chin and stared his lordship down. Which, to her annoyance, was more difficult than usual. She was a tall woman, but the new earl towered over her in a most disconcerting fashion.

Also disconcerting was his casual arrogance. Not to mention those flashing good looks.

"Manners must be at a premium north of the border," she said softly, even as she reminded herself it would be more politic to butter him up.

Her starchy remark made his long, expressive mouth twitch. "If you inveigle yourself into my house uninvited, lassie, you must put up with what you get."

"Rory…" the other man bleated.

Channing arched one sardonic red-brown brow in his direction. "Don't you have some letters to write?"

The man flushed, but to his credit stood his ground.

"I would hate nasty gossip to spoil your arrival at Penton."

Too late for that, Bess could have told them. The villagers weren't far off locking up their daughters and calling in the militia.

Another twitch of his intriguing mouth. Despite everything, that hint of laughter fascinated Bess. Even if she knew quite well that he was laughing at her.

"No need to beat around the bush, Ned. You fear for this lady's safety once you're out of sight."

"Should he?" she asked, suppressing the urge to inform his lordship that she was more than a match for any scurvy Scot, pirate or not.

When those deep-set eyes settled on her, she shivered. With nervousness that made a mockery of her brave words. And with something else she couldn't quite identify.

"I could eat you up in one bite and nobody could stop me."

Her eyes narrowed at the challenge. "I'd stick in your neck."

To her surprise, he laughed with unfettered appreciation. The joyous sound echoed off the bare stone walls as he flung the papers onto an ancient chest against the wall. A glance revealed that they were the letters she'd written since he'd arrived a month ago. "Aye, you might, at that."

"Rory, I must protest," Ned said stalwartly.

Channing ran his hand through his thick russet hair

and regarded his lanky offsider with impatience. "Och, be off with you, laddie. The lady's safe, and she knows it. And so is her reputation. This is the country. We can talk a wee while without setting every tongue in the village wagging." He paused. "Anyway, who's to know?"

"His lordship can be difficult," the man said, turning to her apologetically. "Perhaps it would be better if you called another time."

Bess, who, despite everything, was enjoying this unconventional encounter, smiled. It was much more fun doing battle with his lordship in person than via reams of disregarded letters. "Why would I want to do that, Mr.—"

"White, Miss Farrar. Edward White." He bowed with a politeness so far lacking in the earl. "I'm his lordship's secretary."

"And butler and cook and bailiff. And shipmate of twenty years. It's a good thing you're so deuced indispensable, or I mightn't take kindly to you hovering like an old woman."

"It's taken me four weeks to lay eyes on Lord Channing," she said calmly. "Now I've got him at my mercy, wild horses couldn't drag me away."

"Bravo, Miss Farrar," Channing said drily. "Perhaps you'll join me in the library." He gestured with one long-fingered hand toward the door he'd burst through. "You clearly have plenty to say. I'd prefer to avoid freezing to death while you harangue me."

"How impressively cooperative, my lord." She

matched his tone as she preceded him through the corridor and into the library. The room was bereft of books, but at least contained a desk, some seating, and a fire.

She looked at the cobwebbed shelves in dismay. "I had no idea the house was so neglected. Although given that any remaining staff were dismissed six months ago, I should have guessed."

Channing crossed to pour a brandy from the decanter on the desk. He raised the decanter in her direction. "You?"

She muffled a huff of laughter. If he thought his unorthodox behavior would deter her, he was due for disappointment. "No, thank you."

"I'll have to get some good whisky down from Speyside." He took his drink and wandered across to the fire with a restlessness that stirred the air. There was something breathtakingly compelling about the new earl. A crackle of energy that Bess only now realized had been missing from her life. "Did you know my brother?"

"This is a small community, my lord. Of course I did. He was in poor health in recent years."

"He let the house go to rack and ruin."

"Before he left for Italy, he was a good landlord and very conscientious about caring for the villagers."

"I'm guessing you made sure he was."

She didn't answer. Even if it was true. With her father lost in dreams of Byzantium and the earl an invalid, someone had to stand up for the locals. "My condolences on his death."

Channing shrugged. "I didn't know him. My mother took me away from Penton Wyck as a wee bairn, and after my father died, married a Scotsman with four daughters. She never set foot in England again. George was fifteen years older than me and a real Sassenach. He had little use for his barbarous northern relations."

Bess frowned. Growing up, she'd heard about the runaway countess. But Lord Channing's prosaic explanation brought home the bitterly unhappy family history behind the old scandal.

Perhaps this troubled background explained the earl's wildness. It certainly explained why he sounded like he should wear a kilt, even if right now he was dressed plainly, if untidily in a dark blue coat and buff breeches.

"I'm sure even in the Highlands, a man knows enough to hire a few servants when he moves into a house this size."

"I've taken on the important ones."

"The grooms, you mean?"

He shrugged again and gestured her toward a shabby leather sofa. "Aye. The horses take priority. Ned and I can rough it until we discover the lay of the land."

Gingerly she sat, then sneezed at the cloud of dust that exploded around her. "Roughing it..." She added ironic weight to the words. "...hardly befits your dignity as Earl of Channing, though, does it? You need to set a standard."

He propped one hip on the large mahogany desk covered in papers and regarded her unwaveringly. "You see? That's why you surprised me, Miss Farrar."

"Because I'm bold enough to point out your duty?" She made herself meet his eyes, while some silly feminine part of her wanted to giggle and blush and flutter her eyelashes.

She was too old for such nonsense. Sternly she told herself that sin always came disguised as beauty. That was how it lured you in. But in the stark gray light through the window at his back, Lord Channing was the most spectacular man she'd ever beheld in all her admittedly sheltered twenty-six years.

He shook his head and picked up a silver paperknife which he passed idly from one elegant hand to the other. "No, because given the tone of your letters, I expected a worthy spinster of fifty. Not the prettiest girl in the village."

"The prettiest..." She shut her mouth with a snap. What on earth? Could he be flirting with her? Nobody flirted with her. Everyone was too busy awaiting her instructions. Between the late Lord Channing's ill health and her father's position of authority—a position he blithely disregarded—she'd become Penton's guiding hand. "You're trying to turn me up sweet, my lord. Shame on you."

Another half-smile. The part of her that most

assuredly wasn't an old maid burned to see him smile properly. "A wee bit of sugar always sweetens relations, Miss Farrar. A lesson that wouldn't go astray when you lay down the law to your betters."

Her momentary softening after his compliment vanished. "You're not my better."

He laughed softly and stood. "In every sense except the most worldly, that is undoubtedly true. But a month of nagging was more likely to make me ignore you than do your bidding."

Nagging? The hide of the man. She gritted her teeth and struggled to sound polite. "I thought you'd appreciate some advice about local matters."

His eyes creased with wry amusement. Still no smile. And she'd dearly love to see him smile. "No, you thought you'd run me the way you ran my brother—and it's not going to happen."

"When you're obviously doing so brilliantly on your own," she responded tartly, gesturing around the disorderly room with eloquent derision.

"You are the damnedest lassie, Miss Farrar."

His open admiration touched the same foolish patch of her heart that had warmed to hearing him call her pretty. "Language, my lord."

"Why should I mind my manners? You've hardly been a model of decorum."

She blushed—with mortification, not suppressed attraction. Curse him. He was right. Her father would be appalled to hear her. But then, her father's soul was gentle and meek. Nobody had ever used either word to describe her. On the other hand, her father would dither and do nothing while the world collapsed about him.

"I beg your pardon, my lord," she said stiffly.

"Now, don't go all missish on me. Our frank exchange of views is a refreshing change from the usual English mealy-mouthed rot." To her alarm, he came and sat beside her. The sofa had plenty of room for two. But Channing's robust personality made Bess feel as though he encroached too close. Nervously, she edged away.

She prepared to remind him that he had obligations, but that wasn't what emerged. "How do you know?"

"Know what?"

Her cheeks were on fire. "That I'm the…prettiest girl in the village. You haven't set foot in Penton Wyck."

"I've clearly been remiss, if you're an example of the views I'd take in from the high street. I'm sure people must come from miles around to catch a glimpse of the lovely local scenery."

Her lips tightened at his teasing. Just as nobody flirted with her, nobody teased her either. She wasn't sure she should encourage it. This playful discussion made the hair on the back of her neck prickle. She was a self-willed woman past first youth. She was unused to men treating her as an object of desire. But surely she wasn't mistaken about Lord Channing's interest.

Unless after a month penned up at the Abbey, he was bored enough to flirt with anything in skirts. That lowering thought crushed her stirring excitement. This man had been around the world. Even someone as inexperienced as Bess saw that the girls would be mad for him wherever he went. A staid village maiden wasn't likely to get him in a stew.

She regarded him without favor. "My lord, I'm beginning to think I should have asked Mr. White to stay."

He ignored her remark. Her history with him indicated that he had a great capacity to ignore what he didn't want to hear.

"Miss Farrar, you must be the prettiest lassie in the village, because you're the prettiest lassie I've ever seen," he said softly, and for a resonant moment, teasing receded and something more profound hovered between them.

He smiled fully, just for her. And her heart turned a triple somersault in her chest. It was the oddest sensation. The breath jammed in Bess's throat as she stared into his eyes, drowning in rich green velvet. Somewhere at the back of her mind, a voice warned her that bearding this particular lion in his den was a foolhardy act. The pirate earl was a danger to more than ships of the line.

Suddenly she no longer felt like the wise ruler of her own little kingdom. Instead she felt like an untried girl confronting the eternal mystery of potent masculinity.

She surged to her feet, smoothing uncreased skirts in an attempt to hide her disquiet. "I…I must go."

She expected him to laugh at her again. A man as worldly as this would have no difficulty divining her purely female reaction to him.

Lord Channing stared up at her from the sofa. Unsmiling. Then the predatory expression drained from his face, and he looked almost harmless. Or at least as harmless as a man of his attractions could manage. "Don't rush off. You must have come with a specific purpose, something a letter won't accomplish."

"My letters didn't accomplish anything," she responded shakily.

"Well, perhaps a request in person will achieve what they didn't," he said easily, slouching against the back of the couch. "Come, Miss Farrar…" He broke off. "You signed all your letters E. Farrar. What does the E stand for?"

She didn't even think of refusing to answer. "Elizabeth. But everyone calls me Bess."

She caught a glint of satisfaction in his eyes. "I like it."

Standing up and away from him did wonders for her confidence. Her usual spirit revived. "I can't imagine an occasion where you'll use it."

When his lids lowered, he once more became all sensual threat. "I certainly can."

"Lord Channing—"

"Why did you come here, my charming Miss E. Farrar?"

"Not to be mocked," she retorted. "I came here for the Christmas donkey."

CHAPTER TWO

*R*ory studied the bonny lass standing in front of him, the woman who strangely seemed to imagine she could push him around. Damn her, she had more effrontery than any arrogant officer ordering a humble midshipman to jump to his duties.

By rights, her presumption should be annoying. Instead he was charmed. And intrigued. And attracted in a way he couldn't remember feeling before.

Through his turbulent life, he'd seen more beautiful women than he deserved. He'd desired and conquered, and called himself a lucky dog for the privilege. But he'd never felt so lucky as when he'd barged in on Ned struggling to bring this headstrong female into line.

Poor Ned. Bess Farrar was too heady a brew for his palate. But for a captain who'd sailed the seven seas and lived to tell the tale, she was the perfect fit. That demure gray dress with its high neck and narrow lace collar would fool the rest of the world, but never him. She might see herself as a tame household cat, but he'd immediately read her tiger soul.

"Are you calling me an ass, Miss Farrar?" he asked, and relished the shock in her deep blue eyes.

It was fun to keep her off balance. Every time he set her reeling, she lost that daunting air of determination and looked younger and sweeter. He hadn't missed how flustered she'd been when he'd called her pretty.

Good God above. His compliment shouldn't have surprised her. Every man in Penton Wyck must be in dire need of spectacles.

Because she was pretty. Hell, she was beautiful, with her strong-boned face and haughty nose and stubborn chin. On the ocean, circumstances changed in a second and peril arose from nothing. Dry land, apparently, offered the same challenges.

He immediately recognized that his destiny lay with those pure features under that severely restrained luxuriance of wheat-blond hair. His future had marched into the great hall, bamboozled Ned, then turned her magic on Rory himself.

This woman was meant for him. He wasn't sure yet what he felt about it, but the conclusion was inescapable.

"Pardon?"

If he hadn't been so bedazzled himself, he'd almost

pity the confusion in her spectacular eyes. "You said you're looking for the Christmas donkey."

His nonsense at last cracked her solemnity, and she laughed, a low musical sound that he could listen to for the rest of his life. Miss Farrar delivered an impact mightier than any Atlantic storm. All a sailor could do was batten down the hatches, hold the helm steady, and pray that he reached safe harbor.

"Oh, I really have convinced you I'm the rudest creature in the world," she said. "No, I mean a real donkey. Her name's Daisy, and she's the centerpiece of the nativity play."

"And I own this fabulous beast?"

"Yes. Your late brother let us use her at will. But I didn't want to take your permission for granted."

He spread his arms across the back of the sofa and stretched out his legs. "Hence cornering me in person on this issue, instead of bombarding me with letters as you have about everything else."

She made a helpless gesture. "You probably think I'm exceeding my authority."

He raised his eyebrows. "Probably?"

She blushed most delightfully. "Very well, then, definitely exceeding my authority. But time grows short, and my intentions are good."

His lips took on a wry twist. "Many a fine ship has foundered because of the captain's good intentions. Good intentions never saved a man from drowning."

"Unless that well-intentioned onlooker plucked that drowning sailor from the waves."

He laughed in soft appreciation. He'd known immediately she wouldn't be an easy prize to win. She was clever and used to having her own way. Which only made the game more interesting, by heaven. "I'll give you that point."

She looked surprised again. "Are we counting points?"

"We most certainly are." When he stood, she faltered back across the worn Turkey carpet. She wasn't afraid of him, but at some female level, she recognized the claim he placed upon her. Powerful currents of attraction and resistance eddied between them. He'd need all his skill as a navigator to plot a safe course through these hazardous straits. "You'd better show me this donkey."

"There's no need for us both to brave the cold, my lord. All I need is your permission, and I'll take her into Penton for tomorrow's rehearsal."

Daft lass. As if, having found her, he meant to let Miss Farrar escape so easily. "I have a fancy to see Daisy."

"But it's about to snow."

"Then there's no time to waste."

That lush mouth, a promise of passion if Rory had ever seen one, set in a mutinous line, and she regarded him from across the room as if he represented a strange and potentially dangerous new species. "You're a very unusual man, Lord Channing."

He smiled at this outspoken lassie. "You have no idea, Miss Farrar."

"Is it because you're a pirate?"

For a moment there, he'd felt in control of the situation. The feeling had unfortunately been fleeting. He slammed to a halt on his way to the door and stared at her in astonishment. "What on earth did you say?"

She looked shamefaced and made an apologetic gesture with one hand. "I'm sorry. Perhaps you don't like people to mention your former occupation."

"My former occupation," he repeated very slowly. "As a pirate."

"The story's all over the village."

"Aye?"

"You must have expected people to talk about you. And given you've been such a recluse since your arrival, it's inevitable that rumors are flying."

"Inevitable rumors." Rory paused. "That I'm a pirate."

Miss Farrar studied him and devil take her, understanding filled her lovely face. "Seeing you were free to take up the title, I imagine that you've reformed."

"I wouldn't be too sure about that."

She eyed him uncertainly, but plowed on. He commended her determination. "There's no need to feel awkward about your past crimes, my lord. Here at Penton Wyck, we take people as we find them."

"Is that right?"

"Yes." Her tone firmed. "When we *do* find them."

He sighed and ran his hand through his hair. "You're about to start nagging again. I feel it in my piratical bones."

She made a conciliatory gesture. "I know you think I have no right to lecture you. After all, I'm only the vicar's daughter."

He didn't bother hiding his amusement. "That would sound more convincing if you injected an ounce of genuine humility into your tone."

She cast him an impatient glance. "Penton Wyck is small and isolated and the residents rely on each another. We rely on the lord of the manor most of all."

"If my brother wasn't well, I can't imagine he was a mainstay of the community."

"But he was. All right, he wasn't out amongst us as much as he might have liked, but he played his part. He employed the villagers in the house and on the estate, he supported those in need, he attended church until he was too sick to manage it. We all sincerely mourned him when he passed away. He was a good man."

A horrible thought struck Rory, and he frowned. "Were you in love with him?"

She met his gaze. "I did love him. He was the kindest man I ever knew. Everyone in Penton held your brother in the highest esteem."

Relief flooded him, completely disproportionate to

the length of time he and Miss Farrar had been acquainted. Her feelings for his brother hadn't gone beyond friendship. "I'm sorry I didn't know him."

"So am I."

"Now you're saddled with an unknown master."

Her voice was sincere as she stepped closer. "You don't have to stay unknown."

"And already talk is raging—I'm a pirate, and worse, a pirate from Scotland. I'm surprised the villagers haven't made for the hills. What else are they saying?"

"Isn't that enough?"

Rory could tell from her expression that there was more. He guessed that his unmarried state at the grand old age of thirty-two left him open to accusations of chasing the lassies. Especially when coupled with the ludicrous pirate rumors.

"Now I suppose you want me to fill the house with servants," he said in a long-suffering tone.

Of course he intended to staff the Abbey—even someone who'd spent his life aboard ship understood enough about great houses to see that they needed a crew. But there was something pleasurable in having a pretty girl look to his welfare.

"You certainly need help."

"I like the simple life."

She didn't grace that with a reply. "What happened to all the furniture? The great hall used to contain more than just two uncomfortable chairs."

"The lack of furnishings discourages visitors."

"Not all of them."

"No." If he'd known the woman at the other end of those admonishing letters was so breathtaking, he'd have requested a meeting straightaway. "According to the lawyers, my brother had the place cleared while he was in Italy with the idea of renting it, then nothing came of the plan. There's piles of furniture scattered between the attics and the barns."

"I don't remember the house being this gloomy either. When I was a girl, his lordship often had parties. A highlight was Christmas dinner for the villagers, then a ball that night."

When he'd learned about his unexpected inheritance, Rory had just docked in Portsmouth after a stormy voyage from New South Wales. He hadn't welcomed the change in his circumstances. He'd spent the last month struggling to accept jettisoning a career he loved in favor of landlocked life in an England less familiar than any ocean.

Now he felt a pang that his parents' difficult marriage had turned his brother into a stranger. The late earl had featured largely in recent discussions with lawyers and men of business. But for the first time, listening to Miss Farrar, he gained a sense of George as a man and not just a predecessor. "My brother died at an age when he was capable of siring an heir. In fact, I always assumed he'd married and had children. I never expected to inherit."

"In that case, you should appreciate my advice," she said, humor making her blue eyes sparkle.

He had a sudden, extremely cunning thought, worthy of the pirate king she accused him of being. "You're clearly a resource, Miss Farrar, and one I'd be a fool to ignore."

"Oh?"

The suspicious syllable made him want to laugh. She was quick, this miracle of a lassie. His abrupt change of attitude would strike her as unlikely.

"I'll put you in charge of preparing the house for Christmas."

She straightened and regarded him warily. "Surely a permanent housekeeper is a better solution."

"Is the task too much for you?" he said in a pitying voice intended to lift her hackles. "After all, it's so much easier to give orders from afar than get your hands dirty addressing the problem."

"I'm busy with the play."

"And here you are, telling me Penton Wyck is suffering because I don't employ enough people. I'm guessing with my brother's absence, life has indeed been tough these last few years. That's too bad of you, Miss Farrar. You're either deceiving me about local hardship, or putting your own selfish wishes ahead of your neighbors' needs. What would that reverend gentleman, your father, say? Especially at this time of goodwill to all men." He clicked his tongue and settled a benevolent and innocent expression on his face.

He caught a swiftly hidden flash of guilt. "My father would say that it was inappropriate for an unmarried lady who is no relation to play mistress of a bachelor household."

Ah, mistress was such a bonny word. Although if he wanted Miss Farrar in his bed, he already knew he'd have to persuade her to marry him.

Rory wondered why the prospect didn't make him yelp with horror. He'd always avoided entanglements carrying any whiff of forever. Half an hour of Miss Farrar's company, and he was itching to call the banns.

Until today he'd been sailing rudderless all his life. Now he had accurate charts and the wind behind him.

Did she share this powerful affinity? Their conversation ranged beyond the usual polite nothings one exchanged with an acquaintance, and a respectable lady at that. But he'd learned from her letters that she wasn't the most conventional of creatures, for all her harping on duty and obligation.

"Come, Miss Farrar," he said in a chiding tone. "It's clear that you and my brother worked together for the common good. Won't you extend me the same courtesy?"

"You're not like your brother."

"Surely your reputation will be safe if you're surrounded with a crowd of helpers."

She sighed. "You think I'm absurd."

Rory hid a smile. He thought her instincts right on the money. His intentions were far from pure.

Although he meant marriage, he also meant to gain her gloriously sensual surrender. She was made for his bed. And he aimed to see her there before too much longer.

It wasn't yet snowing, but Rory could smell it on the air as they left the house through the warren of kitchens and storerooms. Miss Farrar strode along beside him with a firm ground-eating countrywoman's gait. She was more at home on dry land than he was. Although he gradually found his feet in this new life he must learn to inhabit.

A flush marked her cheeks. Perhaps because of the chill wind, perhaps because she was with a man who stirred her blood. He dearly hoped the second reason was the right one. He'd lent her a greatcoat for their excursion to catch Daisy, and between that, the scarf she'd drawn from a pocket and tied over her shining hair, and her sensible half-boots, she looked ready to march to China.

"I hope you know where to find Daisy." His breath formed clouds as he spoke. Odd to be so perishingly cold and so overheated at the same time. "It's too cold to go to the ends of the estate."

"Haven't you seen her?"

He shook his head. "I might have. I've inspected so much livestock in the last few weeks that all the cows and sheep and pigs have become a fog in my mind. I'm a man of the sea, not a farmer."

She sent him a sympathetic look. "You'll have to learn fast, or every fellow north of London will try to cheat you. What you need is a good steward."

"Do you know someone?"

"Not in the village. And Banks, your brother's steward, retired last year. His son is working as assistant to Lord Leath's man down in Yorkshire. Perhaps the chance of promotion and a return home might coax him back."

"You see?"

"See what?" she asked and to his satisfaction, didn't withdraw when he took her elbow to help her over a muddy patch.

He'd never touched her before. Her arm was strong and slender in his grasp, and even through several layers of good English wool, he could swear he felt her vitality. Touching her certainly helped to keep out the cold.

She couldn't be further removed from the delicate beauties who had clustered around him when he'd dropped in on London, freshly in possession of his title. He'd been cynical enough to note that ladies who might flirt with a younger son had much more serious plans for a rich, unmarried earl. Not that he'd lacked for gold even before inheriting. He'd taken enough prizes on the high seas to set himself up very nicely indeed.

"It's clear that I need your help."

"I can look into finding you a good housekeeper, too."

"You're the only person I'll trust the house to." He drew in a lungful of winter air and caught her scent. Lavender and lemon. Slightly astringent. Like her. With a base note of sweet honey. Again like her.

The path took them through wintry woods. Dead leaves crackled beneath their boots, and bare trees stretched their branches to the pewter sky. When she turned to study him, the shadowy light turned her into a creature of beguiling mystery. "I'm not sure."

It was better than a no. Especially when he still touched her.

He drew her to a stop. "Can I do something for you in return? A new roof for the church? Repairs to the vicarage?"

"No, thank you. Your brother kept everything in good order."

Again his saintly brother. The laddie seemed never to have put a foot wrong. "Is there nothing I can do to persuade you to help me?"

"Actually…"

"Aye?"

She sent him a quick smile. "You might be sorry you asked."

Rory had an inkling that she might be right. On the other hand, when she set up the house, she'd be under his feet and ripe for courting. She wasn't quite as ahead of him as she imagined. "Try me."

"You can reinstate the village Christmas party."

He regarded her steadily. "That means getting the house into fit state in a hurry."

"Only the public rooms. Just the great hall really."

"Aye, very well. I agree."

His swift capitulation obviously surprised her. "I haven't finished yet."

He'd had a feeling there might be more. Nothing he'd seen so far indicated that she was an easy mark. Although he still held her arm, and that had proven simpler than he'd expected. "What else?"

"Joseph from the play has broken his leg."

Hell's bells. Theatricals had never been his forte. As a boy before he'd gone to sea, his stepsisters in Edinburgh had loved to dress up and playact. He'd preferred to be outside riding or playing a rough game of football. "Joseph?"

"Yes." She shrugged. "If you feel it's beneath your dignity—"

He snorted. "Anyone who's been a midshipman gets all notions of dignity knocked out of him quick smart."

Her brilliant smile made his foolish heart leap like a salmon up a Highland burn. "So you'll do it?"

"Aye, if you promise to bring my house up to scratch and run this Christmas party—and never send me another letter."

"Thank you!" For a moment, he thought she might

hug him, but unfortunately, she thought better of it. She regarded him thoughtfully as they continued along the path. "I hope you'll help me with the house."

"If I must," he said, hiding his glee. Days in Miss Farrar's company. Days to convince her he'd make a deuced fine husband. And all he had to do was put on Christmas dinner for a lot of rustics.

"Excellent."

"Who's playing Mary?"

She met his eyes and at last noticed that they were arm in arm. With a fluster that hinted she was unused to the wiles of determined gentlemen, she pulled free. "I am."

Marvelous. "Then I'd better make sure I have the measure of this elusive donkey."

They emerged into a wide field with a burn running through it. A post and rail fence separated the wood from the meadow. In the distance, an open byre sheltered a wee black donkey.

"Stay here," Miss Farrar said, placing a hand on his arm. "Daisy can be skittish after she's been left to her own devices."

He liked that she touched him so unselfconsciously. "Still giving orders, Miss Farrar?"

She cast him an unimpressed glance. "It's for your own good. She bites."

So do I. "I bow to your local knowledge."

He leaned on the gate and watched as Miss Farrar slowly crossed the grass in Daisy's direction. With seeming docility, the donkey turned to observe her approach. Then when Miss Farrar was a matter of feet away, she trotted out of the byre.

Miss Farrar paused to lift a halter from a hook before she went in pursuit. Again the donkey waited until Miss Farrar was near enough to catch her before she kicked out her hind legs and veered toward Rory. Rory was no expert on donkeys, but it looked to him like Daisy was having a good laugh at Miss Farrar's expense.

Miss Farrar followed with a dogged patience that indicated this game was nothing new. The donkey's ears moved backward and forward, but only when she was almost upon him did he realize that he could hear singing.

And it was a song he knew well.

"Rule, Britannia! Britannia, rule the waves. Britons never, never, never will be slaves."

Rory burst into laughter. "Really?"

Unfortunately his hilarity startled Daisy, and she skipped away.

"Head her off!" Miss Farrar shouted from behind her.

He dived into Daisy's path, but she easily avoided him. "She's a slippery devil."

"Sing to her. She likes that."

He cast the madcap lassie a doubtful glance. "Not from what I can see."

"Try."

Miss Farrar looked enchanting. Cold air and exercise lent color to her cheeks and a shine to her eyes. No red-blooded male would miss how gracefully she moved in pursuit of this she-demon disguised as a donkey.

"Another order."

Miss Farrar forgot herself enough to growl. "Please."

He hid a smile and joined her in the patriotic song. Miss Farrar had a pretty voice, a true soprano with a husky edge that heated his blood in defiance of the frigid air. Their voices mingled in a way he hoped foretold another harmonious joining in the future.

For several eventful minutes—Britannia became less robust by the second—they attempted to corner Daisy. But she was too clever to let them back her against the fence.

Pausing to catch his breath, Rory regarded the donkey with dislike. "She's playing with us."

"Of course she is."

"I'll buy you another donkey."

"That's silly." Miss Farrar sent him the same impatient look he'd given the donkey. "It just takes persistence."

"And singing."

"And singing."

"She doesn't approve of my performance."

"She's just getting your measure."

"I've got hers. And I don't think we should unleash this ruffian on my village."

He stopped, shocked. Well, what did you know? Every day since inheriting, he'd felt like an interloper. He'd never before referred to Penton Wyck as his. Perhaps, thanks to Miss Farrar, he became reconciled to this earl lark.

"Don't tell me you're going to let a mere domestic animal defeat you, my lord. Surely a pirate has more spirit."

He really had to set Miss Farrar straight on the whole pirate thing. But before he could speak, Daisy made a sudden dash for the other end of the field. By the time he'd caught up with her, he had no breath for anything but muffled curses. This last month of living as a landlubber had made him soft.

"*God rest ye merry, gentlemen,*" Miss Farrar trilled, approaching Daisy with the halter hidden behind her back.

Rory wasn't convinced the singing had any effect on the evil beast, but while the song held her attention, he stealthily advanced from the other side. The donkey was closer to a corner than they'd yet managed. At the last minute, he spread his arms and gave a loud halloo. The donkey started and lost her bearings enough to back away.

"Well done, Lord Channing," Miss Farrar said, then resumed singing as she closed in on the donkey crushed against the hedgerow. "Now sing."

"Tidings of comfort and joy, comfort and joy."

Daisy retreated.

Rory edged closer.

Daisy dodged, but he cut off her escape.

"Watch out, she—"

"Bites." He jerked out of reach just in time to avoid those large teeth sinking into his arm. But there was a new rip in his greatcoat. "Are you sure she won't run amok among law-abiding citizens?"

"She likes the play. She knows she's the favorite." Miss Farrar took advantage of Daisy's attack on Rory to slip the halter over her head.

To Rory's surprise, the donkey stood calmly as Miss Farrar caught the lead. "You exaggerate the complexity of her thought processes."

"You'll learn." Miss Farrar led Daisy toward the gate. "I'd advise you not to underestimate her. After all, Joseph is responsible for her on the day."

He rolled his eyes as he followed. "God save me."

When he met Daisy's knowing brown glance, he wondered if Miss Farrar was right about the donkey being a criminal mastermind. Right now, she looked as sweet as sugar, and he almost believed it, until he remembered the chase she'd led them.

His thoughts focused on pursuing a prize much more interesting than a cantankerous donkey. His gaze settled on Miss Farrar.

Elizabeth.

Bess.

No great chore. She was lovely in her odd assortment of clothing and her muddy boots. Running around the field, she'd lost her scarf. The exercise had loosened her hair and curling tendrils of blond framed her vivid face.

Rory opened the gate and stood back to let Bess and Daisy go through ahead of him. "Although I don't believe we've settled terms for her use."

Bess fixed startled dark blue eyes on him. "What do you mean? We always use Daisy. It's tradition."

A rascally smile stretched his lips as he shut the gate. "Aye, but now there's a new hand on the tiller at Penton Abbey—or had you forgotten?"

"But…you helped to catch her. And if you don't let us have her, everyone will be so disappointed." Her voice firmed. "It will make a bad impression."

"I wanted to see her to work out what she's worth."

Bess brightened. "Are you offering to sell her? I'm sure we can set a price."

He propped his back against the fence and folded his arms. "Not sell, rent."

She frowned. "How much?"

Without shifting his attention from Bess, he hooked the heel of his boot on the fence's lowest rail. "Not how much, what."

She looked distinctly uneasy. Again he applauded her instincts. "You're being cursed enigmatic, my lord."

"I'm merely negotiating fair hire for this magnificent animal, Miss Farrar."

Bess looked doubtfully at the small donkey, muddy and unkempt after living outside all summer. "And what might that be?"

"Nothing too ruinous." Wicked triumph flooded him as he stared unblinkingly at Bess. "One wee kiss, and Daisy is yours for the play."

CHAPTER THREE

"K-kiss me?" Bess stammered, staring aghast at the handsome, confident man slouched so elegantly in front of her. She was so shocked that she forgot to hold on to Daisy, but luckily Lord Channing had his wits about him and caught her before she scarpered.

"Aye, that's what I said," he told her calmly, as if he was a civilized man and not a wicked rake. Because surely only wicked rakes went around kissing ladies they hardly knew.

"The gossip was right," she muttered, too rattled to mind her tongue.

"That I'm an opportunist?"

"That you're a…a libertine."

His low laugh sent seductive music rippling across her skin. "Good Lord, it seems I'm providing the locals with plenty of entertainment, even before I play

Joseph."

"Which doesn't mean this particular local has to provide entertainment for you, my lord."

Channing plastered a regretful expression on his face. "Of course you don't. Please forgive me for asking." He turned to open the gate and started to lead Daisy back the way they'd come.

"Where are you going?" Bess asked, bewildered.

"I'm putting Daisy back in her field. I'm sure you'll find another donkey. At a pinch, a pony will fit the bill."

Bess caught a growl behind her teeth. She'd known Lord Channing an afternoon, and already he counted as the most provoking person she'd ever met. Her hands clenched in the greatcoat's voluminous pockets as she stared after his retreating back.

He'd taken another ten steps before she spoke. "I didn't say no."

He pulled Daisy up and turned to face Bess. "You didn't say yes."

"You startled me. I'm not used to rogues demanding my favors in return for agreeing to perfectly reasonable requests."

His smile was careless. "I'm so pleased that I'm broadening your horizons."

His insouciant air ruffled her temper. He was obviously used to kissing women at the drop of a hat. She couldn't be nearly so casual about the idea, even if she'd wager he knew how to kiss a girl until he filled her dreams. "You're proving yourself worthy of your reputation."

"As a Scot, a pirate, and a philanderer?"

"When you lend us Daisy, you're helping the community."

"Considered that way, so are you when you kiss me."

The impudent devil. She wanted to call his bluff. And if it wasn't a bluff, tell him he could keep Daisy, and go away and rot in his shabby, empty mausoleum of a house.

But since he'd mentioned kissing, she couldn't help staring at that mobile mouth. There was something so sensual about the shape of his lips. The precisely carved upper lip, the fuller lower one. The creases at the corners hinting at laughter.

Of course he was laughing at her. He believed he held a winning hand, while she was about to throw in her cards and declare herself defeated.

Unfortunately, he was right.

"One kiss?"

He looked surprised. Then pleased.

Then predatory.

Nerves knotting her stomach, she faltered back a step. Not just because she'd kiss him, but because of *how* she'd kiss him. She very much doubted she was up to his usual standard of partner. This man had seen the world, while she'd never been past Newcastle. And she'd bet that he'd left the girls in all those exotic ports kissed to the point of dizziness.

Thinking about kissing him certainly made her dizzy.

He arched one russet eyebrow. "Is that a yes?"

"You're a naughty man, Lord Channing," she said, unsure if the remark was compliment or insult.

"I promise you'll like it."

She made a dismissive sound, even as the excitement pounding in her blood promised that indeed, she would like it. "For the greater good, I can endure a little kiss."

He snickered softly and walked toward her, towing Daisy. "No need to cower, my wee village maiden. I'll see that your first kiss is memorable."

Cower? She'd show him cower. "It's not my first kiss," she snapped before she could stop herself.

Dear heaven, could she sound any more gauche? Mortified heat flooded her face, making a mockery of the cold day.

"Oh?" Now, plague take him, he looked more interested than ever. "The vicar's daughter has a shady past. How intriguing. Perhaps you can teach me a thing or two."

"Don't be absurd," she said shakily, curling her hands into fists until her fingernails dug into her palms. Daisy started to nibble at the dry winter grass.

"Who was the lucky laddie?" Channing's eyes glinted with devilry. "Or was there more than one?"

"You're not acting like a gentleman, my lord," she said stiffly.

"But I am acting like a Scot, a pirate, and a libertine."

"There's no need to sound so proud of yourself." Mustering every ounce of courage, she stepped up in front of him. "Very well. I'm ready."

He caught her arm. "I wish I had another donkey that I could barter in return for some enthusiasm."

Interrupting Daisy's foraging, he shortened her rein and pulled her toward the woods. He marched across the open grass with a determined step, and because he held Bess's arm, she went, too, more confused than ever. Not least because while she resented Channing cornering her into this disgraceful bargain, she didn't at all resent the idea of kissing him.

She must be losing her mind.

"Aren't you going to kiss me?" She cringed that the question emerged more like a complaint than a protest. He'd touched her earlier but now, with kisses in the offing, she was vitally aware of that strong hand curled around her arm.

"For shame, Miss Farrar. Have you no care for your reputation?"

"My reputation?"

He lowered his voice, although there was nobody except Bess and Daisy to hear him. "If I kiss you in the open, someone might see us."

Curse him, he was right. Even on a cold, miserable

afternoon like this, one of his estate workers might pass by and see them embracing on the edge of an empty field.

Trepidation kept Bess uncharacteristically silent as Lord Channing escorted her into the shelter of the trees. How had she reached a point where the new earl was about to kiss her? How had she reached a point where she *wanted* him to kiss her?

For once, she wished Daisy would act up. But true to her contrary nature, she ambled along behind them as quiet as a lamb. Perhaps, like Bess, the donkey recognized Lord Channing as unstoppable, and she'd decided cooperation was the best strategy.

"Stop thinking," Channing murmured, drawing her off the path into a secluded glade. Even in the middle of winter, the leafless trees crowding around them offered privacy. "I can hear your mind churning like a millwheel. It's putting me off my stride."

"I can't help it," she said unsteadily.

"It won't be as bad as you imagine."

The problem was that she didn't for a moment imagine it would be bad. She was convinced it was going to be very good indeed. The kind of kiss that made a girl yearn.

Mostly Bess was content with her sequestered life. She dreaded the thought of anyone shattering that tranquility and making her hanker for something beyond Penton Wyck.

The earl released Bess in the middle of the small

clearing, and she immediately missed the touch of that large, capable hand. He tied Daisy to a branch, using an impossibly complicated knot that was a reminder of his maritime background. Goodness, he must have been a first-rate pirate. One glance from those purposeful green eyes, and any merchant would quail and immediately hand over his cargo.

She'd always considered herself strong-willed. Compared to Lord Channing, she was a sapling in a whirlwind.

"She'll bolt," Bess said.

"No, she won't. That knot will hold through an Arctic gale." That interrogatory eyebrow arched once again. "Are you planning on bolting, too?"

The donkey nosed idly at the leaves scattered across the brown grass. Bess shifted from one booted foot to the other. "Then you wouldn't let us have Daisy for the play."

"Quite right." The smile in his eyes didn't reach his lips. "If only the villagers knew the sacrifices you're willing to make on their behalf."

"I'd rather they never knew about this…disreputable bargain," she said stiffly, even as her heart raced so fast with sinful anticipation, she felt lightheaded. "Please, get it over with."

She stood up straight, closed her eyes and pursed her lips, then opened her eyes again when Lord Channing burst into laughter.

"Something amuses your lordship?" she asked coldly.

It took him an exasperatingly long time to stop laughing. "You said you've done this before."

"I have."

Twice. A long, long time ago.

"Then you clearly have grounds for complaint."

Her eyes narrowed. "I certainly do now."

His gaze softened, and he studied her face as if he meant to paint her. The prickly, defensive back and forth faded to breathless expectancy.

Bess held that penetrating regard for as long as she could before she shifted her focus to the leaf-strewn ground. Her cheeks heated, and her hands twined together at her waist.

Lord Channing caught her trembling hands. Even through her gloves, she felt the jolt of heat. Her gaze flew up to fasten on his face. He looked intent and unexpectedly gentle.

A smile turned up one corner of his lips. "Believe me, your virtue is safe, Miss Farrar. It's too bloody cold to take our clothes off."

She wanted to object to his language—and to his brazen mention of undressing—but standing here holding his hands, his salty vocabulary was the last of her worries. After all, a pirate would express himself strongly. And he was wrong. Whatever the temperature of the air, she felt ready to go up in flames.

"The deal is one kiss," she reminded him.

"If I put my arm around your waist, are you likely to take fright and run away?"

Suddenly he stood much closer. She'd never been so aware of anyone's height and strength.

"N-no."

"You don't sound very sure."

"I made a bargain, my lord."

He drew her into his body. "I commend your principles, Miss Farrar."

To her mortification, she squeaked like a frightened kitten as every sense opened to his nearness. The air smelled cold and clean, with a hint of autumn leaves. Lord Channing smelled warm and clean, with a hint of salt. Perhaps during all those years of buccaneering, the sea had soaked into his skin.

Before she could stop herself, she closed her eyes and inhaled that splendid essence. A hum of pleasure escaped her, and her backbone curved until she settled against him with the most perfect fit.

Radiant heat surrounded her. Extraordinary how agreeable it felt to stand in a man's arms on a wintry day.

With an aplomb that melted her bones to honey, he tilted up her chin. "Prepare for boarding, Miss Farrar."

Lord Channing's lips skimmed across hers. Warmth trickled through her.

For a moment, he didn't do anything alarming, and through the onslaught of sensation, she admitted this was all quite pleasant. She'd definitely survive the experience. His hold tightened, and he adjusted his stance until she was closer than ever.

Then his lips moved more purposefully, and the world lurched off its axis to go dancing among the stars.

She'd had no idea her lips were so sensitive. Every nerve in her body focused on the coaxing pressure. Not trusting her legs to hold her up, she lifted her hands to his shoulders. His soft sound of approval sizzled through her like lightning.

She drowned in heat—and yearning. This kiss made her yearn. She'd been right to fear him.

Bess gasped when he flicked his tongue against the seam of her mouth. What an odd thing to do.

He did it again, taking advantage of her parted lips. Shock turned to a rush of irresistible response. She stiffened as surprised pleasure turned to uncertainty. This was wickedly carnal and beyond those tentative experiments when she'd imagined herself in love at eighteen.

Her hands flattened on his powerful chest to push him away, but to her shame, Lord Channing was the one to bring the heady interval to a close. He stepped back and released her.

Without his support, she stumbled. He caught her hands to stop her collapsing in a humiliating heap. Her blood raced like a raging torrent, and her lips burned. With a mere word from him, she'd step back into his arms and beg him to do it all again.

She'd had no idea a kiss could turn her so silly. How utterly irritating.

Lord Channing's expression was searching and almost tender. The lids lay heavy over those deep-set eyes. He was breathing unsteadily, but his grip was firm.

Helplessly—and Bess wasn't a woman used to feeling helpless—she stared up at him, wanting to say something clever and dismissive. But that kiss had stolen all capacity for speech.

She trembled to recall those blazing seconds when the silky tip of his tongue invaded her mouth. That should have revolted her. It would have, if he'd told her what he intended. Instead the wanton exploration had melted all defenses. Made her hot. Made her curious.

Made her want…*more.*

At her faint sound of distress, he frowned. "Are you all right?"

No, she wasn't, but pride came to her rescue. Bess straightened and tugged her hands free. She could stand on her own two feet, curse him. Swallowing to ease her dry throat, she told herself she could talk, and walk away, and go on with her life, and absolutely nothing had changed. One kiss from a pirate didn't turn her into a different person. She was still competent, managing, independent Bess Farrar.

Competent, managing, independent, *lonely* Bess Farrar.

She swallowed again and forced her voice to work. It sounded scratchy and out of practice. "Perfectly."

That expressive eyebrow tilted when she couldn't control the hitch in her answer, although she was grateful that he didn't contradict her. She told herself to move away, but she seemed to be planted where she stood.

He brushed his lips over hers. Unable to resist, she closed her eyes and kissed him back.

Something soft and cold brushed her cheek. She opened dazed eyes to see snow drifting from the heavy gray sky.

As he shifted away with unconcealed reluctance, she licked her lips and muffled a groan. She could taste snow—and Lord Channing. How…disturbing.

"The…the arrangement was one kiss."

A twist of that fascinating mouth, even more fascinating now he'd kissed her. "Just something on account." He glanced up at the sky. "I think we need to get Daisy into the barn, don't you?"

The abrupt shift from forbidden enchantment to prosaic reality left her struggling to adjust. "I'll take her back to the vicarage. We've got a rehearsal tomorrow afternoon."

"She can stay in the Abbey stables. Once you start on the house, I imagine you'll be there most of the time, getting things ready. It's only a week until Christmas, my dear Miss Farrar. No time to be lost."

The lingering glow ebbed as practical considerations became paramount. But the soft fall of snow reminded her that only moments ago she'd been lost in his arms. She struggled to sound as if she hadn't just been kissing his lordship with an enthusiasm that made her blush. "You're very highhanded."

He laughed softly. "It comes with the title. I was a perfect lamb when I captained my ship."

It was her turn to laugh. She didn't believe that for a second. "You meant it about holding a Christmas dinner for the village?"

"Of course. You must know by now I'm a man of my word."

One kiss. He'd stuck to his word there, too. With just a little extra in the final moments.

The sting wasn't that he'd kissed her. The sting was that she'd enjoyed it so very much. Too much.

Still, she'd paid the price he asked, and now she got what she wanted. Even if she counted out the price not in pennies, but in sighs of breathless wonder. "I have your permission to staff the house, and provision it, and decorate it for the party?"

"I'll expect you to tell me what you're up to."

That was fair, given he was funding everything. "And you'll come to the church at four tomorrow and play Joseph?"

"I said I would." He paused. "And I'll bring Daisy."

"I warn you that the house will be noisy and messy until I've finished."

He cast her a mocking glance. "Are you trying to talk me out of this?"

She was convinced that entering into this arrangement was a mistake. But she'd look like a capricious fool if she backed out now, when he agreed to everything she asked.

If only she wasn't so sure that Lord Channing had his own agenda, and that agenda included more kisses at the very least.

"No."

When sly satisfaction flashed in his eyes, the clamor of misgivings swelled to a shriek. "Excellent. After breakfast, then?"

CHAPTER FOUR

Rory didn't sleep well. The memory of holding Bess in his arms wasn't so much a torment as a promise of more to come. He felt as excited and on edge as an inexperienced midshipman facing his first battle at sea.

Bess, too, had been inexperienced. Whatever scoundrel had kissed her had made a rum job of it. She must be in her mid-twenties, but she'd kissed like a sweet young girl, all closed lips and caution. Her innocence had touched him, bolstered his wavering resolution not to take her too far.

Although any man of principle would say he'd already taken everything too far, stealing that chaste kiss. She was a virtuous lady, a vicar's daughter, no less. And they'd only just met.

But he couldn't let her go without one small taste. And that taste had been glorious.

If fate was kind, he wouldn't have to wait long to taste her again.

The next morning, his lecherous plans hit a snag. When he emerged from his bedroom—he'd slept later than usual after his restless night—people of all ages milled about in the great hall below. The villagers, he assumed, under the command of the woman he intended to marry.

Ned White joined him at the top of the stairs. "You didn't tell me it was all hands on deck this morning, Rory."

Rory shot his friend an amused glance. "I surrendered to a superior force, laddie."

Ned's attention settled on Bess, all business in her plain gray dress and sensible apron. An impression undercut by the color in her cheeks and the flyaway strands of golden hair. "A fine-looking woman, Miss Farrar."

"Aye."

"An ideal wife for a new earl with local ways to learn and ties to build with his neighbors."

Damn it, Ned knew him too well. That was what came of sailing together for the last twenty years. "She's a lassie with her own ideas. Anyone who took her on would say goodbye to a quiet life and any hope of a meek wee wife to smooth his brow and jump to his orders."

"Yes, well, some might say after a man has crossed the world's oceans, a meek wee wife would seem dull in comparison."

"Aye, some might."

"Your tenants appear to have a lot of respect for her."

It was true. Rory had served with enough captains, good and bad, to mark the notice they paid Bess. Not to mention the affection. Hard to match this capable leader with the bedazzled girl he'd kissed in the snow.

Rory changed the subject. "Did you know there's a rumor abroad that I'm a pirate?"

Ned snorted with laughter. "You?"

"Aye."

"Well, shiver my timbers. When you're not ravaging the Spanish Main, will you hoist the Jolly Roger on the Abbey's flagpole to tell the world the master's home from marauding?"

"You're not funny," Rory said, trying not to smile.

"I think I am."

"You always do." He paused. "How in Hades do daft tales like this start?"

Ned shrugged. "Someone's cousin heard something from someone else's cousin, who heard something from someone passing through on the London coach. You know how these things work."

"Should I say something? Or will that just add fuel to the fire?"

"I suspect it will die down of its own accord when you don't wallpaper the house with maps marked with an X."

"Very droll. And not helpful."

"Oh, you wound me. With your cutlass. Just don't make me walk the plank."

"I can't take much more hilarity, laddie. Shall we make our presence known?"

Ned managed an ironic bow. "After you, my lord."

Rory cast his oldest friend a wry glance and stepped up to the balustrade. "Good morning, everyone."

He was used to addressing his crew through the bluster of wind, wave and sail, so his voice easily cut across the chatter. Silence fell, and as one, thirty faces turned upward.

The expressions were as he expected. Given the outlandish gossip about his exploits before coming to Penton Wyck, wariness was inevitable. But outright hostility was thankfully absent. Instead he read curiosity and interest.

Automatically he sought out Bess. Her expression was harder to interpret. Had she found sleep elusive, too? Perhaps she'd spent the hours since they parted reliving his kiss. He bloody well hoped so.

She dipped into a curtsy and as if her movement released the crowd from a spell, the other women bobbed into curtsies and the men bowed. Rory supposed he'd have to become accustomed to these homages to his rank.

"Thank you for coming through the snow to prepare Penton Abbey for my first Christmas here. It's a grand old house and needs bringing to life." Call him a Frenchman if that wasn't approval in Bess's steady blue gaze. "You don't know me yet, and I don't know you. But working together for a common cause is the best way to discover a man's mettle. I hope by the time we're drinking a toast to the season and the Yule log is blazing in the hearth, you'll consider me one of you and a worthy successor to my late, respected brother." He gestured toward Bess. "Miss Farrar knows where to stow everything, so defer to her. This salty old sea dog has no idea how to rig a landlubber's berth."

As he'd hoped, the self-deprecating end to his speech lightened the solemnity that resulted from mentioning his brother. It even elicited a few chuckles.

Ned stood beside him. "Do you mean to leave them to it?"

"Don't be a fool, lad." Rory sent him a devil-may-care grin. "I've got a vicar's daughter to catch. I'm not letting the comely Miss Farrar out of my sight."

Ned smiled back. "She hasn't got a chance."

Rory remained preternaturally aware of Bess's location. Right now she stood under one of the windows, speaking to an elderly gentleman in black who seemed to hold some authority. "I hope to God you're right."

Ned regarded him in shock. "Well, that takes the biscuit."

"What does?" Rory asked, without shifting his attention from Bess.

"You must be in love with her."

Unfamiliar heat pricked his cheeks. Damn it, Rory hadn't blushed since his first voyage. A boy grew up fast below decks.

"I only met the lassie yesterday." Gossip was right about one thing at least—he had more experience with the fair sex than was good for him. But love? That was uncharted territory.

Ned looked smug. "I never thought to see the day."

"She's a lovely creature."

"Undoubtedly."

"And clever and capable."

"Inarguably."

"A man of property needs a wife. He can't stay the same reckless, self-centered bastard he was in his youth."

"Especially when he falls in love. In all our years together, I've never seen you less than confident of your chances with a woman. It's been deuced irritating. If you're unsure about this lady, it's because she's not just a woman, she's *the* woman."

"White, you try my patience," he snapped. "Come and put that vivid imagination to work moving furniture."

"Aye, aye, sir." Ned had the temerity to salute before he ran lightly downstairs to join a party heading out of the hall.

Rory didn't immediately follow. Ned White knew him better than any other soul on earth. Better than the family in Edinburgh he'd left at eleven and had rarely seen since. So while he'd dearly love to dismiss the fellow's ramblings as sentimental claptrap, somewhere deep in his soul, they struck true.

Instead of joining his tenants, he stood staring broodingly at Bess who continued to pass out instructions. Her blithe disregard for his presence rankled. And the fact that it rankled rankled even worse.

The day sped by in a welter of physical activity that reminded Rory of his days in the lower ranks, toiling like a slave on a warship. Of course, he could retreat to his library and let them get on with it, but where was the fun in that?

He only snatched rare seconds alone with Bess, but he had the privilege of observing her in action. By heaven, she was a fascinating creature. He could happily watch her all day.

If the wind set fair, he'd watch her for the rest of his life.

He didn't realize other people had remarked his interest in the vicar's bonny daughter until he found himself in the library with the black-clad cove he'd noticed earlier. However the house ended up, Rory appreciated this chance to get to know his tenants.

Obadiah Simpson was a retired doctor who had traveled the length of the country. A man of unusual sophistication for this backwater.

"She's a fine lass, Miss Bess," the old man said, stacking leather-bound volumes on the newly dusted shelves. Rory had just brought in another box of books from the barns.

"She is," he said, curious where Simpson went with this. Casually he brushed cobwebs and dust off his sleeves. He'd thought the house was dirty, until he started grubbing around in the outbuildings.

"She's very well liked in the village."

Rory had seen that for himself. "Are you trying to warn me off, Dr. Simpson?"

The old man turned, a book clutched in his veined hand. "Not at all. I'm merely making conversation."

"Like hell you are."

"Well, perhaps not entirely." He fastened piercing gray eyes on Rory. "Are you of a mind to woo the jewel of our small community?"

"That would be a rash decision when I only met the lassie yesterday."

Simpson eyed him steadily. "You strike me as a fellow who makes up his mind without dillydallying."

Simpson had that right. "I don't even know if Miss Farrar likes me."

"She does."

The gratification that flooded Rory made him feel

like a schoolboy mooning after a pretty girl. "Are you matchmaking?"

Simpson's smile was knowing. "I doubt I need to exert myself much to put you two together."

"We've hardly spoken all day," Rory protested.

It was regrettably true. He'd imagined that with Bess under his roof, opportunities for dalliance would abound. He hadn't counted on the crowds swarming through the house or Bess's diligent attention to duty. She was too busy organizing cleaning and repairs and the placement of furniture to flirt.

"But you've looked." Simpson paused. "So has she."

"That's good news."

Simpson frowned. "Now, don't go thinking she's one of your London light skirts. Unless your intentions are honorable, you can set your sights elsewhere."

Rory laughed again, unsure whether to be annoyed or touched at the old man's interference. "Does it occur to you that you're trespassing beyond your rights?"

Simpson gave a dismissive grunt and returned to shelving books. "I've known Bess all her life. Only a fool would mistake her forthright manner for boldness. If that fool did mistake her, she has people who will fight to protect her."

"Including a father," Rory said mildly. "Who surely should be saying these things to me if anyone must."

"Ah, the vicar." Simpson bent to lift another armful of books from the box at his feet.

After a while, Rory realized Simpson intended to

say no more about the Reverend John Farrar. He was suddenly curious about the man he hoped would become his father-in-law. Perhaps he might attend church on Sunday after all. "Mr. Simpson, my intentions regarding Miss Farrar are none of your business."

"That's a pity," Simpson said placidly, continuing with his work.

"Why?"

"Because getting Bess to yourself might go more smoothly if you had some help."

Rory's eyes narrowed on the man. "You don't know anything about me—apart from the wild talk I've got wind of in the last few days."

"You're the most exciting thing to happen in Penton Wyck since Daisy broke loose at the Christmas play five years ago and knocked the Bishop of Durham into the mud."

Despite himself, Rory laughed. "Well, that puts me in my place."

"We tend to take people as we find them here, my lord." Bess had said something similar. The man kept placidly arranging the shelves. "Bess would make you a fine wife."

"Undoubtedly. But would I make her a fine husband?"

Simpson fixed a critical eye on him. "That's up to you. Don't think you'll sway her with your title and riches. It didn't work for your brother. It won't work for you."

Rory frowned, surprised and not altogether pleased, although it made sense. Had his brother kissed her? If he had, he'd taught her deuced little. "My brother wanted to marry Bess?"

"He did. But she wouldn't have him."

Now, that was interesting. "Most women would leap at a countess's title."

Simpson shook his head in disappointment. "There you go, thinking her one of your flighty misses. Our Bess will only marry where her affections lie. And don't imagine your brother was her only chance either."

"There were others?" Of course there were. Rory wasn't the only man in England with eyes in his head.

"Sir Gavin Spiers in the next valley, for one. And Henry Browne, your brother's lawyer, wasn't blind to what a grand wife she'd make either. And that's only in the last year."

"Yet she's unmarried."

"The vicar has a respectable fortune, although you wouldn't know it to look at the poor muddleheaded loon. And Bess's grandmother left her a goodly portion when she passed on three years ago. Our girl can afford to be choosy."

Rory wasn't sure if this was good news or not. Damn it, Ned was right. He'd always trusted to his way with the ladies. Now when it mattered, he couldn't help wondering what he had that Bess's other suitors lacked.

Still, faint heart never won fair lady. If he could sail into an ice storm in the Bering Strait, surely he could woo this redoubtable lassie. "So let me get this straight. You're willing to promote my courtship as long as I behave myself?"

The spark in Simpson's eyes made him look younger—and mischievous. "You only need to behave yourself up to a point. A chap who's been a pirate must know what lines to cross."

"I wasn't—"

"This is where you two are hiding," Bess said, bustling into the library with a broom clutched in one hand.

Rory's heart lurched at the sight of her. A strange sensation, not altogether welcome.

"You're halfway there already, my lord," Simpson muttered for Rory's ears alone.

Halfway there? Rory had a sinking feeling that the wind had blown him way beyond his destination and now pushed him toward the next port.

"We were afraid you meant to give us another job," he said, ignoring the smug old man who thought he knew everything.

"We need to go and work on the play." Her gray dress was creased and grubby, and a streak of dirt adorned one high cheekbone. His breath hitched at how earthy and real she was. She was so alive that she made the air rustle. He wanted to catch her up against him and never let her go.

He managed a theatrical sigh. She didn't need to know how fatally she undermined his defenses. Or at least not yet. "Work seems to be your favorite word, Miss Farrar."

"You'll be glad it is when the house is fit for you to live in."

Rory hoped he went through all this chaos so the house was fit for *her* to live in. He glanced out the window to see a trail of villagers, many of whom he now knew by name, heading down the drive. "Are they all in the play?"

"Some of them. But you're not abandoned altogether—you've now got two footmen and four maids to look after you. And a cook. Mrs. Hallam has taken over the kitchens—for which you'll be mightily grateful, I'm sure."

"That's a devil of a horde to serve one man."

"You'll also need a butler and housekeeper, but those have to come from Newcastle or London."

"More blasted strangers tramping around my house?" He leaned one hip on the desk and folded his arms. This was the longest conversation they'd managed all day. Even knowing that Simpson weighed every word, Rory was in no hurry to end it.

He really was in a bad way. If anyone had told him yesterday that he'd discuss servants just for the delight of a bonny lassie's company, he'd have called them a blockhead.

Rory had a nasty suspicion the biggest blockhead of all was the new Earl of Channing.

The bonny lassie regarded him with disapproval. "Do you really have no care for your domestic arrangements, my lord?"

As long as they included Bess Farrar, he cared greatly for his domestic arrangements.

"Not much." He stood to take the broom from her and prop it against the wall. "Good afternoon, Dr. Simpson. I've enjoyed making your acquaintance."

"Goodbye, Dr. Simpson. Thank you for helping," Bess said.

Simpson didn't look up from the books, but from where he stood, Rory caught the man's smile. "I wouldn't have missed it for the world, my dear."

Rory as a rule didn't appreciate people sticking their oar into his affairs, but the old man had been damned informative. And if local approval of his courtship meant assistance, he'd accept a certain amount of intervention.

When he took Bess's arm, physical awareness crackled through him. Did she share this volatile reaction? She'd given a tiny start at the contact.

"They like you," Bess said softly as he escorted her toward the great hall.

A hint of clean sweat warmed her scent. The idea of her working to achieve his comfort aroused a primitive pleasure. "Don't sound so surprised."

Her laugh was wry. "I wasn't sure they would. Or not so quickly."

His grip tightened as he halted. "What in Hades does that mean?"

"After all the talk."

He really had to address the rumors of his nefarious past, but right now he had more important things to discover. "As long as you like me, I can live with a bit of unfriendliness from the neighbors."

The astonishment in her eyes soothed his brief uncertainty. He didn't lack self-confidence, but events in the last twenty-four hours left him reeling. He'd known he'd marry—an unhappy, nomadic childhood and all those years at sea convinced him of the value of a stable family. But he'd always dismissed the idea of love at first sight as romantic fantasy.

Was Ned right? Did he love Bess Farrar? Devil if he could tell. What he did know was that he'd seen her and known in his bones that she was the one for him.

She frowned. "You can't imagine I go around kissing men I don't like."

"Even if there's a donkey in the balance?"

Her blush charmed him. "Even for Daisy."

He ran his hand down her arm and squeezed her fingers. To his surprise, she returned the pressure. Briefly he considered kissing her again, but the house was infested with domestics.

What he'd give for some privacy, but right now it wasn't to be.

Regretfully he released her when they stepped into the hall. Two young women were polishing the newly replaced furniture, while another poked some holly into a vase on the mantel above a blazing fire.

"Good God," he breathed, taking in the transformation of the formerly barren space. This last month, he and Ned had camped in the house. Now he surveyed the vast room lit through mullioned—clean—windows. For the first time, he thought of Penton Abbey as a home and not just a house. "You've performed miracles."

When he advanced further into the room, the maids curtsied and left. The first step in Simpson's matchmaking?

"Thank you. I hoped you'd be pleased." The sincerity in Bess's voice warmed his heart almost as much as holding her hand had. "Your brother would be so happy to see the Abbey coming back to life."

The brother who had proposed to her. The brother with whom he had more in common than he'd suspected, if they'd both been in thrall to the same woman.

Heavy oak chests and chairs and tables ranged around the walls. Some must date from the days when the house had been an actual abbey. "This is exactly right."

Her smile was approving as she stepped forward to run her hand over the lovely carving on the mantel.

The gesture's inherent sensuality made him long to feel her touch on his naked skin.

"I'm sure you'll want something cozier for the family rooms, but at least the Abbey is no longer an empty shell."

Rory could feel the difference. It was nothing to do with furniture and everything to do with Bess's vivid presence. "Thanks to you."

"I hated seeing the place so rundown," she said. "This house has always been the center of village life."

"The longer I stay..." The longer he talked to Bess. "...the more I feel I know George. That's another thing I have to thank you for. At this rate, you'll earn rights to Daisy into the next century."

The pink in her cheeks deepened. "I...I prefer kisses to housework."

Shock and pleasure vied in his mind. "Are you asking me to kiss you again?"

Her eyes flickered down, and she suddenly looked touchingly young. "Would I be so brazen?"

Which wasn't, he noted with satisfaction, a no. "I'll see what I can do," he said mildly, wanton heat swirling through his blood in a way that wasn't mild at all.

"Not here," she said quickly, subjecting him to a flash of blue eyes before looking down again. Then she straightened and became the woman who had commandeered his house. "And not now. We need to collect Daisy and head for the village. We'll be late as it is."

Not here meant somewhere else. And not now surely meant later.

Rory could hardly wait.

Rory's questions about the vicar found answers on the way to the rehearsal. Penton Wyck included a neat high street with several well-stocked shops, a fine market cross, and rows of attractive half-timbered houses. For a man unused to much fuss for Christmas, a lovely touch was the greenery adorning the houses.

The snow-covered thoroughfare led straight from the gates of his estate through the village to a complex of stone buildings: a Tudor church, he guessed built after the Abbey was requisitioned from the Benedictine monks; a neat rectory dating from last century; various outbuildings; and an impressive and ancient structure with towering doors several stories high.

"It's the tithe barn," Bess said. "That's where we hold our rehearsals."

"Magnificent," Rory said, meaning it. The architecture was simple, but the sheer size of the barn took his breath away. He hauled a recalcitrant Daisy forward. The donkey had been playing up all the way from the Abbey. Only a couple of choruses of "Greensleeves" had kept her moving at all. "The monks must have been rich in their day."

She glanced at him. "They were. That's why those

rapacious Beatons were so determined to claim Penton Abbey when the monasteries were dissolved. That must be where you came by your piratical tendencies."

"It's unfair to blame a man for his ancestors," Rory protested, as a stooped, ramshackle figure in a faded black cassock emerged between the open doors. Only when he came nearer did Rory realize that the man was above average height. The barn's monumental scale had dwarfed him.

"Good afternoon, my dear. Out for a stroll?" Familiar blue eyes drifted over Rory with no hint of curiosity. Rory guessed the man's identity before Bess spoke.

"Good afternoon, Papa," she said. "We're practicing for the nativity play."

"Very good, very good." He smiled vaguely and lifted a thin hand to scratch Daisy behind the ears.

"Lord Channing, may I present my father, John Farrar, vicar of St. Martin's?"

"What's that you say?" the old man asked. "Lord Channing? I thought I conducted a memorial service for him last summer. The choir sang the William Byrd anthem. Most touchingly, too. Dear me, I am becoming forgetful."

"The new Lord Channing, Papa. I told you that the earl's brother had inherited. He's a seafaring man. It took them several months to locate him."

"Oh, yes, yes," the vicar said, and Rory would lay money that he paid no attention.

At least she hadn't told her father he was a pirate.

"You have a lovely daughter, vicar," Rory said, sweeping off his beaver hat and bowing, a complicated process when he had to make sure Daisy didn't get away from him.

"Lovely, yes." The vicar smiled with beatific approval that could mean anything. Rory only realized the vicar had heard and understood when he went on. "Just like her mamma. Her mother was the prettiest girl I ever saw. She could have married anyone. I'm frightfully glad she married me."

"She always said you had the purest heart in the world, Papa," Bess said, her voice warm with affection.

"My lord, welcome to Penton Wyck." The vicar bowed in Rory's general direction. "I don't suppose you have an interest in Byzantium? If you have, I'm writing a paper on Anna Porphyrogenita and the negotiations for her marriage to Vladimir the Great. I flatter myself I've found a few interesting nuggets in the chronicles that haven't been given their full due."

"Not my area of expertise, sir, but I've been to Constantinople."

The cloudiness faded from the vicar's eyes, and he settled an unexpectedly acute regard on Rory. "Have you indeed? I'd love to hear what you saw. I visited as a young man, before I took holy orders."

"I'd be pleased to tell you about my time there," Rory said.

The vicar gestured to the door of the vicarage, only a few feet away . "No time like the present."

"Papa, people are waiting for us. Perhaps his lordship could call another day."

At the change of focus from Byzantium to Christmas celebrations, the vicar's vagueness returned. "Another day. Yes, certainly. Look forward to that. Nativity play and all." He shuffled off, muttering over his shoulder, "Do what you think best, Bess. You always make the right decision. Such a blessing to have you. Such a blessing."

"Good day, sir," Rory said to the retreating back, but the vicar didn't respond.

Bess's expression conveyed a tolerant fondness for her father's eccentricity. "He only hears half of what you say. There's nothing wrong with his mind—he was one of the cleverest graduates of his year at Oxford—but he has difficulty bending his attention to practical matters. He's lost in his books most of the time."

"I'd be happy to talk to him about my travels."

"He'd like that. When he finds a subject interesting, he's a good conversationalist." She paused. "There just aren't many subjects he finds interesting."

Rory watched Bess's father drift across the vicarage's threshold and out of sight. So much became clear that had puzzled him. Dr. Simpson's strange reaction when he'd asked about the vicar. Even more, Bess's position of authority in the village. With the late earl an invalid and the vicar wandering among the ghosts of ancient empires, no wonder she'd found herself overseeing Penton Wyck's welfare.

"Daisy! *Daisy!*"

Bess's urgent shouts pierced his reflections. "Oh, hell."

The donkey had taken advantage of Rory's distraction to stretch out her neck and attack the pretty Christmas frippery decorating the vicarage's porch. What had once been an elaborate arrangement of holly and red and silver ribbons was now a ragged circlet fit for the bonfire.

CHAPTER FIVE

For Bess, the next four days rushed by in a flurry of activity—and a disappointing absence of kisses.

Apart from the bailiff, the butler and the house-keeper, the Abbey was now staffed inside and out. Through all the bustle, Lord Channing proved himself a man of easy manners and quick humor. He'd even turned up at church on Sunday and managed to stay awake through her father's deadly dull sermon about some abstruse point of translation from the Greek New Testament. The villagers already referred to the pirate lord of the manor with pride instead of suspicion.

Bess was less pleased with the way the earl had so swiftly become vitally important to her. Her day only started when he welcomed her to Penton Abbey, and the glow dimmed when they parted in the evening.

Even more frightening, she then spent each night longing to bask in his presence again.

Nobody should become so…necessary so quickly. After all, what did she know of him?

Except the hours working together taught her quite a lot about Lord Channing. Her early attraction soon warmed to respect and admiration, and something that might ripen into friendship.

He wasn't at all high in the instep. He was always ready to share a friendly word with the villagers. His brother had been a good man, but he'd lacked the earl's ability to find common ground with the people around him. Already Bess could tell that the new regime at Penton Abbey would be considerably more democratic than the previous one. If Channing carried his libertarian ideals down to London when he took his seat in the House of Lords, he'd horrify those reactionary old lizards in Parliament.

Not that she approved of all the changes. His lordship might be prepared to listen to advice, but she soon learned that he possessed strong opinions. On some issues she couldn't sway him, the way, curse him, he'd accused her of swaying his brother. Luckily, he had the charm and intelligence to achieve his ends without creating undue resentment in the villagers—or in her.

Perhaps he wouldn't be such a misfit maneuvering his way through Parliament after all.

He must have been a remarkable captain, all steely will cloaked in velvet persuasion. It was a lesson in leadership, watching him turn once wary villagers into allies. She had a nasty suspicion that he managed her just as skillfully.

He'd somehow made his interest in the vicar's daughter generally known. Interest that apparently met the approval of everyone except, perhaps, the vicar's daughter. Bess had soon noticed sidelong glances and sly smiles, not to mention the conspiracy to leave her alone with his lordship whenever possible.

She wasn't sure whether to be grateful for her neighbors' machinations, or resent them. She certainly didn't mind being alone with Channing. If he kissed her again, she'd mind even less.

She and the earl were alone now. They were in the stables and she was grooming a fidgety Daisy for tomorrow's play. His lordship watched them both from the corridor, arms folded on top of the stall gate. The grooms were notably absent, although in the middle of the day, they should be hard at work.

"*Adeste, fidelis,*" she sang when Daisy backed away from the bunch of bright ribbons she held.

Lord Channing snickered. "She objects to the historical inaccuracy of your titivating. I doubt the real donkey was done out like a wee harlequin."

Bess cast him an unimpressed look. "You're no help."

"What if I sing, too?" His teasing smile had her silly heart dancing a gavotte, skipping about like it was spring instead of deepest winter.

"You could try."

"I'd rather watch the battle royal between you and this troublesome beast. It's great entertainment. Daisy's the only creature in Penton Wyck who doesn't jump to your bidding."

Bess draped the ribbons over the edge of the manger and grabbed Daisy's halter to hold her still. "She's not the only troublesome beast I see."

He laughed softly. "Have I not leaped to your merest command, Miss Farrar? I've employed half the village, and now I can't open a door in my own house without tripping over some gormless yokel dusting the china. I've emptied every victualler within a hundred miles to feed your friends and neighbors on Christmas Day. I've stayed up past midnight learning lines for your blasted play—you'd think I was a damned schoolboy sitting his Latin translation exam."

"Language," she said, trying to make her fingers work with their usual deftness as she twined a red ribbon around the harness.

She just couldn't control her shivery reaction to Lord Channing. Never had she been so physically aware of anyone. Nor could she forget how wonderful she'd felt when he put his arms around her.

Damn him—and his deleterious influence on her language—since then he'd acted the perfect gentleman. Even if a gentleman quick to take her arm or touch her shoulder or hold her hand to step onto a ladder. Or catch her waist to lift her onto Daisy's back when she played Mary.

But no more kisses. And while she waited in breathless suspense for him to kiss her again, those teasing little touches were driving her mad.

"It's my house, and I'm a sailor. You'd be disappointed if I didn't let fly with the occasional oath."

He might be right. A wicked part of her thrilled to think of the exciting life he'd led. She loved Penton Wyck. But she wouldn't be human if she didn't occasionally hanker after new horizons. Lord Channing brought those new horizons to her doorstep.

"You haven't got much to complain about. Joseph only has three speeches."

Another smile curled that fascinating mouth. A mouth that she couldn't stop thinking about. Had one taste convinced him she wasn't worth kissing? Had she been too eager? Too clumsy? Did he find her overbearing? This wasn't the first time he'd referred to her ordering him about.

Except she was sure that from the start, he'd followed his own inclinations. He played a deep game —on the surface he might be all cooperation, but in the end, Bess Farrar danced to his tune, not the other way round.

What precisely was his tune? Clearly not kisses, plague take him.

The horrible, shaming truth was that his kiss was the most thrilling thing that had ever happened to her.

Revisiting those heated seconds kept her awake at night and jumpy all day. The fever found no relief. That kiss should have shocked her—after all, they'd only just met, and she'd heard about his reputation—but when it was over, all she wanted was more.

And no good vicar's daughter should devote so much time to thinking about kisses.

Clearly she wasn't good.

Not that Lord Channing did much to take advantage of her sinfulness.

He was talking to her as if he had nothing more important on his mind than the nativity play. "Yes, but Joseph is in charge of Daisy. It's the toughest role in the whole show. You merely need to sit there, looking beautiful."

"Thank you," she said uncertainly.

What the devil was she to make of it when he said such things? If he really thought she was beautiful, why on earth didn't he do something about it?

Like kiss her again.

"Do you want those for anything special?"

"Pardon?"

Channing gestured to where the donkey munched away at the ribbons meant for her adornment. "Oh, Daisy, you rotten thing."

Channing laughed again. "I told you that controlling Daisy was a major effort."

Not as much effort as controlling one pestilential earl. "Sing to her."

"O, my love is like a red, red rose
That's newly sprung in June;
O, my love is like the melody
That's sweetly played in tune.
As fair art thou, my bonny lass,
So deep in love am I:
And I will love thee still, my dear,
Till a' the seas gang dry."

Lord Channing's melodious baritone skimmed across Bess's nerves like silk over glass. The breath jammed in her throat, and she felt giddy and hot. Until she reminded herself that it was just a song, and his lordship didn't mean anything by choosing it except that he knew the words.

He had an annoying propensity to croon love songs to Daisy. They had the same effect on the donkey as on Bess. A strong urge to snuggle up to the singer. Daisy edged closer to the gate and stood transfixed, giving Bess a chance to rescue the mangled ribbons.

Dismayed, she inspected each length of colored satin as that soft Scots voice sang about true love and always returning to her, though it were ten thousand miles. Right now, she wished Lord Channing ten thousand miles away. At least then she might find some peace.

Except she already knew she'd miss him if he left. He drove her insane, he made her restless, he made her want. But seeing him set her world right. She had a sinking feeling that with every day she became more hopelessly infatuated with the roguish new lord of the manor.

She stood motionless and entranced—as entranced as Daisy—while Channing reached the end. And regretted that he stopped.

"I'm not sure I should let you ride Daisy tomorrow."

"Oh?" Excitement spiked, and Bess glanced up from the ruined ribbons she had trouble seeing. That cursed sentimental song turned her vision misty.

Did he mean to steal another kiss before letting Daisy join the play? Bess didn't even care that he went back on his word, as long as he ended this intolerable waiting.

But Lord Channing wasn't looking at her. He studied Daisy, his impressive russet eyebrows lowered in displeasure. "She's a law unto herself. What if she bolts?"

Disappointment, as wicked as it was unjustified, overwhelmed Bess, and she replied on a subdued note. "She never has before."

"There's always a first time."

"With everyone looking at her, she's quite the prima donna." Bess struggled to sound her usual sedate self, an exemplary woman who would never think to barter kisses. "You mightn't believe it, but she always behaves perfectly when she's in the nativity play. Well, apart from two years ago when she ate Mrs. Pickering's new bonnet. And a couple of years before that when she butted the Bishop of Durham.

But nobody likes him so that was almost a public service."

Channing laughed while Daisy's long ears flickered as if she followed each word of the discussion. Perhaps she did. After riding her in ten processions, Bess had developed a healthy respect for the donkey's intelligence, as well as will to mischief. Although as she'd told Channing, Daisy usually cooperated for the Christmas celebrations. She liked the music.

"I could put you on Sparta, my horse."

Despite her confused and disturbing feelings, Bess gave a short laugh. "That black monster in the next stall? He's three times Daisy's size."

"And ten times better behaved."

"Mary didn't ride into Bethlehem on a thoroughbred horse. If she had, I'm sure the innkeeper would have made room for her—even if he had to boot out a guest with less aristocratic transport."

Channing eyed her with curiosity. "I'm convinced you're a revolutionary, Miss Farrar."

Sighing, she gave up any attempt to save the ribbons. "Me?"

"Aye. You have devilish little respect for rank. I've even seen you push an earl around."

Oh, no. She was right to worry. He really did think she was too managing. No wonder he hadn't kissed her again. "I'm sorry, my lord."

He looked startled. "I'm only teasing. No need to poker up."

Channing spoke lightly, but that didn't mean his criticism wasn't sincere. She lowered her head and answered with uncharacteristic meekness. "How you must curse me. I've done nothing but lay down the law. I mean well, but I'm so used to being in charge that I forget other people might have plans of their own."

"I do."

"Forget other people have their own ideas?"

He smiled and opened the gate. "No, I have plans. Lots of them. Now come and have something to eat. Overwork is turning you maudlin."

Bess dredged up an answering smile, although his kindness only reminded her how much she liked him. She didn't want Lord Channing deciding she was unpleasantly bumptious. She wanted him to keep thinking she was the prettiest girl in the village, silly and shallow as that made her.

"At least you must appreciate the cook I found you. Mrs. Hallam is a treasure."

He regarded her searchingly as he stood back to let her out. "I appreciate everything you've done. You and the villagers have made Penton Abbey into a home a man can be proud of. And you've all worked yourselves to the bone to achieve it."

After latching the gate, he patted Daisy in farewell. The donkey's eyes closed in bliss. For Channing, she almost behaved like a civilized creature. Everybody liked the new earl.

Including Bess.

"You're paying them."

He shrugged. "They've done this for more than wages. They've done it for love. And so have you."

Heat stung Bess's cheeks. Oh, Lord. Was she so transparent? How vilely humiliating. Was that why he hadn't kissed her? Because he saw how utterly gooey-eyed she was over him?

"We want you to feel welcome," she said awkwardly.

"I do. I'm even starting to love the old place the way you obviously do."

Such powerful relief flooded her that her head swam. He was talking about her love for the house, not her barely controlled penchant for him. "I'm glad."

Channing took her arm the way he usually did. At first she'd wondered if this was a sign of special favor. But as he never went beyond a polite escort, she'd since realized it meant nothing beyond a friendly gesture. But that didn't stop her foolish heart turning somersaults at the touch of his hand.

"I've never really had a home before."

Deliberately Bess slowed to a stop. She was agonizingly curious about his life before he arrived at Penton Wyck. "Not even as a boy?"

"My mother could never settle in England—or to her marriage to my father. She returned to Scotland, once she'd delivered the heir and the spare as required. With her duty done, she felt free to follow her inclinations. By all reports, my father was pleased to be rid of her. It wasn't a happy union. You must know some of this. The village is a hotbed of gossip."

"Naturally, there were stories. But nobody knew what happened to your mother after she left, and your father certainly wasn't going to tell anyone. It was all such a long time ago."

"That makes me feel old," he said with that flashing amusement that was so much a part of him. To her regret, he released her arm and faced her, shaking his head. "For shame, Miss Farrar."

"You're not old. You're…you're just right," she said, and blushed even hotter than she had when she feared he'd guessed her *tendre* for him.

"Why, thank you," he said, and she knew he was trying not to laugh.

With great effort, she put aside her discomfort. If he was in the mood to confide, nothing would drag her away. "But surely you had a home in Scotland?"

"My mother remarried when I was nine. A rich lawyer from Edinburgh. We lived with him and his four daughters for a couple of years, although Mamma was soon restless and unhappy again. She wasn't cut out for marriage."

"That doesn't sound like much fun."

He made a dismissive gesture. "I liked my stepfather, and it was fun having sisters, when they weren't driving me mad with their giggling. But I was only there for two years. I went to sea when I was eleven."

The quiet stables fostered intimacy. The pleasant

fug of horses and leather and hay lulled Bess into a feeling of warmth and comfort and safety. "What happened to your mother?"

"Ten years ago, she fell from a horse taking a fence that nobody in their right mind would attempt. She broke her neck."

Poignant emotion tightened her throat. He seemed to have nobody. She could hardly believe he'd lived a life so devoid of affection. For a man of his generous spirit, that was a tragic waste. The same lunatic heart that danced at the sight of him urged her to fold him tight in her arms and promise he'd never be alone again.

Bess resisted the impulse. He was a proud man, and her pity would appall him. "I'm sorry."

"So am I. For all her faults, I loved her, and I think I was the only person in the world who came near to understanding her."

She placed her hand on his arm and tried to ignore how the contact made her pulse skip. "Did you see your father after leaving Penton Wyck?"

She caught a fleeting glimpse of long-held and well-hidden sadness. "We met three times, twice when I was a boy, and once when I was in London as a young officer. We were too unfamiliar with each other to form any real bond, despite our blood ties. Did you know him?"

"When I was a child. He was very like your brother. Quiet. Conscientious. Kind. But I was too young to know him well." She squeezed his arm. "I'm sorry I can't tell you more."

"It helps. I feel like I'm drifting in fog. There's so much I don't know—and everything here is so settled and longstanding. I've mostly lived aboard ship. Occasionally a vessel would feel like home, my first command in particular. She was a darling. But—"

"It's not the same as this house where your ancestors have held sway since the Wars of the Roses."

"Exactly. I knew you'd understand." He placed his bare hand over hers where it circled his arm. His touch jolted her with raw shock. "So when it comes to this place, I appreciate your thoughts. I'm used to handling a ship, not a great estate."

They walked toward the stable doors, arm in arm again. "I've run my father's household since I was twelve. I'm rather in the habit of taking charge. After my mother's death, I had to. Papa will happily go without eating for a week when he's on the hunt for some obscure reference about Julian the Apostate."

"Not very exciting for a young girl."

"I've been left to run wild, my aunt says."

"Your aunt?" They entered the snowy yard behind the house.

"Yes, my mother's sister. She lives in Newcastle, along with my four beautiful cousins, all of whom made advantageous marriages."

"She never tried to find you a husband?"

"She brought me out in local society, but I didn't

take." Bess cringed to recall how gawky and provincial she'd felt at the Newcastle assemblies.

Channing's bewilderment went some way toward soothing the sting. "I can't imagine why not. You're utterly charming."

She stopped so sharply that his hand dropped from her arm. "Nobody's ever called me that."

"You've charmed me into fixing the Abbey and holding a Christmas dinner and, most horrifying of all, playacting."

"I made you do all that," she mumbled, even as her heart expanded under his praise.

"No, you made me want to do it. There's a difference."

She studied him. Low cloud hid the sun, but the snow's white glare threw him into stark relief. "You're a kind man, Lord Channing."

It was his turn to look uncomfortable. "Nonsense. It's blatantly obvious that if Newcastle didn't fall at your feet, there's something wrong with Newcastle, not you. How old were you?"

"Sixteen the first time, eighteen the last." In all the busy years since, she'd almost forgotten the ignominy of failing to cut a dash, and of her aunt's bitter and voluble disappointment.

"You're an original, Miss Farrar. Believe me, in London, you'd be the toast of the town. As a humble second son, I'd have been completely below your lofty notice. You'd cut me direct and waltz away in the arms of a handsome marquess with fifty thousand a year."

She laughed wryly. "What nonsense you talk."

Especially as she was positive that even as a humble second son, he'd stand out as exceptional.

"At least my nonsense has made you smile. Did no fellow have the brains to see what a jewel you are?"

Her cheeks heated under his admiration. If they hadn't been in the open, with interruption likely at any moment, she'd kiss him again.

Bess decided then and there that the next chance she got, she'd ask him to kiss her. Surely that light in his eyes indicated that he'd cooperate.

And what if he doesn't want to stop at kisses?

Wicked excitement weighted her belly as she contemplated more than kisses. Although she knew she steered into dangerous waters. "There was a gentleman my aunt favored."

"But you didn't?"

"No. He was forty-five and had six children."

"There must have been someone else."

"How do you know?"

His glance was mocking. "You said you'd been kissed before."

How very interesting. It seemed his mind dwelled on kisses, too. "There was a very nice man without prospects." She hadn't thought of Tom Wilson in years. "He liked me, but he needed to marry money. My portion is respectable, but not enough to restore a tumbledown estate and support an extended family of indigent relatives."

"Did he marry money?"

"I heard he wed a rich widow from York."

"And I'll wager he's spent every day since cursing his fate."

She laughed. "I doubt it. Our little romance was very boy and girl, not something you eat your heart out over for a lifetime. I can't even remember what he looked like, although at the time, I thought he was breathtakingly handsome."

"I'd never forget you. I'm sure he hasn't either."

She tried not to seize on Channing's remarks as a sign that he cared about her. It would be so easy to mistake his kindness for something more. "I hope he has. It was all so silly. Although I convinced myself it was a grand passion and cried into my pillow for weeks when I came home. But after that, I just got on with things here."

"Waiting for your Prince Charming."

Although the joke bit too close to the bone, she forced a laugh. She had a strong inkling that Lord Channing's kiss had woken her from enchanted sleep. "He must have lost my address."

"These princes are deuced careless coves, by God. You'd better stick with earls."

"I'll remember that," she said lightly, telling herself again that she'd be an idiot to lend too much weight to his teasing.

Lord Channing looked strangely pleased with himself as he stood back to let Bess precede him inside. Confused and unsettled, Bess stepped into the crowded kitchen, full of rich, spicy scents as Mrs. Hallam and her assistants baked puddings and pies for Christmas dinner.

Today Bess and the earl had spoken as friends, as equals, and he'd been quick with some pretty compliments. Then the flirtatious, almost bristling banter between them had briefly vanished and they'd touched on something deeper.

Did that mean more kisses, or a different sort of closeness where kisses had no place? And if she chose kisses, would they blight this fragile, precious friendship before it had a chance to bloom?

CHAPTER SIX

ory's boots squeaked as he tramped through the snow, Bess by his side. He tugged a sledge half full of holly, ivy, and pinecones. They were both dressed as they'd been on their first afternoon together, in coats, boots, scarves and thick gloves. Again, Bess had borrowed a spare greatcoat to wear over her own more feminine pelisse.

Around them, the woods were dim and silent. It was midafternoon, but heavy cloud turned the light to gloaming. Senses honed through a thousand storms at sea told him bad weather was on the way. They probably shouldn't stay out much longer, but he was loath to bring these private moments with Bess to an end.

They'd joined a group collecting greenery for the house. Then as had so often happened these last few days, the others had drifted away to leave him alone with Bess. If his courtship failed, he couldn't blame local opposition. The villagers had done everything they could to promote his wooing.

A wooing that left him puzzled and frustrated and enchanted. The more he saw of Bess, the more he liked her. And the more convinced he was that she was the woman for him.

But this burgeoning respect grated against his burning need to have her in his bed. His strongest impulse was to tumble her, then sort out a quick wedding. And she deserved better than that. Not to mention that after all the villagers' conspiring on his behalf, he'd pay them back in false coin if he dishonored their darling.

But the prospect of months suffering at this pitch of desire left him fit to explode.

He wasn't even sure she'd accept him. Aye, she liked him well enough, and she accepted his touch with gratifying ease. But did that mean she wanted him? Even if she did, would she marry him? The discovery that she'd refused a string of eligible gentlemen, including his brother, had dented his confidence.

Damn it, he wasn't used to agonies of doubt—over anything, least of all a woman. But then, Bess Farrar was the first woman who had really mattered. It was impossible to plot his course with his usual unshakable élan.

"There's some mistletoe." She pointed to a high branch. "We're lucky to see any at all. It usually doesn't grow this far north."

If she'd been like every other lighthearted conquest, he'd make a joke about kissing her—then kiss her. Instead he crossed to cut down her find, using a saw attached to a long stick.

"Well spotted," he said, deriding how jolly and avuncular he sounded when he felt so horribly hot and bothered. "I haven't gone out after Christmas greenery since I was a boy."

Bess regarded him curiously as she collected the tangle of leaves and berries from the snowy ground and packed it onto the cart. After a couple of hours, they'd fallen into an efficient work pattern. She was cheerful company. But he already knew that from sharing the Herculean task of setting up the house. She was cheerful company with everyone. It was a humiliating admission, but Rory reached a point where he was ready to go on his knees and beg for some sign that he was special.

He knew he was unreasonable. They'd met less than a week ago, and while he'd immediately recognized the flaring attraction, she was much less used to dalliance. The day after he'd kissed her, she'd hinted that she'd be happy to do it again. But since then, she'd backed away from anything overtly flirtatious. Perhaps closer acquaintance made her decide she didn't want to kiss him after all.

Right now, he'd cut off his left leg for one word of encouragement. For some physical contact she initiated, he'd cut off both legs.

"What did you do on the ship at Christmas?"

He shrugged. "Nothing on this scale. We'd have something nice for dinner and share out extra rum. I'd read the nativity story from the Bible to the crew, and if the men were keen, they'd sing a few carols. And of course, it all depended on weather and the enemy. Once gales off the Azores kept us jumping for a fortnight. Nobody did much celebrating that year."

"What an adventurous life you've led." Her expression was wistful. "You might find things at Penton Wyck dull in comparison."

He picked up the sledge's handle, trudging a few yards deeper into the woods. "It hasn't been dull so far."

"You've arrived at a busy time. Things go quiet now until spring."

"Then I look forward to enjoying my spectacular new house and getting to know my tenants."

One tenant in particular.

She stopped to cut a few branches off a holly bush. Balancing his long-handled implement on the sledge, he crossed to help and noticed her shivering. "It's getting colder. And darker. Perhaps we should go back."

He made the offer reluctantly, because despite the constant hum of frustration, he was enjoying himself. An excursion through the snow with a bonny lassie and the promise of a blazing fire when he returned home made for a braw afternoon. The scent of the dormant woods sharpened his senses, and the air was crisp as a new apple.

Bess peered up through bare branches at the leaden sky. "We probably should. The weather is closing in."

As if to confirm the wisdom of returning, a gust of icy wind whistled through the trees. Rory took charge of the sledge. "Hold on to me so you don't slip."

She immediately hooked her gloved hand through his arm. His blood warmed despite the worsening chill.

After slogging through the intensifying gale for an arduous hour, Rory realized that they were much further from home than he'd thought. And now they contended with snow as well as wind. "It's a perfect day for rum punch. I'll make some when we get in."

Bess smiled, but he noted the worry in her eyes as they pressed on through thickening weather. When he glanced behind him, their tracks had completely disappeared.

"The villagers will enjoy that."

Rory blinked away snowflakes sticking to his eyelashes. "And you?"

"I'm one of the villagers." She shifted closer. He hoped it wasn't just because the temperature plummeted. "I'm sorry. I've brought you too far."

Not far enough, he thought wryly.

The weather deteriorated with alarming swiftness. Only minutes ago, he'd clearly seen the path ahead. Now even the huge oaks on either side loomed as gray, indistinct shadows.

"We need to find shelter until the worst of it is over," he said, shouting through the blasting wind, even though Bess struggled on right beside him. "Is there anywhere?"

"There's a woodcutter's hut near here, if we haven't wandered too far out of our way."

He abandoned the sledge and grabbed Bess's hand. Be damned if having found her, he'd let her freeze to death. "Let's find it."

They forced their way forward against the wind. It made a mockery of his thick clothing, slicing through to freeze his skin. He angled Bess behind him so he took the brunt, but he knew from her uneven progress that she found it hard going, even using him as a windbreak.

Eventually she tugged him to a panting halt. "There should be a track off the path here. Oh, this snow is such a nuisance. I'm not even sure where I am anymore."

"We'll find it." He flung an arm around her shoulders. Through her thick coat, he felt her shaking tension. "I haven't studied Joseph's lines to be stuck in a blizzard over Christmas Eve."

Even through the gloom, he caught her sardonic glance. "Next year, I'll make you the Angel of the Lord. Then you'll know about lines. That part is pages."

He gave a huff of laughter, even as he saluted her courage. Miss Farrar wasn't a girl to have hysterics at the first sign of trouble. "Nobody in their correct mind would cast me as an angel."

"You're right about that. What a pity there are no pirates in the Christmas story."

"I'm not—"

"There it is, the track to the hut."

They turned direct into the frigid north wind, and he needed all his breath to keep going. Bess led as drifts of snow piled up around them, deeper with every minute. He tied his scarf more securely around his stinging ears. Not an easy task one-handed in the middle of a blizzard. But no way in hell would he let go of Bess's hand. And not just because if she got too far ahead, he'd likely lose her.

Rory's logical mind told him the trek was mere yards. It felt like miles. The wind was powerful enough to force him backward, unless he applied all his strength against it. The heavy snow blinded him so that only when he stood in the lee of the hut did he realize they'd reached their destination.

He pushed the door. It didn't budge. His brain was so frozen, it took him several seconds to fumble for the primitive string and nail latch.

"Come on," he said breathlessly, staggering inside and finally releasing Bess.

The room was dark as a coalmine. The wind tore at the wooden building, so it wasn't much quieter inside than out. Through the elements' roar, he heard Bess stumbling around and reached for her.

His hand landed on something soft and round. Even before her startled gasp, he knew he'd touched her breast. Suddenly he wasn't cold at all. For one burning instant, his hand curled to shape her flesh before he snatched it away.

"I beg your pardon, Miss Farrar." It was difficult to sound sorry, but on the other hand, he didn't want her fleeing into the snow to escape his attentions.

After some scraping, a soft glow chased away the darkness. She'd lit a lamp. "It was an accident."

That time, maybe.

Avoiding her eyes so that she wouldn't see how desperately he wanted her, he glanced around the wee hut. It was unexpectedly well set up. Shelving covered the walls, mostly filled with tools, but he saw some food and basic medical supplies. Even better, there was a hearth and a good supply of wood.

"By God, this is a palace."

She laughed, shaking off that awkward moment when he'd touched her breast with an ease that he found disheartening. His hand still tingled with heat.

"Not quite. But the weather here changes in the blink of an eye. Available shelter can mean the difference between life or death."

"I was surprised how fast the snow came in."

"This is Northumberland." She went to check the food stocks. "It's no place for weaklings."

"So we could be trapped for a while?" He hoped he didn't sound too happy about that.

The furnishings were adequate, but basic. A rough table, four spindly chairs with rush seats. And a truckle bed against one wall. Two shuttered windows and the chimney breast.

Rory bent to build a fire as Bess lit a second lamp. And he tried devilish hard not to think about that bed, and being alone with her for hours on end.

"At this time of year, the weather usually blows itself out. In January and February, people can be stranded for days if things turn nasty."

Days? And one bed? It became even more difficult to concentrate on getting a spark from the tinderbox. "We'll miss the play."

"I hope not. I hear a new performer makes his debut with a spectacular turn as Joseph."

Rory laughed from where he kneeled before the hearth. She really was a brave soul. His years at sea had given him a deep appreciation for courage. This lassie would put his stalwart shipmates to shame. "He's good with the donkey at least."

The kindling caught most satisfactorily, the flames licking greedily at the larger logs. At least they were unlikely to freeze.

"He's good with a fire, too."

"I'm no useless aristocrat," he said drily. "Life on a ship prepares a man for any circumstances, including finding himself alone with a beautiful girl in the middle of a snowstorm."

She cast him a mocking look. "And teaches him a smooth line in flattery, too, it seems."

He merely spoke the truth, but if he started telling her how wonderful she was, he didn't trust himself not to offer physical proof of his admiration. "What on earth are you doing?"

She'd wrestled the door open and wind cut through the room. He leaned over the fire to keep the frail flicker of heat alive.

"I'm getting some snow to melt for water. We've got the makings for soup. Are you hungry?"

Yes, and not just for soup. "Something warm would be nice."

She was outside only moments. The door slammed shut behind her as she fought her way back into the hut. He crossed to take the heavy iron pot she'd filled with snow and set it on the hook above the flames.

"I'll have to compliment the landlord on his arrangements." She headed for the shelf of supplies and began to sort ingredients.

Rory didn't smile as he pulled a chair up to the table and sat. When the villagers had conspired to advance his courtship, he'd been amused—and touched. And he'd certainly appreciated any opportunity to have Bess to himself.

But now, because of that conspiracy, potential disaster loomed. At least from Bess's perspective.

"If we stay here all night, there will be repercussions," he said gravely.

"It will be all right." She brought two onions, a heel of desiccated bacon, and a few shriveled turnips, potatoes, and carrots to the table.

He hadn't expected her to collapse into hysterics— his Bess was made of stronger stuff than that. But surely the threat of scandal deserved more attention than she gave to a few old vegetables. "Your reputation will be in shreds."

She returned to the shelves. "We've got barley, too, and split peas. We definitely won't starve."

"Capital. Did you hear what I said?"

She carried a couple of jars across. "There's chamomile for tea, and some sort of liquor. It's probably filthy stuff, but it might help to keep us warm."

Rory caught her wrist before she moved away again. As the room warmed up, they'd both taken their gloves off, so he felt her pulse racing beneath his fingers. She wasn't as calm as she appeared on the surface. "Bess?"

She regarded him wonderingly. "You've never called me Bess before."

He released an impatient breath. "Never mind that. I just want you to know that I'm a man of honor."

Her eyelids flickered down, and she stared at his large tanned hand encircling her pale wrist. "This isn't London or even Newcastle. People here understand that emergencies happen."

"If we're alone until morning, there's no help for what we must do."

She pulled away and returned to the shelf where she rooted out a couple of bowls, a sharp knife, and a ladle. "I'm not going to make a fuss."

"You won't have to."

She looked back, blue eyes deep and serious in the golden light. He realized that she was fully aware of the trouble they were in. "Let's cross that bridge when we come to it."

"We could try to get back to the Abbey. It can't be much more than a mile."

Her lips turned down in dismissal. "In the dark in a blizzard? And both of us on foot and not dressed for this weather? We'd be taking our lives into our own hands."

"It would save a scandal."

"I'd rather stay alive." She began to chop an onion with impressive efficiency. "I grew up in this valley. Trust me when I say this is likely no more than a flurry."

A flurry? The world outside was howling white horror. But he put aside further arguments for now. As she said, there was no point borrowing trouble. They were stuck here until the storm worked itself out.

He'd marry her tomorrow, scandal or no scandal, but she clearly didn't share his enthusiasm for the idea, damn it. "Can I help?"

She looked up with a quick smile. And visible relief that he changed the subject. "I doubt I've got the strength to dice that bacon. Can I give it to you? You might need an ax."

"What time is it?" Bess asked from the table where she lingered over her empty bowl. Rory sat on the bed across the room, legs stretched over the rough mattress.

The improvised soup had been surprisingly palatable, and now they drank herbal tea from tin mugs. The hut was cozy, and they'd both removed their heavy outer coats which lay steaming in front of the fire.

He set down his tea and retrieved his pocket watch. "Nearly eight."

When he'd ventured outside for more snow, he'd fumbled around in pitch darkness. The blizzard still raged, but he'd become so used to the wind, he hardly noticed it anymore.

"It's getting colder again."

"Yes." He extended a hand toward her and hoped he wasn't making a mistake trusting to his willpower. But he couldn't bear to have her to himself, yet so far away. "Body heat is the best way to keep warm."

Pleasure filled him when she crossed to take his hand, kneeling on the low bed. He slid his arm around her and tucked her close into his side, pulling up the blankets until they were cocooned against the wall.

"You're shivering," he said in dismay. He reached for

the flask of homemade liquor he'd put on the floor beside the bed. "Have some of this. It might help."

She sneaked a hand out from under the blanket and took the flask. She brought it to her lips and took a sip, then choked. "That's vile."

He laughed as he took back the flask and tested its contents. Aye, she was right. It was bloody dreadful, but once the fumes had cleared, he appreciated the spreading warmth. "Well, we're stuck here. Any idea how to pass the time? If I had a pack of cards, I could teach you piquet."

"I can play piquet."

He snuggled her closer. He reminded his animal self that he'd offered her body heat, not the heat of passion. Difficult to remember when he touched her. "Miss Farrar, you clearly have a wicked past."

"Not very," she mumbled into his chest. "Your brother taught me."

"Aye?" Ridiculous to be jealous of a dead man.

"When you're ill, you have a lot of time to fill. I used to visit the Abbey to read to him. One day he was bored with the story and suggested cards instead."

Rory struggled not to picture an intimate scene in the same state bedroom where he'd slept alone and longing since meeting Bess. It was much more likely she and his brother had been in one of the public rooms downstairs.

He was a fool to torment himself. If Bess had

wanted the late Earl of Channing, she'd have married him.

"I'll have to make sure all the huts on my estate are stocked with playing cards." He offered the rough spirit, but she shook her head. He braved another taste, then sealed the flask and put it beside the bed.

Despite their dire situation, he felt ridiculously content. Bess was soft and warm in his embrace, and her rich scent, tinged with wood smoke, filled his senses.

He rested his cheek on her shining hair. A hint of wet wool also teased his nostrils, despite the fire drying them out over the last few hours. But beneath that, she was all delicious woman.

With all his might, he strived to behave like a solicitous gentleman, and not a rapacious seducer. After all, her presence in his arms was a mark of hard-won trust. She clearly had no idea how his blood surged at her nearness, nor how he fought the need to drag her beneath him and warm her up the best way he knew.

Since he'd gone to sea, he'd had few dealings with virtuous ladies. The sort of lassie who succumbed to a sailor knew he'd be away on the next tide. Bess, for all her strength and vigor and courage, struck him as so heartbreakingly fragile right now. He loathed the thought of frightening her with his mighty desire.

If she'd been one of his lusty mistresses, he'd tumble her in a blink. But she wasn't. She was a chaste vicar's daughter, and he had no idea how to shift her feelings from cordiality to passion. She was pure and perfect, and he wanted her so fiercely, he felt ready to burst into flame.

"I'm sorry I got you into this."

He emerged from his brooding to meet her solemn blue gaze. "How is this your fault? Unless you've got some influence with the snow gods that I don't know about. If you have, for pity's sake, ask them to lay off."

She smiled, but her heart wasn't in it. "I made you come out cutting Christmas greenery. In fact, I got you involved in having Christmas at the Abbey in the first place."

"Silly wee chit, don't you know yet that every step of the way, I've done exactly what I want?"

She studied him, her brow wrinkling in puzzlement. "Have you?"

"Aye. Unless you'd prodded me out of my bachelor squalor, I'd never have come to know the villagers. Or you."

"Oh." She put more effort into her smile. "I'm glad."

"That I joined in?"

"Yes. And that I got to know you, too."

Dear Lord, he ached to kiss her. To do more. Only with the greatest effort did he resist hauling her up against him. He'd been bold enough to kiss her that first day. Now too much hinged on what happened between them for such recklessness.

Her smile faded, replaced by an intent expression

that corroded his frail self-control. "I know just how I'd like to pass the time."

"We could swap life stories. Although no doubt mine would shock you."

"Perhaps it would." She paused. "And perhaps I want to be shocked."

He didn't understand. "Bess?"

She licked her lips and tilted her chin at a defiant angle. "Lord Channing, would you please kiss me again?"

CHAPTER SEVEN

*L*ord Channing's striking face tightened with shock. His jaw hardened and a muscle flickered erratically in his cheek. He looked like she'd asked him to shoot his best friend.

The bed suddenly felt intolerably small. Sick with humiliation, Bess wriggled to escape the arm she now realized that he'd placed about her for purely practical reasons. Her cheeks burned hotter than his skillfully built fire.

"I'm sorry. I was stupid to ask."

"It's too dangerous to kiss you here." He sounded austere and resolute, and not at all like the lighthearted man who had teased her about her mythical wicked past.

"I told you I won't kick up a scandal."

"But if I kiss you—devil take you, lassie, will you sit

still one wee moment?—it's surer than sunrise that I'll do something worthy of a scandal."

Puzzled, she stopped pushing and studied his somber features. "I trust to your honor."

His lips twisted in self-derision. "Well, that makes one of us."

A deep breath fought her dizziness. "I…I liked it when you kissed me before."

"So did I."

That was something. She seized her courage with both hands and squeezed it until it squeaked. "So why haven't you done it again?"

"Because you're a virtuous woman, and gossip runs through this damn village like a flood down a dry valley."

"People will think we've been kissing anyway."

"People will think a lot more than that," he said grimly. "If I kiss you, they'll be right."

Monumental disappointment crushed her. He tried to let her down lightly, but rejection was still rejection. She went back to trying to escape. "Please forget I said anything."

Despite her best efforts, tears clogged her voice. She'd never invited a man's attentions before. After today's debacle, even if her life depended on it, she'd never invite them again.

But, oh, how it smarted to hunger so desperately, and know Channing felt nothing in return.

"Bess, you make it so impossible." He sounded like she tested him to the ends of endurance.

Still she wouldn't look at him. "I promise I won't embarrass you again."

"What?" The few inches she'd managed to claim back between them disappeared as he caught her with ruthless hands and shoved her onto her back. He loomed over her, big and powerful and, unless she was mistaken, fuming.

She ought to be frightened. But she'd sunk so far into sin since she'd met Channing that her wanton blood surged with female excitement. And a much overdue return of spirit.

"You're to blame. You made me think you like me."

He stared at her as if she was losing her mind. "I do like you."

She raised her chin and glared at him. "I mean...*like* me."

"I do."

He clearly didn't understand. Which was odd. He was one of the most perceptive people she knew. "You kissed me."

"I did."

She frowned as her temper spiked. "If you're not attracted to a girl, it's wicked to kiss her."

"It's wicked to kiss her anyway."

"Exactly," she said, so desperate to score a point against him that she hardly knew what she agreed to.

"And it's wicked to single her out and call her pretty and…and make her feel special."

"You *are* special."

Bess immediately dismissed that as another attempt to soothe her hurt feelings. "It's wicked to touch her, and take her arm, and look at her as if you want to kiss her again."

"The way I'm looking at you now?"

Something in his voice choked any answer in her throat. Confused, she stared up into his face. The unwavering regard of those deep green eyes had her heart performing drunken cartwheels.

Channing indeed looked as if he intended to snap her up like a bonbon between his straight white teeth. He leaned over her, caging her between his impressive chest and the arm he propped against the pillow near her head. Against her side, his body was pleasingly heavy and hot.

"Y…yes," she finally forced out between lips that felt as dry as sand. Her pulse throbbed so hard, it shook her whole body. She began to tremble, not to her shame with fear, but with frantic anticipation. "Just like that."

His eyes darkened in sizzling concentration. Nobody in Bess's whole life had looked at her with such burning focus. Her breath hitched, and her head swam until all she saw was his face. His lips curled in a smile that made her giddy with longing.

If this was more teasing, she'd never forgive him.

"At last, a right answer."

"Does that mean…" she stammered, as without conscious command, one hand slid up his arm to shape his shoulder.

"That I'm about to compound all the wickedness you accuse me of by being very wicked indeed? Aye, it does."

"Oh…" she said faintly, then didn't speak again because Lord Channing's lips stole her breath.

This was shatteringly different from the last time he kissed her. That had been a question. This was a conquest. He lashed his arms about her and rolled to the side so they lay face to face. His warmth and masculine scent surrounded her. That rich essence flooded her senses with the promise of excitement and adventure and daring. And home and lifelong sustenance and safety.

She shouldn't feel safe. After all, he was a pirate and a seducer, and she'd known him less than a week. But none of those good sensible warnings touched her heart. Her heart told her that she was home.

Rory Beaton was her home.

So when his tongue flicked against her lips, she obeyed the silent prompting and parted. He explored her mouth with shocking carnality. She tasted chamomile and raw spirits, delicious when combined with Channing's distinctive flavor.

When she moved her tongue against his, he growled

encouragement. She did it again, and the kiss became an incendiary dance of lips and tongues. A deep pulse pounded in the pit of her stomach, making her feel empty and needy and jumpy. She wriggled to get closer, frantic to ease that hot, painful craving. Every rule she'd lived by tumbled around her like fallen ninepins hit square by the ball. Nothing outside the circle of Channing's arms mattered. All that mattered was the passion flaring between them, and her need to know more, feel more.

He teased at her lips, nipping and licking and taunting her. She caught on quickly and teased him back until he, the worldly rogue, groaned and gave her more of those long, desperate kisses. As if he perished of thirst in the desert, and only Bess offered sweet, fresh water.

She'd told him he made her feel special. When he kissed her as if the world would end if he stopped, he made her feel like a goddess. How could this be wrong?

Shyly, she buried her hands in his thick, silky hair, holding him close for more kisses. He whispered incoherent Scots words of appreciation against her lips and cheeks. The soft burr of his voice turned her bones to molten syrup. Emboldened she stroked his neck and face, feeling the prickling beginnings of his beard on his jaw. Everything he did, everything he was fascinated her.

He rolled her onto her back and surged over her. His mouth traced paths of fire over her face as she looped her hands across his powerful back. He found a spot where her shoulder curved into her neck. Kisses there made her quake, and when he bit down gently, she cried out and clawed at the fine lawn of his shirt.

He rested on one elbow and bent to take her mouth again. She met him unhesitatingly, sliding her fingers into the curls at his nape. He offered such a banquet of different, delightful textures, she hardly knew where to explore next. Somewhere at the back of her mind lurked the certainty that this glorious interval couldn't last, that she had to wring every drop from this experience while she could.

His kiss was so overwhelming that she didn't immediately realize that he'd flicked open the buttons descending from her collar. When air brushed her skin, she drew back to see her bodice gaping over her breasts.

"Channing?" she whispered, more in wonder than protest. She knew she should be frightened, but stronger than fear was instinctive trust.

"Rory," he muttered, sliding a seeking hand under her shift to claim her breast. His palm was warm and confident on her flesh, and when he rolled her nipple between two fingers, heat seared her. The peak tightened with pleasure that verged on pain.

When he slid the frail covering away, his eyes flared at the sight of her bare breast. "You're so beautiful, you take my breath away."

Bess knew she should stop him, but the fire in his

eyes held her acquiescent as he took that beaded point between his lips. When he drew on her, she caught his head in her hands, pressing him closer. Heat blasted her, and she writhed against him, begging for more. She'd never felt like this in her life.

He looked up from her breast and kissed her again. When he slowly drew her skirts up, she murmured consent. He meant sin, but right now, the greater sin was abandoning this passion before she reached its destination.

When he touched her between the legs, she bucked with shock. She greeted his fingers with a hot surge, and whimpered with excruciating need. He was so close to where she ached to feel him.

He lifted his head and regarded her with a searching expression that pierced her soul. She was beyond pretending and made no attempt to hide her impatience. She had no truck with pride or prudence. All she wanted was Rory.

"Please?" she whispered with every ounce of longing in her heart. "Please don't stop."

For one fraught moment, desire's clinging web held them captive. Breathlessly she waited for him to proceed, to initiate her into this ultimate mystery. His hands were hard on her hips. His body was big and powerful above hers. His face reflected her unbearable hunger.

Then in the space of a heartbeat, his expression closed and he turned into a stranger. Behind his eyes, shutters slammed down upon all that heat and desire and need.

"Rory?" she asked shakily, cupping his jaw with an unsteady hand. Briefly, he remained motionless under her touch, and she wondered if she'd mistaken his withdrawal. Then he angled his head away and shifted until his body no longer touched hers.

Ice encased her soul as he reached across and tugged her shift over her breast. "Bess, this can't be. I'm sorry."

As the beautiful unrestrained ardor in Bess's face faded to hurt bewilderment, Rory's heart cramped into a hard nut of regret. Regret was a sour taste in his mouth, too, when only seconds ago, all he could taste was Bess Farrar.

"Why did you stop?" she asked, her face pale where before she'd been flushed with pleasure.

Knowing he couldn't trust himself so close to temptation, he rolled off the bed and stood up. "I had to."

She pushed into a sitting position. Temper replaced the devastation in her eyes. "Is that so?"

"Aye." He backed away until his legs hit a chair. He collapsed onto it. Frankly, he wasn't feeling too steady. "I shouldn't have let everything get so far."

"No, you shouldn't," she bit out.

Shaking fingers making a mull of the mundane

action, she buttoned her bodice. But it was too late. The memory of her breast under his hand would haunt him until he died. He sucked in a jagged breath and battled for composure. And wished this damned hut was the size of Blenheim Palace. Bess remained dangerously within reach, and his honor barely clung by its fingertips.

Rory bowed his head and stared unseeingly at the rough timber floor. Looking at her hurt him.

How he cursed his inconvenient conscience, but he couldn't argue with its conclusions. Every principle he had recoiled at giving Bess Farrar her first sexual experience in a shabby hut with no promises exchanged.

He'd sinned before. Of course he had. But ruining this shining girl was a sin far beyond any he'd committed in his turbulent, swashbuckling life.

When he'd looked down into her lovely face, he'd read unconditional surrender. Once, he'd thought that was what he wanted from her. But it turned out he wasn't nearly as selfish as he'd believed. Caught up in her first taste of passion, she lost all sight of her welfare.

If he took her now, he'd show her pleasure. He'd treat her with respect and care.

It would still be a grievous wrong.

"I hope you'll forgive me. I didn't behave like a gentleman."

Her lips tightened. "In my opinion, you're behaving too much like a gentleman, my lord."

No sweet whispers of Rory now, he noticed, hiding a wince. His refusal of her breathtaking generosity clearly stung. He could endure her anger. Her pain left him feeling like she eviscerated him with a blunt butter knife. Every word he spoke only seemed to widen the gulf between them.

He longed to take her in his arms, but he was grimly aware how precariously he maintained control. If he touched her, Miss Farrar would face tomorrow as a fallen woman. This wondrous, bright, new feeling that grew between them would become a thing of shame and secrets.

He couldn't bear that.

He repeated what he'd recognized when, eager and reckless, she'd begged him not to stop. *Bess Farrar deserved better.*

"Bess…"

She sighed, a sound of such misery, it made him want to howl like a motherless bairn. "I'm sorry. I'm acting like a witch."

Blistering sexual frustration didn't leave him feeling too jolly either. He wondered why doing the right thing made her furious and him wretched. Where was the justice in that? "No."

He'd never seen so much effort put into a smile to such little effect. His hands fisted against the urge to catch her up against him.

Because while he might set out to comfort, that wasn't how everything would end. Damn it all to hell.

"You're trying to be kind." Dull eyes leveled upon him. "You're a good man, my lord."

If she knew the demons of lust warring for ownership of his soul, she wouldn't say that. "No, I'm not."

She managed a choked laugh. "I'm not a witch, and you're not a good man? We can't seem to agree on anything."

She struggled to make the best of a situation which had no best in it. By God, she humbled him. "Please listen to me."

Except what the devil could he say? How could he form a coherent explanation from this churning maelstrom of contradictory impulses? And if he started reassuring her in words that he wanted her and he'd pulled back for her sake, he knew he'd go on to demonstrate that desire in actions. Next time he wouldn't find the strength to stop.

"No, not now." Her voice cracked, and her hands dug into the thick, gray blankets. He loathed that he'd pushed this vivid creature so close to the edge of breaking. "Lord Channing, I'd be most grateful if we didn't discuss this anymore. I find...I find I'm very tired."

"Bess, for pity's sake..."

"Yes, for pity's sake, my lord, please...please leave me in peace."

"Very well," he said grimly. Despite the risk to his control, he ached to talk to her, to explain what had happened, to make her understand. But she looked so exhausted and sad, he couldn't bear to push her.

She flopped down on the bed and turned her back. For a long moment, he stared at her eloquently hunched shoulders, suffering a roiling mixture of longing and remorse. He knew he made a complete bloody mess of this, but he didn't know how to fix it.

Eventually with a heavy sigh, he stood and fed the fire before he tugged on his greatcoat. When his fingers snagged in the rip Daisy had made in his sleeve, he swore under his breath. The reminder of the first time he'd kissed Bess wasn't exactly welcome just now.

He banged the chairs together to form a makeshift bed. Nowhere near as comfortable as the one Bess occupied in bristling silence. But even if she allowed him to sleep beside her, he knew better than to test his willpower.

Rory leaned back against one chair and propped his feet on another. The iron-hard wood beneath his arse served as yet another reminder of the price of virtue. But whatever his wicked self wanted, he knew in his soul he'd done the right thing.

If only Bess thought so, too.

He drew out his pocket watch. It was only just past nine o'clock. He felt like he'd lived a lifetime in the last hour. His thoughts strayed toward those miraculous kisses, but he brought himself up short. Things were difficult enough already, without torturing himself about what he could be doing right now, instead of trying to arrange his long body in a way that wouldn't leave him hobbling tomorrow.

Outside the wind shrieked like a banshee. Contrary to Bess's optimistic predictions, the storm showed no sign of abating. It was going to be a hell of a long night.

CHAPTER EIGHT

The sound of the hut's door opening disturbed Rory from his restless doze. Stretching painfully, he raised one hand to rub his stiff neck. He wouldn't recommend choosing to sleep on two chairs.

"Ned?" he asked wonderingly when his friend came inside, stamping snow from his boots. "What the devil are you doing out in this blizzard?"

"It's now a beautiful night." Ned shut the door behind him. "You've chosen a dashed unpredictable place to live."

Rory realized that the wind no longer howled. "How did you find us?"

"When you and Miss Farrar didn't come back, people were worried, but couldn't go out in the weather to look for you. Once the snow eased, I came after you. When I found the sledge, I knew you couldn't be far away."

Bess had stirred when Ned came in, and now she sat up without sparing Rory a glance. She looked disheveled and exhausted. Rory's gut contracted with stabbing guilt when he saw tearstains on her cheeks. He'd hurt her when he'd brought that wild encounter to an end, and that had never been his intention.

Damn him, he should have let her down more gently, but at the time, he'd been a million miles from equanimity himself.

When Rory tore his gaze from Bess, he caught a speculative glint in Ned's eyes. She looked like she'd survived a blizzard. Unfortunately she also looked thoroughly bedded.

"Are you on your own?"

"Yes, I tried to get here ahead of the crowd. But they're not far behind me."

Ned's words were a warning. Rory and Bess had been alone for hours, and unless he was careful, they'd be irretrievably compromised. He wanted her to marry him, but not because she had to. And he couldn't bear to think of people sniggering about her.

"Good evening, Mr. White," she said, standing and smoothing her hands down creased skirts. "Thank you for coming to find us."

"It's my pleasure, Miss Farrar." Ned liked Bess, and he appreciated her liveliness and competence. Neither of which would save them from scandal, if the villagers chose to interpret this evening's events in a prurient light. Guilt stabbed Rory anew, as he recalled how close he'd come to making any prurient thoughts reality.

"What time is it?" Bess ran her fingers through her tumbled hair and divided it into three strands for plaiting. Her movements were quick and deft as she confined the rumpled golden mass. Rory's fingers itched to touch that lovely mane. His tiresome principles didn't stop him wanting.

"Just past midnight," Ned said, straightening his spectacles.

Rory looked squarely at his friend. "If people know we've been together all this time, there will be the devil to pay."

Bess moved around the hut, tidying away traces of occupancy. Despite their dire circumstances, Rory found her quiet housewifery mesmerizing. Any man would be lucky to come home to such a wife as Bess. Good and faithful and bright.

And right now, a million miles out of reach, even if she stood mere feet away.

"I'll say I saw nothing untoward," Ned said.

"Not good enough." Rory studied his friend's scholarly features. "A lady's reputation hangs by a thread, and I swear Miss Farrar is as pure now as she was when she stepped into the hut."

It was almost the truth. But as she straightened the bed and folded away the blankets, Bess's shoulders stiffened.

"What would you like me to do?" Ned asked.

"Tell people you found me in the hollow of a tree or sheltering under a bank, and you and I arrived together at the hut to find Miss Farrar. I'll say she and I were separated in the storm. All hell was breaking loose, so there's no reason for anyone to doubt our story, especially if you back me up."

"Of course I will." Ned smiled at Bess who had stopped to watch them both with a troubled frown. "I'll never allow anyone to question your virtue, Miss Farrar."

She managed a smile for Ned. Again she avoided Rory's eyes. "Thank you, Mr. White. You're very kind."

Ned turned to Rory. "Go and roll in the snow until your coat's wet. Nobody will believe a word of this story if they see you looking so warm and dry."

Rory bit back a sardonic laugh. If only Ned knew how close he'd come to diving headfirst into the snow after he abandoned Bess at that crucial moment. Grimly he headed outside and tugged at a low-hanging branch. The freezing wet snow that cascaded down his neck seemed suitable penance for his trespasses.

By the time their rescuers arrived, the hut was pristine, and Bess and her two companions sat around the table, the picture of innocence. Only Rory noticed that when she shared a lighthearted narration of her adventures with the villagers, not once did she glance in his direction.

Bess's subdued air hadn't lifted by the time the participants gathered at the Abbey the next day for the Christmas Eve procession. Rory, coming downstairs ready to play St. Joseph, felt a very unsaintly urge to smash something when he saw her drawn, tired features. The woman dressed in Mary's sky blue robe looked like she'd travelled a long, hard road to reach Bethlehem.

She'd been working with his servants this morning, supervising placement of the lush greenery to mark the Yuletide, and checking arrangements for tomorrow's party. But she'd kept at least a room away from him. He could only assume by choice.

Wisdom indicated that with scandal hovering, discretion was the best course, even if he itched to corner her and make her tell him what was wrong. After holding her in his arms, it was torture pretending they were mere acquaintances.

Was she shy after last night? She'd been an innocent after all, and he'd done more than enough to shock a virginal vicar's daughter.

"Miss Farrar, are you all right?" Rory asked under his breath as everyone else crowded around the blacksmith's wife, and her baby who played Jesus in the day's performance.

"Perfectly," Bess said in a flat voice, without looking at him. He was devilish tired of that opaque blue gaze skating across him as if he was another piece of furniture.

Worse. Bess always paid attention to the furniture.

"Are you sure?"

"Perfectly."

"Well, that's…good," he said, not believing her for a moment.

Rory eyed the mistletoe suspended above her head and wondered how she'd react if he caught her around the waist and kissed her. She'd probably say "perfectly" in that polite little voice that didn't sound at all like the woman he knew.

Dr. Simpson, dressed as the innkeeper, approached to ask a question, and she turned to him with barely hidden relief. Rory slouched discontentedly against the wall and observed proceedings with a jaundiced air. He wasn't yet in costume, but seeing he only had to pull a striped robe over his shirtsleeves, he wasn't bothered.

His gaze tracked Bess as she moved around the cast, straightening a crown on a Wise Man, reminding the chief shepherd of his lines, checking with the choirmaster. Children and villagers milled about outside the house. They'd sing Christmas carols accompanied by recorders and drums, as the procession wound its way through the village.

Everything except Bess Farrar was in cracking shape. The house smelled like a forest, fresh and green and sharp with aromatic pine sap. Thank heavens yesterday's foul weather had cleared, and Christmas

Eve dawned clear and cold. Through the open doors, Rory saw how the sun struck the snow to blinding white.

Bess spent several minutes calming the Angel of the Lord who had the longest part. Sally Potts was counted the village beauty, and this was her first year in a speaking role. Perhaps Rory was biased, but he couldn't help comparing her to Bess. Even today, when his darling looked like she hadn't had a wink of sleep, she was still the prettiest lass he'd ever seen.

The only player who escaped a few words of encouragement was the lord of the manor. Did Bess mean to convey the impression that nothing untoward had happened in the hut? This morning he'd noticed a few speculative glances, but so far their story was generally accepted.

He puzzled over her attitude. Bess might be angry with him, or disappointed. Although surely now that the heat of passion faded, she must realize that he'd done the only thing a man of honor could.

Except that what he saw when he watched her—and he watched her as closely as a cat watched a bird fluttering in a bush—wasn't pique, but a valiantly hidden unhappiness that made his gut clench with remorse.

He desperately needed to talk to her, to find out what went on inside her lovely head. Two years with his stepsisters had taught him that when females got a notion, their minds could whisk them away to the edge of doom before a man recognized he'd made a minor mistake.

The hell of it was that even if he could get Bess to accept his apologies, he wouldn't have a second alone with her all day to make them. So he lingered, worried and frustrated, on the edge of a crowd which excluded him, even as it embraced Bess.

"It's time to go outside," she said with a cheerfulness that struck false in Rory's ears. "You've all been marvelous in rehearsal, so I'm sure this will be a special year."

Dr. Simpson smiled at her, then sent Rory a meaningful glance. "It is indeed a special year. We welcome a new earl, and I couldn't be more pleased that his lordship is already an indispensable part of our small community."

To Rory's surprise, everyone in the room burst into applause before a ragged but enthusiastic rendition of "For He's a Jolly Good Fellow" with three resounding cheers to follow.

Touched, he stepped forward. He'd been wrong to feel excluded. His head was all over the place today with the chill between him and Bess. At least she'd joined in the song, he hoped not just for appearance's sake.

"Thank you, Dr. Simpson. I couldn't ask for a warmer reception. I'm happy that I've dropped anchor in Penton Wyck. For my money, there isn't a finer lot of people in England." He paused. "Or in Scotland either, which I never thought a true son of the High-lands would say." Everyone laughed. Even Bess managed a smile. He gestured toward where she stood half a room away. "I'd like to thank Miss Farrar. Without her, I'd never have discovered the joy of preparing for a traditional Christmas, or had a livable house—or met the charming Daisy."

Another laugh and three more cheers for Bess who looked damnably on edge. If she didn't settle down, she'd be the nerviest Mary in history.

Rory signaled to the two footmen standing by the door. Within seconds they were circulating with trays of mulled wine. The players had a long afternoon ahead, mostly in the open. A wee bit of extra cheer wouldn't go astray. The scents of cinnamon, cloves and oranges from the fragrant brew rose to combine pleas-antly with the tang of pine.

"Thank you," Bess said. "Now it's time we set off, or Daisy will go without us. The idea of leaving her to her own devices is too terrifying to contemplate."

Another laugh. Apart from that stormy pool of unhappiness around Bess, a river of goodwill flowed through the room.

Rory noticed that she hardly touched her wine. Which was a pity. If anyone looked in need of liquor's bolstering effects, it was Bess.

Everyone trooped through the open doors. Outside, maids were collecting empty cups, and the festive atmosphere felt like Christmas started early. Even

Daisy looked happy, decked out in ribbons, with her coat clipped and groomed to a shine.

Rory paused in the doorway to savor a sensation he'd never before experienced. That this was home, and these were his people, and he belonged here. His chest felt too small to contain the swelling emotion in his heart.

He'd never imagined his inheritance would change him. But it had. Irrevocably.

Since his arrival—no, in the last week—he'd sent down roots into this rich Northumbrian soil, roots that he hoped would nourish the rest of his life. A mere seven days ago, his fierce longing to step up to life as Lord Channing would have astonished him.

He had one person to thank for the transformation. The one piece missing in this picture of contentment.

Bess Farrar.

Suddenly he couldn't bear to wait to heal the breach between them. He couldn't bear to wait to stake his claim to her.

The maids and footmen traipsed toward the kitchens. Bess lingered behind in the great hall to soothe Sally's stage fright. The girl looked marginally more confident as she slipped the harness for her glittering white and silver wings over her shoulders. Then had to ease sideways past Rory to fit through the door. Sally wasn't the world's cleverest creature, but with her masses of fine fair hair and delicate face, she appeared truly ethereal.

"You look just like an angel, Sally," he said as she passed. "You'll be the star of the play."

Sally blushed bright red and lurched into a clumsy curtsy. "Thank you, my lord."

He caught her and helped her onto the steps before she dislodged the wings. Or worse, tore them. Then before Bess could escape, he stepped back inside, slammed the door shut and bolted it.

"What on earth are you doing?" she asked, astonishment banishing the well-mannered automaton who'd driven him to distraction. "We need to start."

"They'll wait," he said, turning to face her and folding his arms implacably over his chest.

Displeasure lit her eyes. She stood in the center of the hall, exactly where he'd first seen her. He'd known then that she was the one for him.

"Well, that's not fair. And after making such a nice speech, too." At last, she sounded like that spirited lassie who had the nerve to lecture him about his duties.

"I hope this will only take a wee while."

Wariness replaced annoyance in those beautiful blue eyes, and she stepped back. In her long Marian robes, she was a creature from another world. It seemed blasphemous to recall his hand curling around her bare breast. Except that his feelings for Miss Farrar had always contained a healthy dose of carnality.

"What's...this exactly?"

He prowled toward her. "Have you really no idea?"

"No," she said. "And if we don't go outside now, all the gossip we've managed to avoid will rise up and devour us."

He laughed softly, enjoying himself for the first time since he'd kissed her last night. "Don't be a wee goose, Bess. They've gossiped about us all week."

"What? Are you sure?"

"Aye, of course I'm sure."

"They haven't said a word to me." The light through the high window made her look a thousand times more angelic than Sally Potts ever could. If an angel could be confused and irritable and eminently touchable.

"Well, they wouldn't, would they?"

"Just what have they been saying?" she asked suspiciously.

He smiled, delighted with her, delighted with himself for finding her. Who would have imagined his perfect bride was hiding in an obscure corner of Northumberland? "That you'd make me a fine countess."

She frowned. "What nonsense."

"And I'm inclined to agree with them."

Disbelief widened her eyes. "You are?"

"Aye."

To his consternation, just when he thought he set his course for a friendly port, unhappiness returned to sap all the lovely vitality from her face. Her eyes lowered, and she buried her hands in her skirts. Too late. He'd seen how she trembled.

"I know what you're doing," she said in a toneless voice.

"Of course you do. I'm proposing."

"Because you think you have to," she mumbled. Instead of throwing herself into his arms, she marched past him toward the door. "And you don't. Even if there's talk about last night, it will die down when we treat each other the way we always have."

"And how's that?" He stepped in front of her to block her departure.

Bess regarded him with disfavor. "Like...like an earl and a humble tenant."

He burst out laughing. "Och, what utter rot. You haven't got a humble bone in your body, and if you've ever given a moment's deference to my rank, I certainly missed it."

Her voluptuous mouth firmed, and she crossed her arms. "Well, that's how I intend to treat you in future. I'm sorry if I've been disrespectful. I won't be disrespectful again."

"Would you like to place a wee wager on that?"

She frowned, looking less self-righteous by the minute. "You've gone quite mad."

His lips twitched. "That offer to treat me with appropriate deference didn't last long."

She didn't smile. "I'm sorry, my lord."

Last night she'd called him Rory. He vowed she would again before she left this house. "No, you're not.

And anyway, it's true. I've been insane since the day you walked in and laid down the law."

"I'm sorry for that, too," she said sturdily.

He caught her hand. "Don't be. If you hadn't barged in, I'd have missed out on the last week, and that would be a crying shame."

She glanced up at him without trying to pull free. "I'm so glad you've become part of the village. The mulled wine was a nice touch."

Rory stifled a laugh. "I do have an occasional idea of my own, you know. In fact, I have the idea right now that you should say you'll marry me. Then we can save those good people from standing about in the snow, wondering what we're up to."

She regarded him with such distress that he longed to take her into his arms. But some deep instinct told him to tread with care.

"You don't have to do this."

He sighed and tightened his grip on her hand. "I know I don't. I want to marry you."

"No, you don't."

He straightened to his full height and glared down at her as if she was an insubordinate gunner. "The devil, what maggot has got into that busy mind of yours, my bonny Bess?"

To his regret, she pulled away, her face drawn with a misery that made his stomach cramp in denial. Could he be wrong? Could all his hopes come to nothing?

"I don't want to talk about this."

"Too bad. Tell me why you've been wandering around all day like the ghost at the feast." A horrible thought struck him. "Don't tell me you're ashamed of what we did?"

Bess raised despairing eyes to his. "Shouldn't I be?"

He caught her shoulders. "No, blast it, you shouldn't. You're a lovely, ardent creature, and when desire is mutual, it's natural to express it."

Her lips trembled, and to his horror, her eyes glazed with tears. "But it wasn't."

"Wasn't what? Natural?" He laughed. "It most certainly was."

"No, mutual," she muttered.

He frowned, not understanding. He must be the most thick-witted clodpoll in creation. "You didn't want me?"

She avoided his stare, and to his horror, a tear trickled down her cheek. "Of course I did. You know I did."

"I thought so."

"But you didn't want me."

"What utter damned drivel." He fought the urge to prove once and for all how asinine that pronouncement was. "I was desperate for you."

"Then why did you stop?"

"Oh, Bess," he said helplessly, and this time he didn't hesitate. He wrapped his arms about her and kissed her thoroughly. She hesitated before she kissed him back, leading to a satisfactorily passionate attempt to convince her of his interest and affection.

Reluctantly he raised his head. She looked rosy and well kissed and, to his relief, a wee bit happier.

"I thought I must have disgusted you when I was so…so eager," she confessed. "Or I did something wrong that made you stop."

When Rory stepped away after Bess offered him everything, he'd known he hurt her. She'd left herself dangerously vulnerable, and his abrupt withdrawal had to smart. But he'd had no idea his denial had made her doubt herself so profoundly.

What a bloody idiot he was. He'd underestimated the powerful innocence that made her see his barely held restraint as lack of interest. "You were glorious in my arms, a dream. You're everything I desire in a woman. Surely you know that."

"You seemed to want me. And then…you didn't."

"I'll always want you. Even when I'm old and gray, and I need an ear trumpet to hear you call me a blockhead."

When the wee joke roused the ghost of a smile, fresh hope flooded in. With every moment, she looked more confident, thank God. "So you wanted to keep kissing me?"

"Hell, Bess, I wanted more than that—but it wasn't the time or place." His voice deepened into a husky rumble. "I intend to claim you as my wife and my countess in front of the entire world. You're worthy of every honor, not some hole-in-the-corner seduction, no matter how mad I was for you."

"Oh, Rory, what a fool I am." Her eyes glowed with such light that his heart turned over. "You were being noble. I should have realized."

"And hellish painful it was, too." He kissed her quickly to thank her for calling him Rory. "Silly widgeon."

For the first time today, those lush lips curved in a genuine smile. "So you're not proposing just to save my reputation?"

He wasn't given to flowery speeches or dramatic gestures, but this moment called for something memorable. The emotion shining unspoken in her eyes defeated inhibitions.

He shifted back a pace and caught her hand. Then he dropped to one knee and stared up into the bonny face that fired his dreams. "I'm proposing, Bess, because without you my life is incomplete. I'm proposing because from the moment I met you, you've filled my every thought."

"That's better," she said unsteadily. Serious dark blue eyes studied him. "I've only known you a week."

His grip on her hand tightened. "It's been a devil of an eventful week, though, worth more than six months of society courtship where we'd sit over teacups with a chaperone counting every word."

"Would you…would you court me like that if I asked you?"

His blood surged in raging denial. He wanted her now—in his bed and in his life. "Yes."

She raised a skeptical eyebrow. "You don't sound too sure."

He gave her a rueful smile. "I'm impatient to make you mine. But I can wait." His voice rasped as he continued. "Just for the love of heaven, don't make me wait too long."

"A year?"

Good God. He'd be a tattered wreck after a year of burning for her. "So you'll marry me?"

Humor lit her eyes. "So you'll wait a year?"

"Aye, if I must. I'm sure of what I want. I can't expect the same of you." He paused. "As long as I have your promise."

"More than a year?"

He rose and regarded her uncertainly. "Are you really not sure?"

"I'm checking to see if you are." Her smile widened. "I want to be more than just a convenient choice."

He released a crack of appreciative laughter. "You're teasing me, you impossible lassie."

The glance Bess sent him from under her lashes was unmistakably flirtatious. "I might be."

"You don't want to wait a year?" He slid his arms around her waist.

"I dislike tea parties."

She was a treasure. Provoking, but definitely a treasure. "So how long must I wait?"

"How long would you wait?"

"Forever if I have to," he bit out, drawing her closer. "Will you marry me, Bess?"

She clasped her hands behind his neck. Her touch thundered through him like fifty cannons firing a broadside. "I will, my lord."

"You will?" he said stupidly.

Her brilliant smile dazzled him, made him feel like he tumbled through the stars to paradise. "Oh, yes. I was sure from the first, too."

"My darling…" He kissed her with all the reverent joy in his heart. He only stopped when someone knocked on the door, loudly enough to rise above the blood pounding in his ears. Slowly he raised his head and stared down at Bess. She looked completely spellbound.

"My love, our privacy comes to an end." Unable to resist, he kissed each corner of her full mouth. That mouth had lured him all week. The promise of a lifetime of kisses made him ready to throw back his head and shout his triumph to the rafters.

She strained up toward him. "Kiss me again."

Rory laughed and forced himself to step away. How could she have imagined he despised her ardent spirit? Her fiery passion was one of the many things he loved about Bess.

Love…

He loved Bess.

The world stopped turning. Even the insistent knocking faded to nothing.

He loved her. With a love larger and mightier than the ocean.

"Rory?"

He blinked until the great hall returned to focus. But still the everlasting truth hammered at him. He loved Bess. And she'd agreed to be his wife. He could hardly wait.

"We're getting married," he said jubilantly and caught her up against him for another kiss.

This time she pulled free. She turned toward the door. "Dear heaven, the villagers will wonder what's happened to us." She glanced at the tall clock against the wall. "We should have set out twenty minutes ago."

"They'll forgive us once they know why we delayed." Given the efficient flow of information, he'd lay good money most, if not all, of them guessed what Bess and the new earl were doing right now.

"Shall we tell them?" To his delight, she caught his hand.

"I should speak to your father first."

"So today this is our secret."

He was sure that he looked completely moonstruck. Why not? He was. "Aye."

Her hold tightened. "I like that."

He raised her hand to his lips. "You've made me the happiest man in England." He paused. "And Scotland."

"I'm rather pleased myself." Then typically her

attention turned to practical matters. "You need to put on your costume."

Bess Farrar had promised to marry him, and the whole world turned to Christmas. "Just one more kiss."

"We're going to be so late," she said, without her usual conviction.

He edged her back a few paces. "It's your fault. You found the mistletoe."

"Oh, you're a devil," she whispered before his lips captured hers.

Silently he vowed lifelong devotion. He wondered if she sensed his pledge, because when he raised his head, her eyes were misty.

With a tenderness that jammed the breath in his throat, she touched his cheek. "I'm going to love being your wife."

But did that mean she loved *him?* Another rap on the door proved this wasn't the moment to find out.

They had time. Praise heaven, they had the rest of their lives.

"Curse our obligations. I want you to myself." He crossed the room and flung on Joseph's striped robe. Then he unbolted the door. Dr. Simpson stood on the step, looking knowing, while the people lined up in the snow watched with unconcealed curiosity.

"Are you ready?" Rory whispered to Bess when she joined him in the doorway.

"I'm ready for anything as long as you're with me."

How he loved the proud tilt of her chin. "Then let's

hoist our sails and set our course for new lands, sweetheart."

He strode out to join his people, the woman he loved by his side.

Bess slipped out of the crowded, noisy hall onto Penton Abbey's dark front step. Her heart raced with such excitement, it was like having a hundred Christmas candles burning bright inside her.

Carefully she closed the door. She didn't want anyone to follow. Earlier there had been a moon, but now the sky clouded over for more snow. Behind her, she heard the scratch of fiddles and the villagers' whoops and stamping feet as they danced to celebrate Christmas Day. Although by now, it was well into Christmas night. Everyone was having far too much fun to go home after the new earl's magnificent feast.

"Just where are you off to so late, my bonny lassie?" Rory drawled, emerging from the shadows beside the door and catching her hand.

Bess laughed, as much from happiness as amusement, and let him draw her down to stand in the snow in front of the house. "I can't delay. I'm off to meet a pirate, good sir."

"The scurvy rascal will have to wait," Rory said. "I've got plans for you first."

He swooped down for a kiss. Immediate and now

familiar passion ignited. She curved into his tall, strong body, at last free to express her aching longing. It felt like an eon since he'd last kissed her, and she sank blissfully into the heated demand of his lips. This was the first chance they'd had to be alone since yesterday's proposal.

The play had proven a great success, and while she and Rory hadn't said a whisper about their engagement, pointed looks from her neighbors hinted that the village's gossip mill whirred away as usual. Even Daisy seemed to understand that this was a special day, and she'd been a perfect angel. Unfortunately the human angels hadn't been quite so exemplary. Sally Potts had forgotten her lines when she announced her good tidings to the shepherds, and a brawl between Mrs. Hallam's twin boys had disrupted the heavenly host's chorus of hallelujahs.

"I missed you so much," she whispered, twining her arms around him.

"Oh, my darling—" He dragged her up for more kisses. "Damn it, we can't stay long."

"I know," she said breathlessly. "I'm beginning to loathe propriety. When will you talk to my father?"

"Tomorrow." They'd reluctantly decided that Christmas Day wasn't the best time to approach the vicar about his daughter's engagement.

"Early?"

"I'll be there at the crack of dawn if you think it will hasten the wedding."

When she rested her head on his chest, his gallant heart beat steadily beneath her ear. "Oh, Rory, I'm so very happy. I can't tell you how much."

His arms tightened, and he propped his chin on her hair. "I'm the luckiest man in England."

"And Scotland."

"And Scotland. And the rest of the world." He kissed the top of her head. "Merry Christmas, my bonny countess."

She buried her nose in his chest, loving the rich, musky smell of his skin. He was so marvelously warm. "Merry Christmas, my dashing earl."

"I've got the present I want."

Bess raised her head. The light from the house illuminated his strong features—and the roguish glitter in his green eyes. "Perhaps, but you'll have to wait to unwrap it."

Rory gave a long-suffering sigh. "Och, and isn't that just like a blasted Englishwoman?"

Something cold and soft brushed her cheek. With wondering eyes, she stared up at the sky. "It's snowing. It was snowing the first time you kissed me."

He smiled down at her. "Aye, and clearly it's a sign from above that I need to kiss you again."

"Clearly," she said drily, stretching up on her toes to brush her lips across his. Then some instinct made her pull away and glance back at the house. "Oh, dear."

He turned his head to follow the direction of her gaze. The great hall's tall windows were lined with smiling people, craning their necks to take in as much of the view as they could. Bess saw Dr. Simpson, and Ned White, and her father—looking puzzled—and Mrs. Hallam, and Will and Sally Potts, and all the other local people who had worked so hard to ready the Abbey for Christmas.

Rory burst out laughing and flung his arm around Bess's shoulders, hugging her into his side. "I think, my bonny, that our wee secret is out."

CHAPTER NINE

*R*ory knocked softly on the dressing room door before he entered the candlelit bedchamber. It was late, nearly midnight, and he was naked beneath his heavy velvet dressing gown.

He and Bess began their honeymoon at a naval friend's manor on the North Sea near Craster. They'd completed the last hours of the forty-mile journey to this spectacular piece of coastline in the dark. The waves crashing against the shore vied with the thunder in his blood at the sight that greeted him in the flickering golden light.

"My God, but you're lovely," he said reverently, once he'd managed to shift the boulder blocking his throat.

Slowly Bess turned from the window where she'd been watching the starlit sea, and the welcome in her smile made his heart swell with joy. "When you look at me like that, I feel lovely."

Her golden hair tumbled loose around her straight, slender shoulders. She wore a sheer, white nightgown that offered shadowy hints of the curved body beneath.

He swallowed to moisten a suddenly dry mouth. He wanted her so much. "We've got the house to ourselves for a couple of days."

On Rory's instructions, the manor was provisioned and the staff took a paid holiday. Upon arrival, the housekeeper had greeted them with congratulations, blazing fires, and a bottle of champagne, then left them to look after themselves. At the end of the week, they sailed south for two months in Italy.

"I look forward to seeing everything in daylight."

"You'll love it." He'd kept today's destination secret, and she'd been thrilled to discover the sea at their doorstep. The wild scenery made a fitting setting for her vivid spirit. "Do you mind doing without a maid?"

A smile tugged at her lips. "I'm rather looking forward to tending my husband like a proper village wife."

"Och, that's a pity. I'm rather looking forward to my wife being very improper indeed."

He crossed the parquet floor and kissed her tenderly. Her lips parted beneath his, but he didn't deepen the kiss. There would be passion later, but for now, his overwhelming need was to cherish this exquisite creature who gave herself into his keeping.

He drew back and cradled her face between his palms. When they'd stopped for a hurried meal in

Alnwick, by unspoken mutual consent they'd kept their conversation to unimportant matters. So in all the ways that mattered, their life together began here in this room overlooking the cliffs.

"I can't tell you how proud I felt when you walked down the aisle this morning and promised yourself to me." Proud, yet strangely humble.

Her smile was tremulous, and aching emotion deepened her blue eyes to midnight. "You shouldn't say such things. Unless you want me sobbing all over you."

He laughed fondly and kissed her. "That doesn't sound like my indomitable bride."

"Your indomitable bride is feeling a little fragile."

"I'll have to kiss her back to her stalwart self."

"I've missed our kisses," she murmured, leaning forward. "Why did you make us wait a whole month?"

"You threatened me with a year."

"I was only teasing, you know I was."

He nipped at her full lower lip. "My reasons were good."

She sent him an unimpressed look. "I think you're more concerned about propriety than London's strictest chaperone."

"I want to do everything right—even if I suffer for it. And believe me, my love, I did."

Frequently over the last four weeks, he'd cursed this need to show the world how much he honored Bess. With a special license, they could have married within days. But he abhorred the idea of any snide comments about a quick wedding, following that snowy night in the woodcutter's hut. So the vicar had called the banns, and Rory had endured the excruciating delay of a conventional engagement.

"I know." Bess rose on her toes and kissed him. These weren't the sizzling, voracious kisses he'd fantasized about through this whole pestilential month. But her unfettered affection warmed the cold, lonely places in his soul, places he'd never known existed until he met her. "And I've been dreadfully ungrateful."

"Aye, dreadfully," Rory said with a quirk of his lips. "You'd better make amends tonight."

"Only tonight?"

"It's a start. I have a powerful appetite to feed. We haven't had a minute alone since Christmas."

Once they were betrothed, they'd hardly exchanged a private word, let alone indulged in any mischief. The free and easy week of courtship became a memory. When he and Bess hadn't been preparing the Abbey for their life together, she'd been introducing him to the neighbors and the local area. With every day, he'd become more a part of this new life that had felt so alien when he'd arrived in Northumberland. He had Bess to thank for that. He had Bess to thank for so very much.

Having her in his arms now felt like a miracle. Her physical presence beat through him like a great drum. "Then you left me for a week to kick up your heels in Newcastle."

"You know I needed to buy my bride clothes, and order furniture and curtains. Believe me, staying with you, even under a hundred curious eyes, would be much more fun than staying with my aunt."

"I'll wager her nose was out of joint when she discovered you'd captured an earl." Bess's aunt and cousins had attended this morning's wedding in Penton Wyck. They'd been nauseatingly obsequious to him, while barely concealing their jealousy of Bess.

Bess laughed shortly and cuddled closer. Her rich female scent teased his senses. "They made it clear that I didn't deserve my good fortune. But my aunt is very fashionable, and she warmed up a degree or two when we cleared out the shops."

"Dear Lord, you didn't let her bully you into buying a thousand folderols, did you?"

Bess leaned back in his arms, a glint in her eyes. "Frills are all the rage this year."

"Lord help us." He knew she was teasing. Again.

"And then you dragged me away after the wedding breakfast on an interminable journey. We could have stayed the night at Penton Abbey and traveled tomorrow."

He shuddered theatrically. "Good God, we'd never have a moment's peace. The villagers can't bear to let you out of their sight. Simpson would stick his head into our bedroom every hour to check I was treating you right. Sally would badger you with improper questions. Your father would wander in at two in the morning to share his latest theory about some Byzantine princess or other."

She gave a low laugh. "Well, we can't have that."

"The avid interest in the consummation of our vows quite put me to the blush."

"The villagers like you."

"They *love* you." He adopted a wounded tone. "Then when I finally get you to myself, all you do is snore."

Most of the trip, she'd slept curled up beside him in the coach. She'd worked so hard for their perfect wedding. Despite his teasing, he was overjoyed that the day had turned out to be everything a bride could want. Although he doubted the vicar understood that his daughter was now married. John Farrar had stumbled through the service and had needed Bess's prompting when it came to Rory's three Christian names.

"I'm saving my strength for tonight."

He laughed in appreciation and reluctantly abandoned her to cross to a side table where the champagne waited. A couple of deft movements and the cork popped. "Och, you're a bride in a million, lassie."

Bess drifted toward him. "I hope you think so after tonight."

Surprised, Rory looked up from filling two glasses with the frothing golden wine. "Of course I will. How can you doubt it?"

She didn't smile back. "I'm worried about

measuring up. You're a man of the world—literally—
and I've never done this before."

Apparently more than wedding preparations lay
behind her exhaustion. Poignant tenderness flooded
him that she should worry about pleasing him. Didn't
the daft lass know she pleased him just by existing?
"Bess, take my word for it, no woman compares to you.
You're a jewel."

"You make everything sound so easy."

He shrugged and put down the bottle. "If we don't
get everything right on the first try, we've got at least
forty years to practice until we're perfect. Goodwill
and friendship will take us a long way. And desire."

And love.

Was that love he saw in her eyes? They'd never
spoken the words, but tonight some profound and
precious bond united them.

He passed her a glass and sipped from his own. "I
want you quite desperately, in case you haven't
noticed."

Thoughtfully, she took a sip, then replaced her
nearly full glass on the table. "Show me."

"With pleasure," he said, smiling back. He drained
his glass before setting it next to hers. His friend had
been thoughtful leaving them the wine, but right now,
Rory felt so drunk on happiness, he needed no other
stimulant.

Taking her hand, he drew Bess closer to the fire. He

was overwhelmingly aware of the large, heavily carved bed in the center of the room.

He kissed her knuckles with a veneration that turned barely leashed hunger into something nobler and sweeter. He'd never before felt this need to protect and please and cherish.

Bess hadn't done this before. In the most essential sense, neither had he. They would both emerge from this winter night changed forever.

Her eyes were as blue as the ocean that had been his mistress in boyhood and youth. Now he dedicated himself to a new cause. Silently he promised his love and loyalty, his courage and strength to this woman.

Rory started gently, almost tentatively. Transfixed with wonder, he stroked her luxuriant hair. He touched her face, her shoulders, her arms, her hands, feeling the vital life beneath her skin. This was a lassie full of fire and vigor. And he thanked God that she was. He wanted an equal on his journey. Bess had matched him from the first.

She was trembling. His caresses, subtle but sinfully purposeful, aroused her. When his hands glanced over those magnificent full breasts, she made a stifled sound in her throat. He returned, caressing her until her nipples stood proud against the cool lawn. He took one beaded peak between his lips, making her cry out. She arched into him, burying her fingers in his hair, urging him on. Dizzy with her scent, smoky lemon and lavender and honey, he moved to the other breast. The nightdress was so fine, it was almost like touching her bare skin.

When he finally raised his head, she was flushed and shaking, and her eyes were heavy with desire. "Don't stop," she said, as she'd said once before.

When he had stopped. For her sake.

"We've only just started." He seized her for a deep passionate kiss, thrusting his tongue into her mouth. She met him without shyness, although he'd seen shyness in her eyes.

He caught her nightdress around her hips and lifted it over her ruffled golden head. She raised her hands in swift modesty, but something in his face must have reassured her. Raising her chin with familiar courage, she stood naked and proud before him.

"You're perfection," he murmured in awe.

As if he touched something sacred, he skimmed his hands down her slender arms, feeling her warmth without lingering. Some mad corner of his mind couldn't quite believe she was real. He'd dreamed of this moment since he'd first seen her.

He caught her hips to hold her still, and kissed her with every ounce of unspoken love in his heart. She wriggled nearer, hands trailing over him, pushing his dressing gown away from his chest, learning his body as he learned hers. He backed her toward the bed, whispering encouragement between kisses on her lips and along her throat.

"Rory…" she sighed when he scraped his teeth up her neck. She shivered. "That makes me feel…"

"Good?" he muttered, curving his hands over her lusciously round buttocks.

"More than good."

He laughed softly, and returned his attention to that sensitive spot under her ear until she squirmed and whimpered. How he loved her wild responses, but these sweet preliminaries already melted into the next step.

Holding her shoulders, he lowered her to the bed. Then with sudden ruthlessness, he flung away his dressing gown. Her eyes widened in shock—and curiosity.

"Heavens above. Are you sure this is going to work?"

He laughed as he kneeled over her. "I'm sure, my love."

With a naturalness that slammed his heart into his ribs, Bess stretched out beneath him and linked her hands around his neck. "I hope you're right."

He kissed her again. She was taut with uncertainty, but under his gentle persuasion, she gradually turned soft and liquid once more. He cupped her breasts, squeezing the plump flesh until she shook. She gasped when his eager hardness pressed into her belly.

"It's all right," he crooned, running his hand down her side. "Trust me."

"I do," she whispered, and lay with lovely looseness

as her knees rose in invitation. Female musk filled the air until he felt like he drowned in Bess.

His hand glided lower, tracing the silky plain of her stomach, following the voluptuous curve of her hips, brushing the feathery hair that covered her sex. She jerked, and a husky moan escaped her. Her hands tightened on his shoulders, and she nibbled an incendiary trail down his neck. This innocent boldness stirred him to desperation.

He slipped his hand between her legs. She was hot and sleek, and when he explored the slick folds, she jolted with surprise.

"That's wicked."

"Should I stop?"

"Oh, no, never," she murmured, and spread her legs to give him better access.

Rory teased at her center, until she was panting and restless, but he kept her from tumbling into climax. When he slid one finger into her satiny passage, she was tight. His heart gave a mighty thump, and his head swam with the need to claim her. But he clung to patience. Just.

When she adjusted to the careful invasion, he tested another finger. He worked her until she cried out in agitation and clung to him.

"Don't make me wait," she choked out. "I want you so much."

He kissed her, clumsy with overpowering need.

This slow awakening tantalized him to the edge of madness. "I want to please you."

"You will." She bit his shoulder hard enough to hurt. "You do."

Rory raised his head to meet eyes glassy with arousal. It was time. Feeling like his life hung in the balance, he angled her knees higher and carefully lowered his hips.

Bess watched him steadily. Her lips were red and swollen from his kisses, and a hectic flush marked her cheekbones. He pressed through glorious resistance.

Slow. Slow.

He couldn't bear to hurt her. Even as his blood pulsed with the command to take, to seize, to own, he held back.

When her body opened sumptuously to his, his restraint received its reward. Every shift, every touch, every sigh, all etched themselves on his soul. Bess was exquisitely hot, so marvelously responsive. The urge to thrust flayed him like a whip.

Her fingers dug into his shoulders. "I won't break, Rory."

What a bride fate had delivered. "Are you sure you're ready?"

Despite the moment's extremity, she managed a broken laugh. "I feel like I've been ready for a month."

"Oh, my darling," he groaned, and unable to resist, he thrust home.

Bess bit back a cry as Rory possessed her body. But much as she tried to hide her reaction, he must have felt how she stiffened. He abruptly stopped moving and under her hands, his back went as hard as stone. As hard as that large, intrusive part of him pressing inside her.

He sucked in a shuddering breath and surged up on his powerful arms to stare into her face. "Dear God, Bess, I'm sorry."

"Don't be," she said huskily. She'd been unprepared for the act's stark physicality, the way her wedding vows about becoming one flesh would feel in reality.

His smile was wry, although she read aching concern in his eyes. "I'd cut my throat before I hurt you."

She raised one unsteady hand to his cheek. "I'd much rather have you alive and with me, Rory, thank you very much."

"It will get better, I promise."

When she shifted to ease the pressure, he settled more firmly. She was overwhelmingly conscious of the throbbing weight, but with every second, the initial pain ebbed. And there were things she liked about what they did. She liked being so close to him. She'd definitely liked the way he'd touched her before he'd taken her. That had been wonderful.

Recalling those intoxicating caresses, she bowed up

to kiss him. His fervent response banished trepidation. When she relaxed against him, he groaned and jutted his hips forward. Unexpected pleasure ripped through her, and her hands curled into his damp hair, bringing him closer into the kiss. He reared over her, deep-set green eyes unwavering on hers.

As Rory pulled away, her body clung to him. Her gasp this time expressed unconditional delight. When he slid into her again, she greeted him with a liquid surge.

"Oh, I see," she sighed.

"You will."

Closing her eyes, she gave herself up to him. The universe closed in, so that all she knew was Rory's potent scent, the deep rumble of his praise, the sublime connection of his body moving in hers. A new sensation rippled through her, grew stronger and stronger. Until it was mighty enough to crack the sky.

The unearthly yearning coiled tighter. Surely she must shatter. It was the way she'd felt when he'd so shockingly placed his fingers inside her.

But this was…more.

Frenzied with the mysterious promise beyond the striving, she bit his shoulder again. He swore softly and changed the angle of his thrust.

The world tilted and flared into blinding light.

Bess cried out as she shuddered through the transcendent fire. He moved more purposefully, then with one fierce plunge, he flooded her with heat. Rocketed to heaven, she closed her eyes and clutched his back with frantic fingers.

Eventually the wildness receded, and the world stopped reeling. She drew her first full breath in what felt like a year and opened heavy eyes.

She and Rory lay on their sides wrapped in each other's arms. They both breathed in gasps after those volcanic moments when she'd lost contact with everything but Rory and what he made her feel.

After that extraordinary union, her body ached. She'd never felt as close to another person. And because the honesty between them cut sharp as a knife, she could no longer hold back the simple, eternal words.

"I love you, Rory," she whispered, placing a tender kiss on his bare chest.

He rolled her onto her back and rose over her. "What the devil did you say?"

Her stomach knotted with dismay as she struggled to read his expression. He didn't look pleased. He looked like someone had hit him with a plank.

Under that searing gaze, the lovely glow receded. "It doesn't matter," she muttered.

They'd never discussed love, although he'd made his desire more than clear. But desire wasn't love. And the stark, painful truth was that she wanted Rory to love her. She wanted it more than she'd ever wanted anything in her life.

"Bess..."

"You don't have to love me back," she said, wishing desperately she'd kept her mouth shut.

"Well, I'll be damned." To her astonishment, that devil-may-care smile curled his lips. "You love me."

Her pulses careered into a drunken gallop, and suddenly she didn't feel nearly so bereft and uncertain. "Of course I do. Why else would I have married you?"

Rory frowned as if he only just made the connection. "I'm a complete numbskull. Of course that's why you married me."

"Did you think I wanted your fortune?"

He shook his head. He still looked surprised, but happy surprised now. Like a man out on a morning stroll who had stumbled over a pot of gold in his path. "No, I knew it wasn't that. Otherwise you'd have accepted my brother."

Her lips flattened with annoyance. "People have been talking."

"Aye, they certainly have." The teasing light in his eyes confirmed that he was far from displeased to know she loved him. That was good. Even better would be if he loved her back. "They've been saying something else, too."

She sighed. "That I'm besotted with you, I suppose."

He laughed softly and kissed her. "I never heard that. I wish I had."

"So what have they been saying?" It was hard to keep her mind on the conversation after that kiss which, while swift, had been thorough.

"That the new Earl of Channing took one look at the vicar's bonny daughter and fell head over heels." He settled between her legs, and she became aware of some very interesting things happening to his body. "Bess, I'm trying in my clumsy way to tell you that I love you."

Dazed she stared up at him. "You do?"

"Aye, I most certainly do." The tenderness shining in his eyes convinced her more than mere words could. His brogue was thicker than usual. "You blazed into my life like lightning, and I never wanted to live without you again."

"I felt…I felt the same," she confessed, and her elation in becoming his wife expanded until she felt ready to burst with the glory of it all.

"Will you tell me again?" he asked softly.

She brushed back an unruly lock of auburn hair that tumbled over his forehead and studied those beloved features. "I love you, Rory."

Rory kissed her again, gentler, sweeter. He slid up on the pillows and settled her in his arms. "And I love you, Bess. Forever."

"I'm so happy," she whispered, resting her head on his chest. "I thought I was happy before. But knowing I love you and you love me, I can't tell you how wonderful that feels."

"I'll devote the rest of my life to keeping you this way."

She kissed his bare shoulder. "I never thought I'd

fall in love with a pirate. Until you arrived at Penton Wyck, I've always been revoltingly well behaved."

Even before he spoke, she felt his sudden tension. "Actually that's something I've been meaning to talk to you about."

She tipped her head back to study his expression. When they'd exchanged their vows of love, he'd looked incandescent. Now he looked troubled. And a tad sheepish.

"You don't need to make any dreadful confessions, my love." She paused, savoring the endearment on her lips. "What's done is done. I love the man you are now, whatever your murky past."

"That's very understanding." Rory's lips turned down in self-derision. Bess had sounded so very proud of herself when she'd professed her love for an outlaw. How he hated to blight her pleasure. "But I'm afraid there's one dreadful confession that won't wait."

Her eyes wary, Bess sat up and tugged the sheets higher to cover her breasts. "Rory, what is it?"

He caught her hand and regarded her ruefully. "Gossip isn't always as accurate as it was when it spread the news about my yen for you, bonny lass."

"What do you mean?"

"It means, despite all the colorful tattle, I'm not and never have been a pirate."

She peered into his face, clearly seeking some sign of his familiar teasing. But on this occasion, he was deadly serious. "Not a pirate?"

He shook his head and admitted the shameful truth. "I went into the Royal Navy as a boy, and spent the next twenty-odd years fighting most respectably for king and country. In fact, since the end of the French wars, I've devoted the majority of my time at sea to catching pirates."

A faint frown drew her brows together. "So you're a law-abiding citizen?"

"I'm afraid so. I'm terrifically sorry, my darling."

She still looked as though she didn't believe him. "But how on earth did the story spread?"

He shrugged. "My guess is that a Scots sea captain was already such an exotic addition to this secret corner of England that stitching piracy onto his history meant only an inch more embroidery. In people's imaginations, it's a wee step from navy man to lawless buccaneer, I suppose. At least it is in landlocked Penton Wyck."

"Why didn't you tell me before?"

"I tried a couple of times. But I must admit, on other occasions…"

"You couldn't resist leading me on?"

"I couldn't help myself." He couldn't interpret her reaction. She was back to avoiding his eyes. "Are you *very* disappointed? I'm sure I could launch a career as a pirate, now that I've retired from the navy, but it would mean going back to sea. And I'd much rather stay here with you."

She sighed as heavily as if she'd slept through Christmas and missed all the fun. "I thought I was being so adventurous when I fell in love with you."

"I know."

"I'll just have to face the painful truth and struggle on." She raised her chin and at last, he caught the laughter in her face. "It's too late to reject you and find a real pirate."

He should have realized before this that she'd learn to accept his vilely unblemished past. He wasn't the only one who liked to tease.

His eyes narrowed. "My dear Lady Channing, let's get one thing straight—you'll seek no pirate lovers while you're married to me."

She tilted her head. "Or what?"

He dragged her under him. "I'll put you in the brig."

"You could." To his delight, she linked her hands behind his head and arched up until her breasts brushed his chest. She'd clearly forgiven his lack of piratical history. "But I might get lonely there."

"Well, that won't do." He dropped a kiss on the racing pulse at the base of her throat. It seemed he wasn't the only one getting excited. "I could maroon you on a desert isle."

She pouted and tugged at his hair. "Even lonelier than the brig."

He trailed his lips up the silky length of her throat

and felt her shiver in quick response. "Not if I shared the island, too."

"I...don't like coconuts," she said unsteadily as he nipped at her earlobe.

"Then that won't do either. That settles it." He smiled down at this woman he adored. He knew he must look completely pudding-brained with love, but he didn't give a tinker's damn. "I'll just have to make every day of our life together an adventure, my bonny. Starting this very minute."

EPILOGUE

Christmas Eve, 1823

*B*ess, Countess of Channing, emerged from the doors of Penton Abbey to survey the crowd assembled for the nativity play. This year, Sally Potts was a much more confident angel. Dr. Simpson was, as always, the innkeeper. Daisy pretended to be a biddable beast, but Bess didn't trust the way she eyed Melchior's crown. Ned White made his debut as Caspar. Last autumn, old George Morrow, who had filled the part for fifty years, had passed away peacefully in his sleep.

She smiled as her gaze traveled over her friends and neighbors dressed as shepherds and angels. Some new faces. A few old ones missing.

The year had brought so many changes to Penton Wyck. Not least the wholesale acceptance of the new earl. Her smile widened as her attention focused on the tall, russet-haired gentleman playing Joseph—and also keeping a wary eye on Daisy.

When she'd married Rory, Bess had been sure she couldn't love him more. But a year had deepened her understanding and respect for her brave, openhearted husband. Today she watched him doing his best to appear at ease in a striped woolen robe, and she felt like love filled her whole life from corner to corner.

Sensing her observation, he raised his head and sent her an answering smile. She loved this preternatural connection they shared.

The footmen, now augmented to six, moved through the throng, serving the hot toddies that had proven so popular last year. Then an expectant silence fell as Rory raised his cup.

"This is my second year as part of this splendid Christmas pageant. I'd like to thank you all for your hard work. We look forward to another grand success. I'd also like to express my gratitude to the woman who is the heart of this community, my beloved wife. Bess, thank you for making me part of your world. When I arrived in Penton Wyck last year, I had no idea I'd found my true home. But you—and everyone here— have made me feel like I belong. I doubt there's a more contented man in England..."

"Or Scotland," Ned said, just loudly enough to raise a scattered laugh.

"Aye, or Scotland today. I give you my wife, my countess, and the woman I love. Lady Channing."

Three energetic cheers broke out, ringing through the cold air. It hadn't snowed this year, but Ralph Thompson, the oldest man in the village, swore there would be a heavy fall tonight.

Snow had fallen the first time Rory had kissed her. Ever since, Bess had been sentimental about a white Christmas.

"To you, my bonny lassie," Rory said.

Bess blinked back tears. She was disgracefully emotional these days. The villagers' cheers, not to mention Rory's beautiful speech, left her wanting to bawl like a lost calf.

"Th...thank you," she said unsteadily, meeting Rory's bright green eyes. "And I'd like to say a special thank you to my wonderful husband. Penton Wyck couldn't ask for a better master, and I couldn't call a better man my lord."

They were usually playful with each other—passion and laughter made for a stimulating life. She rarely spoke with such unalloyed sincerity. In homage, she sank into a deep curtsy, struggling a little with the straight cut of Mary's blue robe.

Rory understood. Of course he did. His tender expression warmed her to the bone. Over the last year, their bond had deepened and stabilized, until love was the very air she breathed.

"You do me too much honor, my lady," he said, mounting the stairs to take her hand as she rose. He turned to the crowd. "Let's make this the best play ever. Then the merriest Christmas in the history of Northumberland."

He escorted her to where Daisy waited in line behind the Three Wise Men. After that glowing tribute, Bess could no longer contain the news she'd intended to give Rory as a gift after the midnight service in St. Martin's.

"Rory, wait a moment," she whispered before he lifted her into the saddle.

"What is it?" he asked in quick concern. "Aren't you feeling well?"

She'd been sick that morning, but she felt marvelous now. She stretched up on her toes to murmur into his ear, "Mary is with child."

Rory caught Daisy's bridle before she could do any damage and his attention was on the disgruntled donkey. "Of course she is. With the Baby Jesus."

Bess laughed and placed a hand over her belly. "No, although perhaps with the next Earl of Channing."

Rory abruptly dropped the bridle and whirled on her, his face pale with shock. "What did you say?"

She glanced around. Nobody was watching. The players were all too busy taking their places for the procession. "I'm going to have a baby."

The brilliant happiness that lit Rory's eyes threatened to split her heart with joy. "Truly?"

"Truly. Anne Coe says in June." Bess had visited the village midwife yesterday to confirm her suspicions.

"My dear, dear love." He caught her up against him and despite being in public, he kissed her soundly. When he raised his head, Bess was blinking back more tears. If she made it through the day without dissolving into floods, it would be a miracle of biblical proportions.

"Well, really!" Bess's aunt exclaimed from the steps behind them. "Such behavior."

"What else can you expect from a pirate?" Bess's starchy cousin Priscilla sniffed in disapproval beside her mother.

"Bess told me he wasn't a pirate, but a captain in the navy," Bess's slightly nicer cousin Phoebe said from the doorway behind them.

"Now he's turned respectable, of course that's what she'd say," Aunt Henrietta retorted dismissively. "I know a renegade when I see one."

Rory caught Bess's arm before she could confront her relatives. "It doesn't matter."

Bess laughed wryly. He was right. Her relations' nastiness didn't matter. "It seems the legend of the pirate earl of Penton Abbey is indestructible."

He tilted that sardonic auburn eyebrow. "Come on, admit it—you like the idea of being a buccaneer's lady."

She traced a finger along his jaw, ignoring her

aunt's gimlet stare. "If you're the buccaneer in question, I'm proud to call a pirate my husband."

He kissed her again and carefully placed her in the saddle. Bess fumbled for the reins, but she was too late. Daisy took advantage of Rory's distraction to snatch Melchior's crown.

"Oh, Daisy!" Bess said in frustration as Melchior shook his fist at the unrepentant beast munching the painted cardboard circle. "You are the absolute limit."

Rory laughed. "Penton Wyck abounds with unruly women."

"And you wouldn't have it any other way," Ned said, offering Melchior his crown as a replacement.

This year, the Three Kings would present themselves to the Infant Jesus without one diadem. Drums and recorders burst into the introduction to "The Holly and the Ivy," and the parade set off at a jaunty pace for the village.

"Amen," Rory said, taking Daisy's rein and turning back to smile at Bess with such love in his eyes that she felt ready to fly up into the sky with happiness.

Her life brimmed with blessings. A home she loved. Dear friends. A husband she adored. And now a baby. How could any merely human heart contain this overflowing gratitude?

The 1823 Penton Wyck nativity play was memorable

on a number of counts. A lovely performance from a very pretty Angel of the Lord. Some particularly fine singing from the heavenly host. A mere two kings graced with crowns. A Joseph losing control of the donkey at a crucial moment so the manger ended in a hundred splintered pieces, and Baby Jesus had to make do with half a beer barrel for a cradle.

And a Mary who cried like a waterspout all the way to Bethlehem.

ABOUT THE AUTHOR

ANNA CAMPBELL has written 10 multi award-winning historical romances for Grand Central Publishing and Avon HarperCollins, and her work is published in 22 languages. She has also written 23 bestselling independently published romances, including her series, The Dashing Widows and The Lairds Most Likely. Anna has won numerous awards for her Regency-set stories including Romantic Times Reviewers Choice, the Booksellers Best, the Golden Quill (three times), the Heart of Excellence (twice), the Write Touch, the Aspen Gold (twice) and the Australian Romance Readers Association's favorite historical romance (five times). Her books have three times been nominated for Romance Writers of America's prestigious RITA Award, and three times for Australia's Romantic Book of the Year. When she's not traveling the world seeking inspiration for her stories, Anna lives on the beautiful east coast of Australia.

Anna loves to hear from her readers. You can find her at:

Website: www.annacampbell.com

facebook.com/AnnaCampbellFans

twitter.com/AnnaCampbellOz

bookbub.com/authors/anna-campbell

goodreads.com/AnnaCampbell

ALSO BY ANNA CAMPBELL

Claiming the Courtesan

Untouched

Tempt the Devil

Captive of Sin

My Reckless Surrender

Midnight's Wild Passion

The Sons of Sin series:

Seven Nights in a Rogue's Bed

Days of Rakes and Roses

A Rake's Midnight Kiss

What a Duke Dares

A Scoundrel by Moonlight

Three Proposals and a Scandal

The Dashing Widows:

The Seduction of Lord Stone

Tempting Mr. Townsend

Winning Lord West

Pursuing Lord Pascal

Charming Sir Charles

Catching Captain Nash

Lord Garson's Bride

The Lairds Most Likely:

The Laird's Willful Lass

The Laird's Christmas Kiss

The Highlander's Lost Lady

The Highlander's Defiant Captive

The Highlander's Christmas Quest

Christmas Stories:

The Winter Wife

Her Christmas Earl

A Pirate for Christmas

Mistletoe and the Major

A Match Made in Mistletoe

The Christmas Stranger

Other Books:

These Haunted Hearts

Stranded with the Scottish Earl

Maggie Carr has worked as a housekeeper at isolated Thorncroft Hall since her beloved mother died five years ago. No matter how often she tells herself she's accustomed to being poor and alone, Christmas always stirs poignant memories of a time when she had a place in the world and a family to love. But this Christmas, a handsome stranger bursts into her solitary world and makes her feel like a desirable woman. Maggie has already lost so much to cruel fate. Now as the season advances and she finds herself in thrall to the man who challenges her loneliness and turns winter nights to sultry summer, what price will this irresistible passion demand of her?

Will the Yuletide enchantment vanish with the season's decorations? Or have Maggie and her Christmas stranger discovered a magic to sustain them through a lifetime of happiness?

~

The Winter Wife

Will a chance meeting on Christmas Eve...

Alicia Sinclair, Countess of Kinvarra, cannot believe that fate has been so cruel as to strand her on the snowy Yorkshire moors with her estranged husband as her only hope of rescue. During their rare encounters, the arrogant earl and his countess act like hostile strangers. Now that Alicia has fallen into Kinvarra's power, will he seek revenge for her desertion? Or does the dark, passionate man she once adored have entirely different plans for his headstrong wife?

...deliver a second chance at love?

Sebastian Sinclair, Earl of Kinvarra, has spent ten wretched years regretting the mistakes he made with his young bride, but after long separation, the barriers between them are insurmountable. Until an unexpected encounter one stormy night makes him wonder if the barriers of mistrust and thwarted desire are so insurmountable after all. When winter weather traps Sebastian and his proud, lovely wife in an isolated inn, could the earl and his headstrong countess have a Christmas miracle in store?

A Christmas of confusion lies ahead! Will mistletoe magic lead the way to a happy ending?

Kisses and Christmas Bells

Two Romantic Regency Novellas

Mistletoe and the Major

The Major is home from the wars at last...

Edmund Sherritt, Major Lord Canforth, has devoted eight tumultuous years to fighting Napoleon. Finally Europe is at peace, and he can retire to his estates and the lovely wife he hasn't seen since their brief, unhappy honeymoon. The innocent girl he loved from the first moment he saw her, but who shied away from him on their wedding night.

The beautiful woman who greets him at Otway Hall on Christmas Eve is no longer the sweet ingénue he remembers. This new and exciting version of his beloved countess is strong, outspoken, and independent, and she's willing to stand up for what she wants. The question is—does she want the husband who returns to her arms more as a stranger than a spouse?

Now the real battle begins.

Felicity, Lady Canforth, has had eight long years to regret that she sent her husband from a cold marriage bed to face brutal combat, danger and hardship. The only child of elderly parents, Felicity came to marriage innocent and ignorant, and unable to conceal her shock at the sensual power of the earl's caresses. Before she found the nerve to offer Canforth a more generous welcome, he was called away to war. The Major left behind a countess who was a bride, not a wife; a woman unsure of her husband's feelings, and too timid to confess how fervently she desires the man she wed.

Fate has granted an older, wiser Felicity a second chance to win her husband's heart. Now nothing will stop her from claiming victory over the famous war hero. This Christmas, she'll deploy every ounce of courage, purpose and passion to seize the life and love she's longed for, ever since Canforth left to serve his country. Whatever it costs, whatever it takes, she'll lure the dashing Major back into her bed, where she means to show him he's the only man she wants as her lover —and her love.

After years of yearning and separation, will a Christmas miracle heal the wounds of the past and offer the earl and his bride a future bright with love?

~

A Match Made in Mistletoe

A mistletoe wish...

All her life, Serena Talbot has been in love with the handsome boy next door, Sir Paul Garside. She always eagerly looks forward to Paul's visit to her family over the Festive Season, even if he usually brings along his dark, sardonic friend Lord Hallam. This year, Serena is determined that Paul's kiss under the mistletoe will lead to a proposal. Even if she has to enlist every ounce of Christmas magic she can get her hands on to make that happen.

But the mistletoe gets it wrong!

When Serena slips a sprig of mistletoe from the village kissing bough under her pillow, it's not Paul who turns up in her dreams as the man she's going to marry, but brooding, intense, annoying Giles Farraday, Marquess of Hallam. Still more annoying, once everyone arrives for the annual Christmas house party, she can't stop watching Giles, and thinking about Giles. And kissing Giles, whether there's mistletoe about or not. Now Paul wants to marry her, and Giles wants to seduce her–and Serena has a bone to pick with the old wives who came up with all this superstitious nonsense in the first place.